THE Jean Harlow
BOMBSHELL

THE *Jean Harlow* BOMBSHELL

MOLLIE
COX
BRYAN

MIDNIGHT INK
WOODBURY, MINNESOTA

FIRST EDITION
First Printing, 2019

Cover design by Shira Atakpu

Midnight Ink, an imprint of Llewellyn Worldwide Ltd.

This is a work of fiction. Names, characters, places, and incidents are either the product of the author's imagination or are used fictitiously, and any resemblance to actual persons, living or dead, business establishments, events, or locales is entirely coincidental.

Library of Congress Cataloging-in-Publication Data
Names: Bryan, Mollie Cox, author.
Title: The Jean Harlow bombshell / Mollie Cox Bryan.
Description: First edition. | Woodbury, Minnesota : Midnight Ink, [2019]
Identifiers: LCCN 2018059335 (print) | LCCN 2018060789 (ebook) | ISBN
    9780738759036 (ebook) | ISBN 9780738758695 (alk. paper)
Subjects: | GSAFD: Suspense fiction.
Classification: LCC PS3602.R943 (ebook) | LCC PS3602.R943 J43 2019 (print) |
    DDC 813/.6—dc23
LC record available at https://lccn.loc.gov/2018059335

Midnight Ink
Llewellyn Worldwide Ltd.
2143 Wooddale Drive
Woodbury, MN 55125-2989
www.midnightinkbooks.com

Printed in the United States of America

Dedicated to my grandparents, Paul and Irene Carpenter,
and in honor and memory of our famous relative, Jean Harlow.

In 1937, Jean Harlow was the hottest film star in Hollywood. Some of her blockbuster movies include Dinner at Eight, Red Dust, and China Seas. She was the first "blonde bombshell" in Hollywood. On May 29, while shooting the film Saratoga with Clark Gable and Myrna Loy, she complained of feeling sick. At first, she was diagnosed with influenza, which was a major error. Over the next few days, her body began to bloat, she slipped into a coma, and at 11:37 a.m. on June 7, Jean Harlow died of kidney failure. She was buried in a crypt in Glendale, wearing the gown she wore in Libeled Lady, and, according to newspaper reports, a huge 152-carat star sapphire ring given to her by William Powell. She was just 26.

One

As I squeezed through the tables of tea drinkers, the scent of jasmine, orange blossoms, and saffron heavy in the air, I spotted Justine tucked into a deep curtained booth. Even at this distance, her peculiar bearing alarmed me.

A woman who fidgeted and fussed, never sitting still, Justine sat motionless. Was she ill? Upset? Was there a problem with the Jean Harlow book? She wouldn't say why over the phone, but she insisted I meet her here at Layla's Tea Room, one of the oldest establishments in the city. A place of fading glamour.

God forbid we meet at a fast food restaurant or quaint coffee shop, something more my style. But Justine was accustomed to calling the shots. Always.

The tea room was too dark, sunlight peeking through spaces in the tired silk drapes on the windows and tables lit only by candles. I had once imagined this place as a charming British tea room, but all Layla's needed was a few opium pipes and colorful plush pillows scattered on the floor and it could be straight out of Morocco.

I hurried to Justine as fast as I could, given the dimness of the room, and almost tripped over a large handbag that had slipped from someone's chair. After stepping through the obstacle course of chairs, tables, and purses, I considered arriving at Justine's booth a victory.

She never glanced my way.

"Justine?" I managed to say.

Decked out in a lavender suit complete with a hat shadowing her face, Justine ignored me. She had that thousand-yard stare I knew so well. She was in Justine-land.

I sat across the table from her, shoving aside a heavy crimson velvet drape.

"Oh," she said. "You're here." With every silver hair in place, curled around her jawline in a page-boy cut, she lifted her chin in acknowledgment.

"Of course," I said, sliding my bags along the curved booth seat. "You sounded upset. Is everything okay?"

"No," she said, pressing her hand to her scarf-draped chest. "This Harlow book has brought all the kooks out!"

The server sauntered over and glanced at me. "Can I get you something?"

"Alfredo, you remember Charlotte, my assistant," Justine said, sweeping her arm in my direction.

"Yes, of course. Peppermint tea?"

How did he remember? Justine claimed he remembered everybody's favorite tea and cakes. One of the co-owners of the place, he must have been in his seventies.

I nodded. "Yes, thank you."

"Don't forget the honey cakes," Justine said and winked.

"Sure thing, gorgeous," he replied.

"He's fishing for a good tip." Justine's ruby-colored lips curled into a grin. The fringe from her aqua-and-silver floral scarf splayed onto the table. She drank her tea and fussed with her scarf. "Is it warm in here or is it me?"

"You're drinking hot tea and your scarf is draped over you," I said, reaching over the small circular table. "Loosen your scarf." I stretched over to help her untangle herself and found the fabric drenched.

"Stop fussing over me, would you? I need to talk with you," she said, pulling the fabric from my hands.

"What is it, Justine?"

As she leaned over and the candlelight caught her face, making it clearer, her pallor alarmed me. She fanned herself with her hands and her eyes slanted. "Did you see the man who just left?"

"Man? Do you mean Alfredo?"

She shook her head. "No. Not him."

Her chin quivered, as if she were frightened or confused, completely unlike her. Just what was going on with the Harlow book? What man was she talking about? It was rare for Justine to be so mysterious, so unsure of herself.

Sweat beads formed on her upper lip and cheeks.

"Let me get you a cool towel or something," I said.

She reached out and grabbed my arm. "Please don't fuss," she said, glancing around at the nearest tables.

"But you don't look well. Are you okay?" I pulled away from her.

She shrugged. "I'm as okay as any woman my age with a bad ticker." She cackled and lifted the tea to her lips with a trembling hand.

I stood from the table. "I'll be right back." She didn't want to cause a scene, but she was not well. I needed to do something.

In the ladies' room, I found a tiny linen towel and ran cool water over it. I squeezed the excess from the towel and hurried back into the tea room. Justine was slumped over half of the table. Had she fallen asleep? Damn, she was worse off than I imagined. I slid across the U-shaped booth next to her and pressed the cool towel to her head, figuring she'd snap to attention and warn me off.

But she didn't.

Alfredo walked to the table and placed the honey cakes and a pot of peppermint tea at my spot. He perfected the setting, then glanced up at us and leaned forward. "Justine?"

"She's not feeling well," I said, pressing the towel to her face. She slumped even further. I pushed her back and shook her gently. Her mouth dropped open.

Alarmed, Alfredo motioned to another staff member.

The booth's curtains whooshed and closed around us. In a flash, Justine and I were enclosed in the private booth. Alfredo then reached for her wrist. Another server promptly appeared through the curtains.

"What are you doing?" I asked.

"Pulse," he said, frowning.

Pulse? My heart thudded against my rib cage. Why had they closed the curtains? Justine needed to breathe. I tried to open the curtains.

"No," Alfredo said, sniffing. "She's gone."

"What? What do you mean?"

His lip curled downward. "Justine is dead."

"No," I said, shaking her. "Justine! Wake up!"

Alfredo shushed me as he choked back a sob. He turned and mumbled something to another server, gestured, and leaned toward me. "He's calling the authorities. Perhaps it's best if we wait in the back."

I steadied myself, my arm still around her, as the towel slipped from my other hand. "I'm not leaving her," I managed to say in a voice I barely recognized, a shivery whisper edged in the panic creeping in my throat. A primal scream bubbled in my guts. I swallowed it for now. Instead, I sat next to Justine in silent vigil. *She shouldn't be alone.*

Nobody argued with me.

I stayed next to her even after a woman appeared, examined her, and pronounced her dead. She introduced herself, said something about being a death investigator. Doctor something-or-other with bright orange punk hair...I struggled to make sense of anything. Death investigator?

"Heart failure," she said to the police officer sidling up beside her.

"She have a history?"

Icy cold, my teeth chattered when I answered. "Yes," I said. "Justine had a serious heart attack five years ago."

The death investigator pulled the curtain aside. "You're in shock. Can we get a blanket?"

"Was she feeling sick?" a Daniel Craig look-alike asked me. He wore the uniform of the NYPD, dark blue with gold medals and patches.

"Yes," I said. "She was hot, sweating, like a lot. I ran to the rest-room for a cool cloth, and when I came back, she was slumped over. I didn't even know she was dead. She wasn't clutching her chest or anything like that."

Even as I spoke the words, it felt like someone else was saying them. Justine was dead. And she was sitting next to me.

"Heart attacks in women sometimes present differently. Sweating. Nausea." The orange-haired death investigator draped a blanket over me. Its weight pressed on my shoulders, but where was the warmth?

"What is your relationship with the deceased?" the police officer asked. My eyes went to his name tag. Sergeant Den Brophy. An Irish cop with a Brooklyn accent. Eyes as blue as a jay's wings.

"I'm her assistant," I said, still chattering. "Charlotte Donovan."

"I need your phone number, address, and hers as well," he said. "Closest of kin?"

Willing away the fog in my mind, I remembered her cousin. "Yes, she has a cousin in Florida. Judith, I think her name is. Yes, Judith Turner."

Sergeant Brophy scribbled notes on his pad. The death investigator shifted her weight, hooked her thumbs in the pockets of her pants.

"So the deceased had a history of heart problems, and, given her age, her death is not exactly what we'd label suspicious, even though it happened in a public place," the sergeant said. "Are you certain she was alive when you left the table?"

My mouth went dry. I licked my sandpaper lips. *Was she?*

"I think so, but I turned my back when I ran to the restroom," I said.

"So you're not certain?" he asked.

I shook my head. "I guess not."

"Understandable," the death investigator said.

Was this really happening? Was I sitting next to my dead boss? Was this some kind of bad dream? I blinked hard.

"Are you certain you're telling us everything?" Sergeant Brophy said.

Was I? Was I leaving something out? Think, think, think. Justine shaking, frightened, talking about Harlow kooks and afraid of some man who'd been sitting with her before I arrived.

"Wait," I said, no longer shivering. "There is something I found odd. Justine said a man had been at her table."

"And?" The officer's head cocked in interest.

"She seemed frightened of him. And we were supposed to have a private meeting. Nobody else was invited."

He wrote on his notepad. "Did she say why she was afraid of this man?"

I swallowed a sob. *No.* "She didn't get a chance to tell me."

Sergeant Brophy stepped out for a few minutes, and the death investigator fidgeted around with papers on a clipboard. I maintained my vigil. *Oh, Justine.*

She glanced at the officer when he returned. "And?"

"We're in luck. The place has security cameras, and we're getting a description of the man from the server," he said and turned his focus to me. "Your story has been corroborated, Miss Donovan. We'll call you as soon as we know something."

Know something? The air whooshed out of my lungs. Did they think the man hurt her?

"Do you think that—" I stammered.

He lifted his hand. "We just want to talk to this guy. He's a person of interest at this point. Nothing more."

But my heart thundered in outrage.

Sergeant Brophy leaned across the table. "Here's what's going to happen now, Miss Donovan."

I lifted my face and studied Sergeant Den Brophy. His posture and attitude oozed cop, and his voice soothed me with its concerned tone, like a strong but honeyed hot toddy on a cold winter night.

"We're going to open these curtains," he said. "When we do, you'll see a huge partition. The staff placed it there while we were talking. The other customers think there's a plumbing problem. But we're going to shut the place down now. Potential crime scene. So we want to handle this as fast as we can. Understood?"

"Yes," I said. *Partition. Plumbing. Crime scene. Fast.*

"We're also going to take Justine away from you."

A hollow pang erupted in the center of my chest. "No," I said, blinking away tears. "Please, no."

I knew it was ridiculous. I knew Justine was dead. But if they took her away, I'd never see her again.

"Look," he said in a lowered voice. "I understand you want to stay with her. But you just can't."

What was I going to do without her?

When they pulled her body from the crook of my arm, cold and emptiness swarmed through me. They advised me to look away as they placed Justine on a stretcher with a body bag and secured her. But I couldn't. The efficient, calculating sound of the zipper, the glint of the reflecting candlelight on the metal teeth, and the crinkling, milky gray bag melted as I tried to stand before everything blackened.

Two

I heard the voices first.

"How long is she going to be here?" a male said. Impatient.

"As long as it takes," a female voice replied. No nonsense. "I told you not to move her."

"I've got a business to run," he snapped.

"Not today you don't. Potential crime scene trumps your tea and crumpets."

Gentle pats on my face forced me to open my eyes. I was no longer in the booth. Not only had they evacuated Justine with promptness, but they'd managed to whisk me out of the public space as well.

"Charlotte Donovan?" the orange-haired death investigator asked. I recognized her but wondered why she was hovering over me. "Remember me? I'm Doctor Sweetwater. You passed out and I wanted to make sure you were okay. We've called your mother to fetch you."

"My mother? Damn!" I said before I had time to think. Of course, she wouldn't come herself. She'd send someone. My mother never came into the city. In fact, she hardly left our home on Cloister Island.

Besides, I'd left her that morning in a drunken stupor watching *I Love Lucy* reruns.

"Oh boy. Maybe that was a mistake. The police said she was listed as your emergency contact in your wallet." *I need to switch it to Kate.* "Sorry." She paused. "You've had quite a shock. How are you feeling?"

"I'm fine," I said, trying to sit before a wave of sickness overtook me. She held a trash can while I heaved. *Perhaps I wasn't fine.*

"Sorry," I said after emptying my stomach. The Taco Bell lunch I'd grabbed on the way to Layla's had tasted better going down than coming up. My mouth and throat burned.

"No problem," she replied, reaching for my wrist and cupping it in her hand, checking her watch. "I think you're going to survive." She smiled with reassurance. Then she turned. "She's to stay here until she feels up to leaving. And she's not to leave alone."

"Okay," said an unconcerned male voice in the background.

"I need to run," she said.

When she left, the man came into view. He said nothing to me in the awkward silence.

"Alfredo?" I asked, lying back, sinking further into the pillow.

"He's a bit torn up. He and Justine were friends."

Surprising. She didn't have many male friends.

In a hushed tone, as if he'd just remembered his manners, the man added, "I'm Sam, by the way. I'm sorry for your loss. Were you close?"

Close? I didn't know how to answer. Some days I hated Justine Turner, other days I loved her, and some days I did both. Close? Yes, perhaps, so I nodded as tears pricked at my eyes and ran down my cheeks in a hot stream. She was my boss, I wanted to say. But she was much more to me. She taught me everything I knew about writing, researching, and pulling together a book. Hell, she even taught me more about life than anybody I could think of, even my mother. Eleven years ago, Justine had the heart to hire an intern who was struggling with Lyme disease. "We'll work around it," she'd said. "I like you, Charlotte Donovan."

At the same time, she held my financial life in her hands and wasn't beyond letting me know it on a regular basis.

My muddled brain attempted to form coherent words and sentences. Was it the Lyme? Or was it the shock? I'd been taking my meds and taking care of myself, but sometimes it wasn't enough.

I gazed around the cluttered room. A wall hanging detailed the Heimlich maneuver. Another wall held a poster on the correct method of hand washing. A chart detailed tea varieties. Sam sat at a desk with papers scattered haphazardly on top of it.

"How long had Justine been here before I came in?" I didn't know why it mattered to me. But it did.

He frowned. "We've been trying to figure that out. She ordered a pot of Darjeeling and saffron tea cakes. The pot was half drunk, and the tea cakes were gone. I assume she or her first companion ate them."

"A man?"

"Yes, a man. They're going over the security tapes now."

Our meetings were always private, which is one reason Justine liked the place and her secluded booth. No press milled about to glean any leads on Justine Turner's newest project. They simply were not allowed into the establishment.

"Justine was meeting me. She didn't mention anybody else joining us," I said. Did she? No, I didn't think so. My brain still wasn't operating at full capacity. I must be in shock. "Besides, Justine distrusted men." She insisted all of her editors were women—her doctors, her lawyers—she didn't want to support the "patriarchy."

"Pardon?"

"Let's just say she found men difficult."

11

He rolled his eyes. "Don't we all?"

I sniffed in response. Justine was dead. Dead. Right in the middle of writing a book. How would the book get finished? I stared at the pear-shaped water stain on the ceiling as if it held answers.

"How long have I been out?" I asked.

"About fifteen minutes. Thank God the paramedics slipped Justine out the back. All we need is the word to get around that someone died here."

But someone did. A hot rush of humiliation, tinged with anger, moved through me. *Justine didn't mean to die here, asshat.*

The sound of a turning doorknob and heels on the tile floor interrupted my contemplation.

"Good Lord, woman," a voice I had known since childhood said. "What did you do to yourself?"

"Kate? What—"

"Your grandmother called me," she said. "I'm to bring you home."

Grandma. Of course. She'd probably been fielding calls while Mom slept off her bender.

Kate was one of my few friends in the city. We'd grown up on Cloister Island together. Her parents assigned her the name "Karl" at birth, so in her newly transitioned female identity she was over-the-top feminine, finally allowed to be herself. She stood before me in a floral 1970s yellow chiffon dress, with high platform shoes and shiny cobalt blue beads draped around her neck.

"Home to Cloister?" I couldn't imagine making the trek back now. Not the way I was feeling. A jammed subway train was hard for me to take, even when I was well. Too many people in the city had no sense of personal space. I wasn't sure I could make it to the ferry and across the often-choppy waters. Besides, I planned to meet someone later, which Kate didn't need to know about. She was like a sister, and I hated keeping secrets, but I didn't need another lecture.

Yet at this moment, I longed for my bed in my family's falling-down seaside cottage, and my bedroom view, which mercifully lacked people.

"That's my orders from headquarters," she said. Her jaw was set firm, but the spark in her eyes said volumes. "But I figure if we get you as far as my place in Chelsea, we'll be lucky. You don't look so hot."

"Excuse me if I'm a mess, but my boss just died, sitting at a table in a crowded tea room," I said. *And maybe someone hurt her. Killed her. No, that couldn't be true.*

Kate walked over and helped me sit up. I dizzied, but held fast, not passing out and not throwing up. Success. "I'm so sorry about Justine. Did you hit your head?" Kate asked.

"I don't think so," I said, turning my face toward Sam.

"No," he said. "Your head landed on the, uh, body bag."

I groaned. *Really, Justine? Not only did you die during our meeting, but I also had to pass out on top of your body?* My face fell into my hands as I imagined falling into Justine's body bag.

Dead. Justine was dead.

"You always were so graceful," Kate said, smiling, helping me to stand. She handed me a roll of breath mints. "Just for you. I thought you might get sick."

Thank God for Kate.

"Now where is your bag?" she asked.

Sam reached for my bags.

Kate grabbed my purse and my overnight bag, making eye contact, letting me know she was on to me. My overnight bag was stuffed with clothes, along with my hopes of meeting up with the smoking hot cop I met online.

"Thank you, Sam," I said.

"Oh, don't forget these," he said and held up keys.

I reached for them and examined them. A diamond-encrusted Chanel key ring and a gold Eiffel Tower sparkled next to Justine's keys. They must have fallen out of her bag or jacket. I dropped them into my purse.

"Take care, Charlotte," he said and then ushered us quickly out the back door, past huge unpacked boxes of tea and sacks of flour and sugar, giving me the impression he wanted us gone as soon as possible. I didn't blame him.

After the door closed with a loud clank from behind, Kate and I paused for a moment, getting our bearings. We stood in a narrow backstreet alley, surrounded by dumpsters overflowing with trash and misspelled graffiti on the grimy walls. Traffic noise muffled in between the building and the trash cans.

"Is that supposed to be the word motherf—" I said.

"I always knew we'd end up in an alley together," she interrupted.

"Ha!" I replied. The sound of heels clicking on the ragged side-walk prompted me to turn my head. A woman with a swath of platinum-blonde hair, a tight A-line skirt, and silver pumps rushed past, from one corner of the alley to the other. Her face turned our way for a nanosecond. My heart pounded against my ribs—I swore Jean Harlow herself glanced at me and dashed off.

This Harlow book has brought all the kooks out! Justine had said.

I grabbed Kate. "Did you see that woman?"

"Who?" she said, distracted by her necklace getting tangled with her handbag strap.

"Never mind," I said. The woman had vanished. Kate would never believe me. Hell, I didn't believe me. I blinked. My mind was still in a muddle. *Great, now I'm seeing Jean Harlow look-alikes. Could this day get any worse?*

But with Justine's words fresh in my mind, I ran to the corner and looked down the street.

"Charlotte! What are you doing?" Kate yelled and trailed after me, trying to catch me in her platform shoes.

I realized the woman was gone. I had no idea how she'd vanished so quickly. I caught the scent of her lilac-scented perfume or soap—welcome over the rank trash odor surrounding us. A cold tingle ran up my spine. My grandmother always said that strange feeling meant someone was walking on your grave. Whatever that was supposed to mean.

"What is your problem?" Kate said as she caught up.

I leaned against the building. How to explain?

"There was this blonde," I said between breaths. "She looked like Jean Harlow. And Justine said the book had brought out all the Harlow kooks…and I wondered if she knows something…anything…anything she could tell me about the book…or the man at the tea house…Justine…I don't know. It just seems too weird to be a coincidence after everything Justine said, and then she died, like, right after she said all that." Or maybe I was grasping and delusional, clutching at clouds. Tears came flooding and a big ugly cry overcame me. Kate dropped her bags, opened her arms, and held me as I sobbed.

After several minutes, she peeled me away from her and held me by the shoulders. "Aw, hon, you need to get ahold of yourself. You're just not making any sense. Let's get you some food and a drink or two." She turned and waved at a taxi, which drove by as if she didn't exist.

While we stood there trying to hail a cab, Kate held up my large bag. "It's an overnight bag, isn't it?"

I didn't answer.

"Were you off to meet someone?" Her green eyes slanted, her jaw firmed. Those high cheekbones, perfectly sharp, tilted at me. "Another cop? I don't know about you, woman. You and cops."

"So? Please let's not talk about this. I can't even think right now." I was sore all over from the fall, and my head throbbed. *And I think I just saw Jean Harlow.*

15

"Precisely," she said, grabbing my arm and pulling me down the sidewalk.

"Wait, wait, wait," I said, stopping, dizzy. "Okay, you're right. I'm not up to a date. But give me a moment to text the guy, so he doesn't think I stood him up." I pulled out my phone as we moved over to the building, where it was less crowded, then held it up and grimaced.

"How did this happen?" My shattered phone was dead. Exactly like the rest of my life right now. With Justine gone, I hadn't a clue how I would survive. As I held it up, my hand trembled. Kate noticed.

"Taxi!" she yelled, and this time succeeded.

"We need to get you out of here," she said. "You can call him later. And we're not going to some cop bar, my friend. I know a place with great boneless wings on the Upper East Side."

Sapped and shaky, I didn't argue, even though I hated cabs. And the Upper East Side was expensive.

As we climbed into the back seat together, an oddly familiar fragrance wafted through the cab. Where had I smelled it before? Another chill moved through me as I recognized that the lilac scent was the same one the blonde wore.

I rapped on the plastic seat divider. "Cabby?"

He glanced at me in his rearview mirror.

"Was there just a gorgeous blonde in here?"

He shrugged his shoulders and gestured with his hands. "Sorry, no English."

I grabbed my dark brown hair and pulled it. "Hair. Blonde."

He shrugged again.

Annoyed, I turned to Kate. "You smell it, right?"

"Smell what? The only thing I smell is pleather seats and cheap air freshener."

But my sense of smell always trumped Kate's. Even though I tried to concentrate on the other scents in the cab and the cars lurching by us, the lilac scent lodged in my mind like an unwanted visit from a ghost.

Three

*A*lexandra's Eatery brimmed with the upscale homespun
ambiance that grated on my nerves. But tonight, the doilies
on the table didn't offend me, and the bright floral tablecloths almost
soothed my eye. I still must be in shock.

We found a table next to an outlet to charge my phone and it
buzzed right away when I sat down. "Hello."

"Charlotte Donovan?"

"Yes."

"This is Sergeant Den Brophy of the NYPD, getting back to you
about the security footage. It shows that a man did indeed sit at
Justine's table. When she looked away to speak with the server, he
clearly dropped something in her tea."

A server came up to our table and Kate ordered for us while I
attempted to make sense of what Sergeant Brophy was saying.

"What? What did he put in her tea?"

Kate's eyebrows arched.

"We don't know that yet. We'll be running a tox screen to find out. I'm sorry to inform you this way, but there's a good possibility Justine's death is suspicious."

He didn't say the word "murder," but that's exactly what he meant. Murdered? Justine? The country's most beloved celebrity biographer? Flabbergasted, my mouth dropped open.

"We need you to come up with a list of possible enemies. We also need you to come down to the station to view the recording to see if you recognize the assailant. It's not a great picture, but you may recognize him."

"Okay," I said. "I can do that. I'll come to the station tomorrow afternoon." It came out faster than usual. My nerves were not just frayed, they were ragged and splitting. Justine? Murdered?

I clicked off my cell phone.

"What's wrong?"

The server brought my brandy and sat it in front of me. I took a long pull before I uttered the words.

"The police think Justine was murdered." My voice trembled as I swallowed a sob. A sad end for Justine.

"What? That's crazy. The cops just like to stir things up. Who'd want to kill Justine? Everybody loved her."

I sipped my brandy, trying to will away the dread, wishing Kate was right. "Not true. She's been through several lawsuits and has had plenty of hate mail."

"Hate mail? What kind of hate mail?"

The brandy warmed me. "People who didn't like what she wrote. Some fans feel an ownership over their favored star. Sometimes distantly related relatives of the stars wanting money or threatening a lawsuit."

Kate sipped from her wine glass. "Why do they think she was murdered?"

I relayed what I'd learned and Kate was at a loss for words, which didn't happen often.

About midway through my second brandy and our third order of boneless hot wings, I steadied. The fog was lifting.

Ideas crystallized as my head cleared. Justine's words echoed: *"This Harlow book has brought all the kooks out!"* I willed away the blonde, brushing it off, telling myself I hadn't been able to get a good view if her. Of course, Harlow was on my mind, and the woman was a platinum blonde. A trick of the mind.

But what exactly did Justine mean by *Harlow kooks*? Obsessed fans? Collectors?

As I considered it all, sitting at the bar, I hoped my exhaustion was from the shock of the day and not another bout of Lyme creeping up on me. I decided not to haul my weary body all the way to Chelsea, let alone Cloister Island—not a mere subway ride away, but also a ferry ride. I wondered if I could sneak my way into Justine's place, which was a few blocks to the north. Would her cousin from Florida mind? Would the management? Did they even have to know?

I needed to find a place to lay my head. I'd never been inside Justine's place and had no idea what to expect, but it seemed like the best option. I felt like a zombie, hollow and lifeless. I'd pushed myself too far.

I reached into my bag and found the glittering key chain. "Justine's keys," I said, holding them up. "Let's stay at her place tonight. It's right around the corner."

"Are you crazy?" Kate asked. Her eyes were as wide as the moon. "You're on your own," she said, lowering her voice. "I'm not sleeping in a dead woman's apartment."

"You're kidding me, right?"

She shuddered. For all her wise-cracking ways, she was such a chicken sometimes. But then again, Kate was always a more stereotypical girl than I was.

"I don't think it's legal to camp out in a dead woman's apartment," she said in an almost-whisper.

"Probably not. But I'm her assistant and can claim ignorance if I'm caught. It's just one night." The key chain sparkled in my hand. One night in a luxurious apartment. Justine's apartment. The idea of being surrounded by her things somehow comforted me. Besides, perhaps I'd find answers to this crazy day there.

"I'll walk you to her place, but I'm not going inside," Kate said and shivered.

∞

Opening the door into Justine's home was like opening a crypt. A layer of dust covered everything with a gray, murky glow. The maid must be due to visit. Or Justine hadn't actually been living there recently. Odd. But sometimes she escaped the city and wrote elsewhere. I made a mental note to check on it, along with the countless other details Justine's death had undoubtedly left me with. Which didn't completely surprise me.

Almost twelve years of fact-checking, researching, and tending to her schedule had left me nearly in charge of Justine's day-to-day life. Why should it be different in her death? For the past three years, I'd also been writing more under Justine's name. All hoping that someday, I'd write my own books—real biographies, not the pop biographies Justine wrote.

No, I wanted to write thick, wordy, almost academic tomes.

"Who the hell is going to read an eight-hundred-page biography of Hildegard Von Bingen?" Justine's words rang in my ears.

"Who indeed?" I said out loud and walked over to the window.

A few minutes earlier, I had successfully entered through the back door of the apartment building. The security guard never glanced up from behind the desk. The doorman was busy with a crowd of rowdy partiers in the lobby.

The address: the exclusive L'Ombragé, which was in the same tony Upper East Side area where many celebrities lived, such as Madonna, Steve Martin, and the like. But, of course, Justine was one of them. She would never admit it. She liked to think she maintained a journalistic distance from these folks. But when you dined with Meryl Streep regularly, how could you be objective when writing about her? *"Objectivity? Who has time for objectivity?"*

While Justine's specialty was the movie stars of the '30s and '40s, she released a contemporary biography every few years. Her biography of Meryl must have netted her somewhere in the millions. Rare among writers of any breed.

So I understood she was wealthy, but I had no idea how she lived her life. I'd only been as far as the grand marbled lobby, where I would drop research off for her. Contrary to what many people think, not all research is online, so I sometimes found myself in the stacks of some mildewed library, making copies of old books or checking out films and journals.

Now I wandered through Justine's apartment, surprised by more than the fine layer of dust over the heavy drapes, bookcases, and furniture. Obviously, nobody had been here for a while. Where had Justine been the last few weeks of her life? Why didn't she mention that to me? Or had she and I'd just forgotten? I struggled with memory at times—a fact of my Lyme disease.

The expansive apartment, which took up the entire fourteenth floor, made me feel like Alice in Wonderland, roaming halls and rooms, not quite knowing where to go next. The long, shiny tiled hallway seemed too vast to explore now as weariness overtook me. A floor-to-ceiling painting of Greta Garbo greeted me as I turned back. Satin glass sconces, with fine crystals dangling, set off the face of the woman who'd begun life as a pauper in Stockholm. Justine would not write about Garbo. She claimed she could not objectively write about her. *"Or at least that's what the press would say. She was a huge lesbian icon. Sort of like I am now."* Then uproarious, stomach-jiggling laughter.

I walked into a library and imagined Justine sitting behind the desk, gazing up at me from beneath her heavy, round, red-rimmed glasses. I moved toward the chaise longue in front of a floor-to-ceiling window with top panes of stained-glass pink roses—so delicate it almost made me cry. I'd barely explored the place, but this spot drew me in.

Could I get away with staying here? My heart thudded in my chest. I was too tired to worry about it. Tonight this overstuffed chaise was mine. Though I could muster the bravery to stay here, I didn't think I could sleep in Justine's bed and had no energy to find the guest room.

I undressed and lay on the chaise, pulled a soft throw over me, curled into a ball, and fell into a deep sleep. I dreamed of Justine and, of all people, Jean Harlow.

Jean Harlow's life read like a shallow, tragic Cinderella story. She became a star, but not by hungering for it and clawing her way to the top. She was someone's idea of beautiful and happened to be in the right place at the right time. But here's where one of the few interesting personality traits of Jean came into play. She didn't rest on her sexy laurels. She was aware of her lack of acting skill, and once she was a star, she worked hard at becoming a better one. Now, that interested me. The fact that her mother managed her career, and life up to a certain point, was commonplace. It was a cliché. Many young starlets' mothers managed their careers. But what was it about Jean that prompted her to work so hard? Midwestern values? Overcompensation for guilt at being lucky? What?

When I awakened, thinking of my dream, Jean, and the blonde on the street, it reminded me that I hadn't heard back from Maude Verez, the psychologist we sometimes worked with to help piece together personalities of our subjects. I was waiting on an email from her about some questions I had about Jean Harlow.

I stretched and reached for my phone, now charged and working. Unfortunately. Another missed call from my mom. I ignored it. I wasn't up to her drunken tirades. Not today.

After I found the bathroom and the coffee and figured out how to work the fancy coffee maker, I took my daily elixir into her office.

My fingers pecked at Justine's keyboard, and I felt thankful that we'd updated her passwords when we talked on the phone a week ago. I had more than every right and reason to be here. But my nerves were jumbled, sitting in my ex-boss's home, in what was her private office on her private desktop computer. Where was her laptop? I shook off the chill moving along my spine, and the image of my grandmother crossing herself.

I drank my strong, black, soothing coffee.

As I jiggled the computer mouse, Justine's screen filled with unanswered email. Most of which were typical junk messages, except the notes from her publisher. Sorting through her email would take hours. My lungs squeezed with a sudden lack of air. How would I handle everything?

First, I needed to inform her publisher and agent of her death. I hesitated. It seemed so final.

"The big D: nothing more final."

Opening my laptop, I wrote and sent off the two emails, then continued scanning Justine's inbox on her computer. Something odd caught my eye. A word—"kill." Right in the subject line.

"I'll kill you," it said.

What was this? Who would write such a thing to Justine? My attention zoomed in on the email and my pulse quickened. I clicked on it. The date? Two days ago.

"I swear if you go public with this I'll kill you," it said.

I scanned further.

Justine had responded once. *"You don't scare me."* Typical of her.

I shuddered. Who was this? What was going on here? The rest of it had been encrypted. There was nothing left to read.

Why hadn't Justine told me about this? Sure, she had gotten threats from people over the years, but not like this. This person was threatening to kill her, not sue her. And it was two days before she died.

Which subject was she being threatened about? Jean Harlow? What mattered so much in the Jean Harlow story that someone would threaten Justine's life?

I mentally sorted through the past twenty-four hours. Justine had insisted I drop everything, meet her at Layla's, and not tell anybody. When I arrived at the tea room, she was distraught. Despite what Kate said, I thought it was in fact possible that this mysterious man killed her. He'd sat at her table and placed something in her tea. She'd mentioned Jean Harlow kooks. Now, this. Someone *had* threatened her life. I understood now that Justine had been in trouble. Hard to ignore with the word "kill" on the dark blue computer screen.

Four

I scanned Justine's computer files for any more threats. I found nothing. But knowing Justine, if there were more, she either deleted them or printed them off to stick in her files.

Her paper filing system was as haphazard as her computer filing system, but at least it should be alphabetical. I opened the creaky wooden file cabinet and tucked in, found the H's, searched through the H folders, and Harlow was not there. Might she have used Jean? I examined the J's. Nothing about Jean.

What the hell?

How about T for threats?

D for death?

No success.

I sat down in her desk chair, considering emptying the file cabinet and launching an all-out hunt. No death threat file was one thing, but the Harlow research files? Research on her work in progress? There should be scads of material. I'd delivered some of it myself. Where was it?

My cell phone's beep interrupted my thoughts. I could barely make out the caller ID on my shattered screen.

"Hey Kate," I answered.

"How are you feeling? Better?"

"I don't know," I said. "Something's off. I can't find any Harlow files, and it's just a mess."

"Have you eaten anything?" Kate asked after a beat.

"No, but I've had plenty of coffee. My brain is functioning, thank you very much."

"Let's have lunch and then we'll talk. You never do well on an empty stomach. Who does?" Kate said and laughed a bit.

"Okay." I was suddenly famished, as if the mention of food reminded my stomach of its emptiness. A late lunch might be just what I needed. "Where do you want to meet?"

∞

I spotted her right away, standing on the sidewalk in her canary-yellow pantsuit. I smiled warily. Kate's eyes swept up and down, taking me in. "We should duck into the bathroom. You need some cold water and a touch-up. Or something."

We walked into Petey's Pub, a darkened bar, wood-paneled, brass sconces with kelly green shades, and found the ladies' room, where Kate preened over my face with her makeup. It was like applying a tiny band-aid over a gaping bullet wound.

Kate was unaware that one of the busiest cop bars was next to this place. Okay, maybe I did know too much about the local cops. Some women like kinky sex, some prefer grand romantic gestures or dark, swarthy men. Me? I liked cops. Almost every man I'd ever dated was a cop. Of course, I'd dated a few others, but I always preferred the cops. Still, Kate made too much of it.

Kate sighed. "It's the best I can do. Your mom was right about you. You can't hide when you don't feel well. Even with those gorgeous blue eyes of yours."

I blanched at the mention of my mom, who I'd left passed out on the couch yesterday and hadn't called back. Most of the time, I tried to sober her up before I ventured into the city. But when Justine called, her urgent tone had prompted me to leave the house in a rush.

"Get here as soon as possible," she'd said. "And don't tell anybody where you're going. Do you understand?"

Justine could be a little dramatic. *"I'm a drama queen. I admit it. So what?"*

"Now, let's find a seat," Kate said, dropping her eyeliner into her bag and leaning on the chipped Formica counter "My feet are killing me."

"Welcome to the sisterhood," I said, and grinned as we walked off in search of seats.

I ordered a beer with a burger and Kate ordered a salad and wine. I had to admit, the food was doing me good. My mind cleared even more from yesterday. I was convinced something was wrong. "I think the police are right. Someone killed Justine."

"You said that, but what would the motive be?" Kate emptied her wine glass with one more swallow. "She was ancient. Didn't owe anybody any money. Wasn't involved in shady enterprises."

"Can I get you ladies anything else?" the bartender asked. A large man with a rough face, a crooked broken nose, and botched plastic surgery, he moved like every step hurt. I imagined he was a fighter. Everybody in New York City had a day job while chasing their dreams. Acting. Writing. Fighting?

"I don't think so. Let's settle up," Kate said, then turned to me. "I know you had a weird day yesterday. Do me a favor and get some rest. Don't go off on some research junket and stay up for days."

"Not likely," I said. Kate understood me. I functioned most of the time with my Lyme. Sometimes it overcame me. But when I was on task, I was single-minded. Research was my jam. "Back to Justine. Something was very off. She also talked about Jean Harlow kooks."

Kate shook her head. "Don't try to make sense of this. Remember, she was either in the middle of a heart attack or drugged. The blood might not have been getting to her brain. She may have been hallucinating."

"True," I said and drank my last bit of beer. I just wanted it to all go away.

"Okay," Kate said. "So if she was threatened and killed by the same person, the cops will find them. It's out of your hands. It shouldn't matter to you."

"It does!" I almost yelled, then quieted. "I want to see justice for her. Besides, nine chances out of ten I'm going to finish the Harlow book. I need to know why she was threatened."

Kate leaned closer to me and cupped my hand in hers. "You need to talk and think about something else. Seriously. Let's get your mind off of all this." She paused. "Let's talk about your mom or Cloister gossip or cops. Yeah, cops."

"What? Why?" But I was already smiling.

"I've got five hundred bucks that says you can't stay away from cops for a month," she said with an ornery grin.

"What do you mean, stay away?"

"Don't sleep with any cops for four weeks. Bet you can't do it."

"Of course I can. What's this about?"

I half expected Kate to go off on me. Instead, she quieted. "Because, my friend, you're searching for your father and you're never going to find him in the arms of a guy who just happens to be a cop."

"Are you a shrink now?" I said. Why did she have to bring up my cop father? A man I barely remembered. A man who'd disappeared when I was six years old and who we now presumed dead.

If his disappearance was influencing me at all, it would be just the opposite. I should hate cops. At times, I wish I did.

The bartender's back was turned to us as he fussed with the cash register. A grizzled, blond, surfer-dude-looking guy sidled up to Kate and studied her. Overtly. His eyes swept along the length of her several times. She ignored him, leaning closer to me.

I glared at her. I enjoyed men, and if they happened to be cops, so what? It wasn't as if all my dates were one night stands, but even if they were, I failed to see Kate's issue with it. She'd had plenty, both before and after her transition, and with both men and women.

Leather-clad men with amplifiers and instruments gathered near a corner platform as the crowd thickened and the lights dimmed. Several women dressed in the shortest skirts I've ever seen grouped in a circle near the band.

Kate continued. "Prove to yourself you don't have a daddy issue. Don't sleep with any cops for at least a month."

"I can do it," I said. Still, the bittersweet burn of humiliation waved through me. I didn't know why.

The bartender gimped up to the bar and placed the bill down. Kate stretched for it. The man next to her ordered a beer. "Can I buy you ladies a drink?" he said.

"No thanks," Kate quipped and turned even further toward me. She plunked her red-leather bag on the table and slipped her hand inside for her credit card. "Are we on?"

"Hell yes, you're on!" I dug into my bag and searched for Justine's keys. The easiest five hundred dollars I would ever earn, and man, I could use the money. I still owed thousands on my last hospital stay. *And I just lost my job.*

"Are you two sure I can't buy you a drink?" the man asked again.

Kate stood and towered over him. "We said no, okay? Back off."

"What a bitch," the man grumbled into his beer.

"What did you call me?" Her voice rose as she shoved aside her bar stool. Kate was a deep-voiced woman, and when she was pissed, it deepened more.

"Hey, hey, hey!" the bartender said, nodding his head toward the door. "If you ladies are leaving, it's best you go now."

Kate pulled her bag to her shoulder and waltzed off with me trailing her. "What an asshole. The world is full of them, isn't it?" She turned to hug me. "I've got to run. Late meeting with Japanese buyers. Where are you off to?"

"I'm heading to the police station, remember?"

She laughed and pointed her finger at me. "Remember our bet!"

"How could I forget?" I said as she sashayed off to talk fashion with the Japanese.

My gaze dropped to my red sneakers. *Feet, don't fail me now.*

Thirteen short blocks was nothing back in the day, before my diagnosis, when I lived in the East Village with three roommates and a closet-sized bedroom. After retreating to my childhood home on Cloister Island, and several hospital stays, my Lyme was now manageable. Today, I'd stop and rest every few blocks as a precaution.

I edged along the Central Park sidewalk, glimpsing the Jacqueline Kennedy Onassis Reservoir, trees and flowers in bloom, sunlight streaming through thick brush. It might have been the perfect spring day, except for the word "murder" fresh on my mind.

Five

The officer behind the counter clicked away at his keyboard, spotted me, and held up a finger. I nodded.

When he finished, he glanced up at me. "How can I help you?" He was young, early twenties, uniformed, and had soft brown Bambi eyes.

"I'm here to see Sergeant Den Brophy. My name is Charlotte Donovan," I said.

"Hold on a minute, Ms. Donovan," he said, picking up the phone.

I peeked around the small reception area. Clean, institutional-white bricked walls held trophies, encased badges, and awards. Papers, metal pipes, and white-and-red metal boxes donned the walls too, along with reward posters.

"He'll be right here," the officer said and turned back to his keyboard.

Soon the door opened and Sergeant Den Brophy shot me a smile, which landed in places in me I willed myself not to think about. *Not today.*

"Ms. Donovan, please come in," he said.

He led me through a snaking path between cubicles and desks. The scent of stale coffee and industrial lemon soap hung in the air. We landed in a darker room with a monitor and another uniformed officer—a woman. "This is officer Grace Callahan," Den said. "She's an intake specialist and will take another statement from you. Then we'll review the security footage, okay?"

I shook the officer's hand, realizing then how sweaty my palms were. What was I so nervous about? It wasn't as if I'd done anything wrong. But my heart raced. My skin heated. Was it warm in here? Or was it just me?

"Another statement?" I said as Den gestured for me to sit. I sat on a metal folding chair, which made an unpleasant squeaking noise.

"It's just procedure," Den said, taking the seat next to her. "Okay, let's start from the beginning."

The woman smiled at me. "Go on, please." Her fingers hovered over at the keyboard.

I recounted the day and Justine's death and answered their prompts and questions as best I could.

"Would you like some water? Coffee?" Den asked me after I gave my statement.

"Water, please," I said.

"I'm finished," said Officer Callahan, standing up after closing her lap top. She stretched her hand across the table to shake mine again. "Pleasure meeting you. Good luck."

"Thank you," I said.

Den brought a miniature water bottle in, his thick fingers making it appear even smaller. "We're doing these little bottles now. More environmentally friendly." He handed me the bottle.

I sipped from it. Never had water tasted so good.

He reached for a remote and flipped on the monitor.

My heart lurched into my mouth. For there was Justine, sitting at her table, facing the camera, checking her cell phone, smiling up at Alfredo, drinking tea. So alive. Less than twenty-four hours ago. I drank my water. It did little to quench my thirst.

"Are you okay?"

"Yes," I said. My voice a hoarse whisper.

Then a man walked up on camera. He faced Justine, so his back was to the lens. His arm reached across and patted her on the shoulder—a quick gesture. But as he took his seat across from her, Justine's face showed, and her distress was obvious. Her face was red with anger as she clutched at her chest. Her eyes darted back and forth—she never wanted to cause a scene. I read her lips as she said, *"Get the fuck out of here."*

He didn't move. Alfredo came up to the table and offered him tea, took his order, and Justine gained her composure. The man sat for a few more minutes, blocking Justine's face, but at one point his face turned to Alfredo and the other half caught on the camera. Just a slice of it.

"There," Den said, pressing the pause button. "Does he look familiar?"

The man's upper face hid in a shadow, but not his distinct pointy chin and a jagged scar along his lower left jaw. I shivered and studied the grainy image for something, anything, familiar about that chin, that scar. "No, not at all."

"We have a composite one of our artists came up with. It's conjecture, but based on what we can see here, he may look like this," Den said, sliding a paper toward me. "We've faxed a copy to the tea house as well."

Lizard-like, the man in the drawing stared back at me as if mocking me. I'd never seen him before in my life and was sure I'd have remembered if I did. If the drawing was a good rendering.

I shook my head slowly. "I'm sorry. Not in the least bit familiar."

"You've worked as her assistant for how many years?"

"Eleven."

"You've never seen him?"

"I've never seen half the people she works with or knows. I work from home." Images of my makeshift office in my family's rundown cottage poked at me. "Cloister Island."

"I want you to be certain you've never seen him," Den said after a few minutes. His mouth narrowed, his dimples pronounced.

"I don't have a very good memory sometimes. I suffer from Lyme disease. But I do have a pretty good recall for faces, and that face? I'd remember."

He studied me and grinned slow and sideways. If he looked at me like that in a bar, I'd be all over him. Maybe I was misreading, but the spark of attraction was mutual. Even in this rather unappealing environment. Still, his blue eyes sent shocks of electricity-like waves through me. Kate's face and poking finger flashed in my mind's eye.

I wanted to tell him about the death threats on Justine's computer. But I wasn't sure I should be staying at Justine's place; in other words, if it was legal or not. The more I mulled it over, the more I thought Kate was right. So I kept the nugget of information to myself. For now.

"Did Justine have any enemies?"

"How much time do you have?" I said and laughed nervously.

He grinned. "Okay. Then let's pick the top three. We'll move down the list as methodically as we can."

"It's hard to imagine any of them would kill her. I mean, the people I can think of are writers, Hollywood types, and collectors. Not exactly your murdering kind."

Den frowned. "I wish there were a kind. We see everything. Everyday people going off and killing their neighbor, their lovers ..."

The word "lover" hung in the air and vibrated between us. I dropped my gaze.

"Severn Hartwell would be at the top of the list," I said, lifting my eyes, attempting not to watch his lips as he spoke. Intellectually, I had this. But my hormones had dirty little minds of their own.

"Who's that?"

"He's another pop biographer. Justine's biggest competitor. He wanted to write a Jean Harlow biography but she snagged a contract and made a big announcement, thwarted him." I couldn't help but smile. *Justine*. I dug through my purse for my phone. "I have his number right here."

Den slid a white sheet of paper across the table, along with a pen. I copied down the relevant details. "Okay, who would be the second on your list?" he asked.

I mentally sifted through the possibilities. "There was a Hollywood collector...what was his name?" I scanned the contacts on my phone, searching for the email I'd saved because I'd found it deliciously funny. He was a man who collected the underwear of starlets, especially those from the Golden Era of Hollywood. "Ah, yes. Here he is, Kevin Jonquil."

I wrote down the contact information. "I don't have his number, but I'm sure you can find it. But there's his email."

"A collector?" Den smirked. *Oh. That sideways smirk.*

"Yes, it's a thing," I said. "This guy wouldn't give up. He insisted that he knew about Justine's secret collection of Greta Garbo underwear. He wanted it and was prepared to pay top dollar."

"Underwear?" Den whistled, lifting his left eyebrow. "Damn."

"But she didn't have it, and he threatened her. Didn't believe her."

"Sounds, I don't know, creepy."

I thought a moment. "It is. And it's sad. So many of these people have more money than they know what to do with and they become obsessed and will do anything to acquire an item with the right provenance. I'll never understand it."

My own grandmother could get a bit obsessed, but not over Hollywood items. She owned an antique store on Cloister Island that did a brisk business, especially during tourist season.

"And the other person?"

"Kyle Anderson," I said.

"The Hollywood producer?" Den's voice rose a decibel.

I nodded. "Yes indeed." I wrote his numbers and email address on the paper. I'd memorized it years ago. "He became such a nuisance that we had to get a restraining order." I paused and handed him a card. "Here's one more. Gregory Horvath, a member of Hollywood Cartel Collections."

"I gotta hand it to you, Ms. Donovan—"

"Please call me Charlotte."

"Okay, Charlotte. All this is very helpful. You must have been one kickass assistant."

Damned straight. "I'm glad to help. If Justine was murdered, I want to see justice done," I said.

"Keep in touch, Charlotte," he said as I stood to leave. He handed me his card. "If you need anything, or think of anything of relevance, anything at all, please call."

My eyes met his, and a gleam sparked between us as his left eyebrow hitched. Kate's five hundred dollars beckoned, so I reserved my "come hither" expression for another day.

Six

As much as I hated to, I needed to check in with home. Not sure my mom was in any shape to hold a conversation, I called my grandmother while I sat at a café near Justine's apartment building and waited for the police to leave. I was certain they were searching her place, as they should be. Scents of some sweet concoction baking in the café's kitchen poked at me, but I had no appetite. Highly unusual for me.

"Charlotte Donovan, where have you been?" my grandmother said.

"Justine died and I've been stuck in town," I said, running my finger along the edge of the saucer holding my tea cup.

"We know that. I'm sorry to hear about her death," she said, and paused. I pictured her crossing herself. "Are you okay?"

Scuffling noise came over the phone. She was probably cleaning as she spoke to me. Perhaps sweeping the floor.

"I'm holding up," I said. "But I'm going to need to stay in town a while longer." I lifted the cup to my lip and drank my tea.

"Oh sweetie, how will you manage? Everything's so expensive."

"I'm staying at Justine's place."

She didn't respond.

"At least until we know what's going on with the funeral and so on. I need to be here." I didn't want to tell her that Justine was murdered. No point in upsetting her. "How's Mom?" I asked, and then exhaled.

"She's sober for now," she replied. "She's been asking for you. She said she called."

"I'm sorry, Gram, it's been crazy here. Please tell her I'm okay and I'll be home as soon as I can be," I said. "I'll call her soon. I don't want to talk with her if she's drinking." A young woman sat down at the table next to me with a huge blueberry tart. The scent of it was giving me a sugar high.

"I don't understand why you need to be there," Gram said in an accusing tone.

I swallowed the last of my peppermint tea, which was quality, some of the best peppermint tea I'd ever had. You'd think all of it was the same. But it's not. "I'm Justine's assistant. I need to take care of things." My voice cracked.

"Oh Charlotte," Gram said in a sympathetic tone. "I'll never understand your devotion to that woman."

Gram didn't care for Justine or her treatment of me. Sometimes, I agreed with her. But now that Justine was murdered, and I'd been there when she died, none of it mattered. Everything else about our relationship fell away. She didn't deserve to die like that. Nobody did.

I remembered Sergeant Den Brophy and my list of possible murderers. *Add my sweet little Gram to the list.* Oddly enough, the thought made me smile.

"Like the best caviar or champagne, I'm an acquired taste."

One of Justine's favorite expressions, which spoke to the way she lived her life, was "never ask for permission." *"If I waited for permission, I'd never get anywhere."* As a younger woman she'd waltzed right into places she shouldn't have in order to get the interview or the research she wanted. *"The trick is to blend in and act like you're supposed to be there. If you get caught, be polite and act stupid. Works every time."*

I certainly was testing her motto by staying in her place. But just to be on the safe side, I'd wait until dark before I entered through the back door of the building again. And I'd wait for the cop car to leave. I rose to my feet and slid my bag onto my shoulder, then walked out of the cafe and stood for a moment, with the noise and bustle all around me. A line of cabs trailed on the street. A sausage vendor yelled at a pedicab driver as he whizzed by. I caught the whiff of something sour and rank. It vanished as quickly as it came.

I turned toward Central Park, walking along the clean, wide sidewalks and catching glimpses of the setting sun between buildings. The Upper East Side, with its chic high-rise apartment buildings, classic brownstone neighborhoods, and elegant architecture reminded me of my youth and my dream to be a famous writer like Justine. I imagined I'd live here after writing my first bestselling book. But after my Lyme diagnosis, the city was too much for me. While at one point it had inspired and energized me, after I became sick it did nothing but drain me.

A woman dressed in a short, stunning, peacock blue silk dress walked by me with long leggy strides, the silk fluttering around her. I moved to the corner to cross the street. The light changed, and I marched. Suddenly a bright silverish smear of hair flicked in the sunlight and caught my eye. I followed the gleam. There she was. I was certain of it! The same blonde from the day before, moving at a brisk pace up Fifth Avenue. Spotting this woman twice in two days? More than a coincidence.

I picked up my pace and headed in her direction. Who was she? Did she know anything about Justine's murder? A surge of energy and adrenaline zipped through me and I moved like a linebacker, dodging swiftly through the sidewalk crowds. "Hey!" I yelled at her. She didn't turn her head, but her stride hastened to almost a run.

"Watch it, lady!" a man said as I ran by him. Even at that speed, with my short legs I might not have reached her. But I wasn't ready to give up. I inhaled deeply. My surge of energy was diminishing. I estimated I might make it another block. But wait—where was she? She'd vanished. Probably ducked in to an alley or restaurant. But where?

Sweat poured from me as I found a wall and leaned against it. After all that, she'd disappeared. Once again.

Seven

After my unplanned sprint down Fifth Ave, I headed to Justine's apartment, spent. Good thing the cops were gone.

Once again, I had no problem getting into her place. And once again, I took up residence on the chaise longue, not having the ambition or heart to explore.

I examined the apartment and noted the police hadn't seemed to touch anything—or if they had, they had already replaced things.

I tossed and turned, slipping in and out of sleep, the face of the platinum blonde haunting me in my dreams and my waking. Finally, after exhausting myself, I suppose, I fell into a deep sleep, only to be awakened by my cell phone's ring.

When I was alert enough to find it, it had stopped ringing. I started to fall back asleep after glancing at it to see the time, through the cracks on the screen. I truly needed to get my screen fixed. Who would be calling me at the ungodly hour of eight a.m.? I didn't recognize the phone number. Just as I drifted off, it rang again.

"Hello," I managed to say.

"Ms. Charlotte Donovan?" the official-sounding female voice on the other end of the line said.

"Yes."

"I'm Susan Strohmeyer, Justine Turner's attorney."

Already?

"I've been trying to reach you since yesterday. I'm so glad to get through to you."

"I'm sorry. It's been crazy, as you can imagine," I said, lying back into my pillow. No need to uncurl myself from the blanket. "How can I help you?"

"First, I'm very sorry for your loss," she said.

I paused, choking back a sob. It was too early in the morning for such a harsh reality. But it was true. Justine had died sitting at her favorite table at Layla's. She was murdered. I'd harbored a tiny sliver of hope that it was all a bad dream. "Yes, yes. Thank you." My voice trailed off. I swallowed the burn creeping up my throat.

"I'm going to cut to the chase," Susan said. "Justine left a lot of instructions on the funeral. All the planning has been taken care of. This is so typical of her, isn't it? In any case, the few decisions left to be made are yours to make. She had careful instructions about it."

"Me?" I blinked, trying to wake myself up if I were dreaming. Where was I? Clothes were scattered haphazardly across a chair. I was surrounded by floor-to-ceiling dusty books. The desk was full of papers, folders, and red pens. Always red. Okay, I concluded, this isn't a dream. I was in Justine's library-office.

"You're aware, of course, that she had no family. Only this cousin in Florida, but they weren't close."

My chest filled with a hollow pang. I didn't reply. I couldn't. Waves of darkness pressed on me. I pulled my blanket in tighter. *I might stay on this chaise all day.*

"So you've got some decisions to make. Once Judith arrives in town later today, we'll be reading the will. Even after it's read, it will take some time to settle matters. But Justine asked that we get this taken care of within a few days after her death."

I inhaled and found it hard to exhale. *Wills. Death.*

"Are you still there?"

"Yes." I let out a slow breath. My heart kicked in, rapping hard against my rib cage. I stared up the paneled ceiling.

"It's going to take some time to sort through all of it, you understand. There are stocks, savings, other investments. Sometimes the paperwork in probate is astounding. Let's schedule an appointment soon. I appreciate that this must all seem like it's happening very quickly, but maybe it will help to know this is what Justine wanted. As I say, it's going to take time to sort through. My assistant will call to set up an appointment with you, very soon."

"Yes, okay," I said.

I sat up, flung the covers off, and stood on the parquet floor, glimpsing my bare feet on the tile. *Those are the very ugly feet of a competent woman, a woman who must attend a will reading, take care of matters. For Justine. I can do this.*

"Do you mind if I bring a friend with me?" I asked. I paced between the desk and one of the bookcases.

"Not at all."

After we hung up, I made a pot of coffee, sat down at the desk, and flipped open my laptop, half expecting emails from Justine. Of course there were none for today. But there were several from a few days ago. I wasn't sure I could read them. Not yet.

Just like that, there would never be any more emails from Justine.

My chest squeezed with loss as I sat there, surrounded by her things. Eventually, I'd have to go home and leave this luxurious little hideaway of mine. But still, I was at loose ends. What was going to happen with the Jean Harlow book? I wasn't even certain it would be published without Justine. But we were about halfway there and

I found myself itching to dig in. Once I found the work in progress, that is. But I stopped myself. I wasn't being paid anymore, was I? Who knew what was going to happen?

I should be searching the help-wanted ads. But I had no idea where to even begin. I drew in a breath as I scrolled through my email. Of course, there were return emails from Justine's agent and editor.

From her agent, Natalie Vega:

"Dear Charlotte,
I'm heartbroken. Please advise about the arrangements. Let's chat about the book soon.
Natalie"

Let's chat about the book soon? What was there to chat about unless they wanted me to finish the book?

From her editor:

"Dear Charlotte,
I'm so sorry to hear about this. We'll be in touch soon.
Lucille Everheart"

Reading between the lines, I assumed the project was still a go and started to click on my work files, but then Justine's voice rang in my mind: *"Not one word until there's money in the bank."* Her number one rule. She was such a mercenary. She'd write about anyone, anything, as long as she'd get paid for it. *"Don't ever work for free,"* she'd told me on countless occasions.

"Okay," I said out loud. "I'll wait."

But in the meantime, the Jean Harlow twin haunted me. She wasn't a part of the Jean Harlow project. But she kept turning up. Did she know Justine? Who the hell was she? I typed "Jean Harlow look-alike" into Google and got nothing of any relevance at all. Only one Jean Harlow impersonator for hire, who didn't even resemble the real deal. A blonde wig and a slinky gown wasn't going to do it. Sorry, folks.

The woman I'd seen twice was disturbingly twin-like. Sure, I hadn't gotten a close-up view, but the second time was better than the first. The shape of her cheeks was exactly that of Harlow's. Plump and doll-like. She was much taller than Harlow. Jean was a tiny woman, standing at five feet one inch.

Imagine being born resembling Jean Harlow. What would you do with that gift?

My phone beeped. It was Kate.

"Hey," I said.

"Hey yourself. Where are you?"

"Justine's place."

Silence. Then, "You're crazy. You know that? What if someone catches you?"

I gazed around at the office where I sat: the chandelier, the books, the deep wood panels and floor-to-ceiling windows with the lovely, delicate stained-glass rose. "It would be so worth it."

Eight

Justine's last wishes were not ordinary. This didn't surprise me.
But the opulence of the Club Circe, where her memorial and wake were being held, was more than surprising. It was shocking. I'd read about these private women's clubs in the city, of course, but never imagined I'd be inside one.

"Jesus," I breathed.

"He's not going to help you now, honey," Kate said, sliding her arm through mine.

We were at least thirty minutes early and the place was already packed. I searched for Den or any of his ilk—but true to his word, I couldn't spot him. "I'll be like a fly on the wall," he'd said. *Den. So hot. A little over three weeks left until my bet with Kate is over. But who's counting?*

A huge, softly lit but sparkling chandelier hung from the center of the grand foyer. A circular pattern with, I assume, the goddess Circe was on the floor—mosaic tiles, pink and gray. Two sets of red-carpeted stairs curled upward and led to a central upstairs space.

"Which way do we go?" Kate asked.

"Let's follow the crowd."

Although the room was full of people, the ambiance was quiet, hushed, reverent, as if we were in a cathedral. Someone blew their nose. Another person sniffed. A nervous laugh erupted.

Then, seemingly out of nowhere, a woman dressed in a tuxedo approached me. "Charlotte Donovan?"

I nodded.

"Right this way, please," she said, waving her well-manicured fingers donned with at least two sparkling green gems, which I think were emeralds.

She led us down a black-and-pink-tiled hallway flanked with ornately framed paintings of women I probably should have recognized. Historically important women. Powerful women. A whiff of a floral fragrance caught my nose. Then I smelled leather. Old leather. If these walls could talk, they'd speak about the secrets of generations of wealthy, educated, powerful women.

"You are to be seated in front," she said, with a slight British accent I hadn't noticed earlier.

My heart raced. Why? Why had I agreed to this? Why did it have to be this way?

I glanced at Kate, who smiled and nodded. "You've got this."

Not only had I agreed to finish the Jean Harlow book, but I'd also conceded to a very public announcement about it—during her memorial service. "Part of the deal," Justine's editor, Lucille, had said. "It's the only way to go." The publisher would pay me the rest of Justine's advance for me to finish writing the biography.

I sucked in air. Justine had faith in me. I wasn't going to let her down. As uncomfortable as the public aspect of this made me, I was up to the challenge of finishing the book. I wanted to finish it. Unfinished business was not going to fly—it would pick at my more than slightly OCD nature. But why did they insist on making this announcement at Justine's service?

Kate and I took our seats. While others were being seated, I tried to take it all in without gawking at all the celebrities. I searched the crowd for a man with a scar and a pointy chin—the man who'd killed Justine by dropping poison into her tea. Would he dare show his face here? How stupid would that be?

"Most criminals are not that bright," Den had said to me. "A lot of them would just get off on being at the funeral of someone they killed. In fact, many of them do."

At least, that's what the police were banking on. The place was full of undercover cops—along with celebrities, movie producers, publishers. Justine was respected and admired in film and publishing circles. Unless you'd gotten in her way or were a competitor.

From where I sat in the front of the room, it was almost impossible to be nonchalant in trying to spot the suspect, which required cranking my head around and making it obvious. I tried to play it cool, but Brad Pitt had just walked in, sending little ripples of excitement through me. I blinked nervously, and he disappeared into the crowd behind me.

"Pitt's alone. Do you think I have a chance?" Kate joked.

Judith Turner, Justine's cousin, and her entourage came through the door and sat in the front seats at the other side of the aisle. She didn't even glance my way.

Susan Strohmeyer, Justine's lawyer, had informed me that Judith couldn't make it to the reading of the will, so that event had been postponed until the next day. We still had no idea who'd inherited Justine's wealth or which of the many charitable organizations she'd helped would receive it. But we'd find out soon enough.

I glanced up at the stained-glass dome ceiling—once again, a goddess depicted in the sparkling, vibrant colors. The surrounding walls were papered in velvet. Velvet walls, for God's sake.

My pulse raced as the place quieted. A woman took the small stage and cleared her throat. Sweat pricked at my forehead. I just wanted to get out of there. The stately room suddenly closed in on me.

Kate reached over and grabbed my hand. "It's going to be okay," she whispered. "All you have to do is stand up when they call your name."

Tell that to my quivering knees.

I had no idea what the woman said—or who she was. Justine Turner this, Justine Turner that. It all became blurry and hard to focus on. And then my heart nearly jumped out of my chest when I heard my name. Kate poked at me. I stood.

"Charlotte Donovan, Justine's assistant of almost twelve years, will be finishing the Jean Harlow biography," Natalie Vega announced.

I started to sit down, but then her voice prompted me not to.

"Turn around, Charlotte. Let them see you."

Oh for fuck's sake.

I turned and nodded. I glanced over the crowd. A redhead wearing a black hat with a net over her face caught my eye. I blinked. The face of Jean Harlow was beneath that net.

Crazy. Brad Pitt. Meryl Streep. Billy Joel. My eyes swept over the celebrity-filled crowd. But in the center of the sea of faces was this redhead, with the face of Jean Harlow covered by a black net hanging from a hat. Was I hallucinating?

I swayed. My knees jelled. Kate stood and gently helped me sit down.

"Are you okay? It looks like you saw a ghost," she whispered.

I nodded. My mouth was dry. I couldn't find the words to tell her, *I think I just saw a red-haired version of Jean Harlow.*

At the depth of my Lyme disease, I'd suffered wild, fevered hallucinations. I wondered if this could be my reaction to all the stress.

Losing Justine. Sneaking around to stay in her apartment. Trying to help the police find her killer. Now the biography was on my plate, with a pressing deadline. I considered walking away from it all, but I desperately needed the money.

True to Justine's wishes, the service was quick. She was not a religious woman, nor even spiritual. She wanted no "celebration of life" nostalgic overviews. Just a few words were spoken by the president of Club Circe. I had already cried myself to sleep missing her, but several people who were there were sobbing and sniffing. Justine would be missed.

This part of the service was over, and now the reception in a ballroom in the club would begin. I couldn't stay. A profound, dark weariness crept over me. I wouldn't care if Clark Gable himself rose from the grave to escort me. I needed to get back. I needed a bed. Or a chaise longue, as it were.

"I need to get going," I said to Kate as the crowd began dispersing and filing out of the room, presumably making their way to the ballroom.

"I'll come with you," she said.

"But—"

"No buts about it. You're paler than I've ever seen you. Have you been keeping up with your meds?"

"Yes," I said. "It's just the stress of the day, I think."

As we walked out of the room, a man with an oddly shaped beard caught my eye. Something about his gaze freaked me out. It was a kind of glare, tempered by an attempt at civility. Those beady eyes reached out to me. He was vaguely familiar. But my mind was a muddle.

Kate pulled me along until we escaped the swanky, old-school woman's club.

We took up residence in the café across the street from Justine's place, with Kate insisting I eat before I lie down. As we sat there, I forced myself to eat even though I was queasy. I glanced out of the window as a throng of people passed by, and as a bit of an opening between head and bodies occurred, like the parting of the sea, the redhead from the funeral appeared across the street.

I grabbed Kate. "Look at her."

Kate followed my finger.

She was standing near the L'Ombragé. Sobbing.

"Who is she?"

"I have no idea. She was at the funeral. Look at her face," I said.

Kate stood and leaned further into the window. "I can't see her face. Just red hair."

But the redhead slipped into a cab and pulled off, leaving both Kate and me in a state of perplexed disbelief.

"Are you certain that was the same woman?"

I nodded. "Yes, and she looks exactly like Jean Harlow."

"Not that again, Charlotte," Kate said.

Nine

*W*ading through my emails had become a nightmare. Overnight, the explosion of interest in Jean Harlow—and in me—had reached strange proportions.

I scanned down the list. One at a time. One at a time.

There was an email from a psychic who claimed she had a connection with Jean and had a message for me. *Oh boy. Delete.* There was another message, from a dressmaker in Hollywood, who wanted my measurements because she could see me in a Jean Harlow-like silky gown. *Not on your life, honey.*

There was a reminder about Justine's will reading later in the day. *Thank you.*

I opened an email from a collector who wanted to meet with me.

"Dear Ms. Donovan,

Please accept my condolences on the loss of Justine Turner. It is a great loss, to be certain. I've been in contact with her about Jean Harlow's sapphire ring, which I believe she was planning to sell to me. Forgive my impertinence, as she has just passed away, but these things tend to slip off if we don't secure them. Might we meet to discuss terms?

Yours Truly,

Chad Walters"

I could take care of this right away. I wrote him back with the only factual information I had about Jean Harlow's ring: it had not been seen since her death. The ring's significance was that it had been given to her by the great love of her life, William Powell. But it was gone. The most viable theory was that she was buried with it on her finger.

Walters emailed me back immediately, as if he'd been sitting there waiting for my response.

"I'd like to take you to lunch to discuss, as I'm aware that Justine had the ring."

As if I'd meet a complete stranger to chat about a nearly mythical ring. If Justine had the ring, I was sure I would have known about it. It would have been a great coupe for her and she would not have kept quiet about it. What was this man about?

The ring in question was a 150-carat cabochon sapphire engagement ring from Powell, according to the Natural Sapphire Company, one of my sources. For all the interest in the ring, the star sapphire itself was not gem quality. William Powell was cheap, and despite its size, the ring he gave Harlow wasn't expensive. I'd read an interview with Jean Harlow's jeweler. When she showed him the ring, he examined it and thought, "This is nothing."

Justine and I had examined Jean Harlow's probate records, and it wasn't listed in the contents, even though other valuable pieces of jewelry were.

The only thing adding value to the ring was that it had belonged to Harlow, which would be difficult to prove. If it were found, and a person could prove that it had belonged to her, the ring would, perhaps, be priceless.

I didn't respond to the man's email and moved on to the next. Most of them were junk. But there was an email from Maude, the psychologist we worked with, telling me I should call her. I'd inquired about a particular aspect of Harlow's personality I found intriguing: her work ethic.

I dialed. Greetings were exchanged, along with remembrances of Justine.

"Do you think her work ethic came from her Midwestern roots?" I asked.

"It's not as simple as that," Maude said.

"But she did have a work ethic, despite having grown up in a kind of upper-class family," I said.

"Yes, of course," Maude said. "Which was odd enough in itself, I suppose. But Jean Harlow was a very complicated woman."

I snorted. "Okay. I'll bite. What was complicated about her?"

"Children of divorce, even today, have the same feelings of worth-lessness. Back then, it was highly unlikely that she knew any other children whose parents had divorced." Maude paused, then exhaled into the phone. I imagined her puffing on a cigarette. "She didn't feel good enough. She overcompensated with her over-the-top nice personality and her workaholic tendencies. That's her psychological profile in a nutshell."

I felt a twinge of something—a sliver of inspiration reached out to me then. Something recognizable. A way into my subject.

"And the sex?" I said. But I knew what she was going to say, didn't I?

"Who knows how much sex the woman actually had? I mean, Jesus Christ, does it always have to be about the sex?" Maude exhaled again. "But let's say she had a higher than average sex drive. She was married at the age of seventeen. Once again, all of it fits into the un-worthy feelings she had. It was exacerbated by the culture, of course.

I mean yes, she starred in some films during the pre-code era, but the code attitude permeated the culture. You know, good girls didn't have sex, and if they did, they certainly didn't enjoy it."

That goddamn code. The Hays Code that gave us a plethora of forced happy endings and anesthetized movies. All for the sake of "decency."

"So was Jean Harlow a sexy vamp?" Maude went on. "Maybe. But more likely she was a normal woman with normal desires and had been branded as a vamp just because of her roles and her appearance. Which was outrageously sexy."

"What about the no underwear thing?" I asked. "That would lead me to believe that she wanted to lure men in."

"Of course she did. Don't we all?" Maude said and laughed. "I think it was simply that she didn't like it. So she didn't wear it. Other people placed their own meaning on it. She wasn't the first actress to go without underwear, I assure you."

No, that was true. Norma Shearer often didn't wear undergarments. It was never made a big deal of. I wondered why.

Shearer had been gorgeous and ten times a better actress than Harlow ever was. But you never even heard of her these days—unless you were a student of film. Yet Jean Harlow had become a cultural icon. Time was a tricky prankster.

"I've got to go in a few minutes. Is there anything else?" Maude said.

I thought a moment. "Well, this is going to seem like an odd question."

"My specialty," she said and laughed. She had a generous, rolling laugh.

"What kind of person would want to be a Jean Harlow imitator?"

"Now that is an odd question," she said. "What's even odder is Justine asked me the same thing a few days before she died."

My heart nearly stopped.

"What I told her was that I think there's a part of all of us that would like to be Jean Harlow, or at least resemble her. But for someone walking around pretending to *be* Jean Harlow? That could mean any number of personality disorders, as well as an extreme form of psychosis," she said.

Her words sent my pulse racing. Justine might have known about the woman who seemed to be hovering around me like an unwelcome ghost.

"Did Justine say she knew someone like this?" I managed to say.

"No, she didn't say." Maude hesitated. "But I had the feeling there was something she wasn't telling me. I worked with Justine for years; I knew the woman very well. She was going off on a tangent about a Jean Harlow look-alike. Justine Turner did not do tangents. You know that."

I grunted. "Yes," I said.

"Look, what's going on? Why are you asking about the Jean Harlow look-alike? Do you mind my asking?"

I filled her in about the woman I'd been seeing on the street—and then again briefly, I was sure of it, at Justine's wake.

There was a silence on the end of the phone. "Listen, doll, I'm late for my next appointment. Let me think all of this over and get back to you. I might have something for you to chew on."

We said our goodbyes.

What would make someone want to be another person? Where did the impulse to slip inside someone else's skin come from? Did this woman have something to hide? Surely not. You wouldn't become Jean Harlow if you wanted to slip into the shadows. You became Jean Harlow if you wanted attention—and plenty of it. I didn't need a PhD in psychology to figure that out.

Or had this person just been born resembling her?

I was getting off track. This person had nothing to do with the biography. I needed words on the page about Jean Harlow, not about some impersonator running around the city.

I tapped out some notes from my conversation with Maude, then checked over my email again.

"I insist on seeing you about the ring," Chad Walters emailed me again.

I was fueled with coffee and gleaned he wasn't going to give up until we met. Besides, if he knew anything about the ring that I didn't know, I'd pry it out of him. I wrote him back, giving him the address for the café across the street. I also needed to get it through to him: Justine did not have Jean Harlow's ring.

Ten

The trouble was, he didn't believe me. His eyes spoke of disbelief as he sipped his Earl Grey.

"I'm certain Justine knew nothing about the ring as well," I said. "Only that it's been missing since Harlow's death. That's all any of us know."

A chubby man with ruddy cheeks, Chad Walters' bushy eyebrows rose as he leaned forward. "I'll pay you double what it's worth."

I could not figure out if he was daft or dangerous. "Look, Mr. Walters, I'm unaware of the ring showing up recently or at all. And if Justine knew something, why wouldn't she tell me? I was her assistant and knew everything about the woman. She wouldn't have kept it a secret."

"You recognize that lost things turn up every so often," Chad said. "Take the Tino Costa painting, for example." He was talking about the life-sized painting of Jean Harlow that was lost for over fifty years, then suddenly found belonging to a collector in the middle of the country somewhere. It now resided in the Hollywood Museum with a number of other Jean Harlow items.

I shrugged and sipped my tea. *This is a mistake. I never should have agreed to this meeting.*

"Playing dumb is not going to help your cause," he said with a sneer.

"Excuse me?" Was this guy for real?

"I traced the ring to Justine and have spoken to her about it. Are you certain it's not in a lockbox or safe deposit box somewhere?"

My intuition pricked at me, sending tingles up my spine. If Justine owned either of those, what concern was it of his? What made him think I'd divulge that information? I sipped from my peppermint tea, inhaling the fragrance to calm myself.

Chad Walters pursed his lips. "I'm getting nowhere with you."

"Excuse me?" I said for the second time, setting my teacup in the saucer with a clank.

"If you don't let me buy the ring, there will be consequences. For both of us."

"Are you mad? Because as I've told you, it's nowhere to be found," I said. "Even if I wanted to give it to you, I couldn't." I balled my hands into fists, now on my lap. Was this guy going to attack me? I'd be ready for the fat bastard.

His fleshy ears reddened and the color spread through his face.

"I'm leaving, Mr. Walters," I said and stood. "Please don't bother me again."

He seethed in front of his porcelain teacup and I turned to walk out, not acknowledging the chill racing up and down my spine. Fuck him. Who did he think he was?

As I walked along the street, heading toward Central Park, it occurred to me that I should alert Den to this guy. If he were threatening me over a non-existent ring, it wouldn't be too much of a stretch to imagine him as a killer, or someone who'd hire one. He definitely was not the man in the video, who'd been thin and tall.

Nevertheless, he was definitely one of the "kooks" Justine had alluded to during our last conversation. This particular collector hadn't been on my list of suspects at all.

I passed two police officers dressed in uniform, and I have to admit I lost my focus for just a moment as they were both gorgeous Hispanic guys, built.

Even though I would be getting paid to write the Harlow book, I still needed every cent I could get to pay off my hospital and doctor bills. Not only that, but someday I'd like to have my own place. So I ignored my baser instincts to flirt with the uniformed hotties and made my way to a bench and dialed Den, who was completely untouchable, or at least in my mind he was. I had a bet to win.

The day was an almost perfect spring day, and I breathed in the brisk air as I sat on the first empty bench I found, facing the reservoir. Water called to me. Perhaps it was because I'd grown up on the island. Gazing at the water always soothed me, helped me to think, and got my creative juices flowing.

"Sergeant Den Brophy speaking."

"Hi, this is Charlotte Donovan."

"Yes, what can I do for you?" he breathed into the phone. He wasn't flirting, was he? It was probably dreaming on my part. But something about the tone in his voice made my insides pop.

"I just had the oddest experience," I said.

"Tell ya what, it's about time for me to take off outta here. Maybe we could chat in person. What do you say?"

"Ah," I said, not my most articulate response.

"It's just that I'd rather see you in person, and I'd like to catch you up on what we've found. I kinda hate the phone."

"Oh," I said. Still articulate.

"Let's meet at Charley's on West 72nd. Do you know it?"

"Yes," I said. Of course I did. It was one of the many cop bars in the city. I hoped I didn't run into any of my other "interests." Of course, I'd not seen any of those cops in a while. I'd most recently been dating a few from the Lower East Side.

I wasn't good with changes in plans or spur-of-the-moment meetings. But I had enough time to consider it and feel good about it. Even though Den was off-limits to me at this point, I wanted to tell him about Chad Walters the collector and to find out where the investigation stood. So despite myself, pangs of anticipation moved through me.

I headed toward the subway. The L'Ombragé Apartments came into view, along with a familiar figure—Walters, milling about just outside the building.

I was certain he didn't see me, but it unnerved me. What business did he have there? Did he know I was staying there? My heart raced. I needed to tell Den about this—but it would mean confessing that I'd been staying at Justine's place.

For the first time since I'd been living there, I was glad there was security at the door. I hoped Walters wasn't aware of the back door.

I took one last glance at him before descending beneath the streets. A woman elbowed me as I became part of the monster of moving parts of people heading downward.

Eleven

I walked into Charley's, which wasn't as busy as I'd expected. I examined the small crowd to make certain none of my cop friends were around. The coast was clear.

Den sat straight on a bar stool, wearing jeans and an untucked dress shirt with a leather jacket. He hadn't spotted me yet, so I took a moment to enjoy him. Short, cropped reddish-blonde hair, blue eyes, high cheekbones, and dimples. One in his chin.

He set his drink down, moving with lion-like power, grace, and assurance. He sat back on the stool and crossed his arms, which made the jacket tighten. I could only guess those arms were ripped.

"Hey, Den," I said.

"Charlotte!" He stood and shook my hand, briefly placing his arm on my shoulder. Electricity. Fire. I so wanted to climb into bed with him, wrap myself around him, forget about my day in his arms. Not yet. Not only did I have a bet to win, but I also had the meeting with Justine's lawyer in a couple of hours, for the will reading.

He led me to a table and a server followed. "What will you have, Charlotte? I'm off duty." He lifted his beer.

"I'll have a stout." One stout. No more.

"Coming right up," the server said.

His elbows on the table, Den leaned closer to me. "I gotta tell you, Charlotte, all of those names you gave me check out. They all have sound alibis. Of course, we're checking into the alibis even further. People have been known to lie to the cops."

"I've got a new name for you. Chad Walters."

The server brought my thick, dark stout with a perfect foamy head on it. I lifted the brew and drank it in.

"What's his story?" Den's eyebrows gathered and his chin tilted to the side.

I relayed the story to him, leaving out the part where I was staying at Justine's. But I noted that Walters was loitering outside her apartment building as I passed by.

A group of men, police officers I assumed since the place was so popular with them, laughed loudly, and Den turned his head momentarily, then back to me.

"Excuse me," he said. "I'm going to text the name in." He pulled out his phone, texted, and turned his focus in my direction. "We went into Justine's place and downloaded all the files on her desktop computer onto a jump drive. Our cyber unit is going over everything in detail. God, they sometimes take forever." He took a sip of his beer.

Well, that was good to learn. They would now have the crazy emails I'd read. Whew. I breathed a sigh of relief. For now.

"The weird thing is, my crew could swear someone is staying at her place." He lifted an eyebrow.

My heart thumped. Okay. Was he going to bust me? I remembered Justine's advice about acting stupid.

"That would be me," I said. I took another sip of the creamy bitter drink.

"You?"

"Yeah. I've been staying there since Justine passed. I'm her assistant. I couldn't be running back and forth between the city and Cloister Island. It wasn't feasible right now."

Den set his glass down and grinned. "This is highly unusual. I'm not sure you should be there."

"It's not a crime scene."

"True, but I think it's best we keep this between us for the time being. Though I'm glad you told me."

"You see why I'm so worried about Walters hanging around."

"Have you noticed anybody else? Press?"

"I don't think so." I sipped my stout. "But there is another person I've seen that makes me feel like I'm losing it."

I explained about the look-alike woman I'd been seeing—first a blonde, then a redhead. I wasn't sure they were the same person.

"She was standing outside the apartment building sobbing the day of the memorial," I said. "And she was definitely at the service."

"We had the place under surveillance. I'll see if I can find her on the footage. In the meantime, I wanted to ask you about this guy." He pulled out his phone and clicked around. He held the phone up. "Does he look familiar?"

A chill moved through me. "Yes. I noticed him. He was one of the few people I actually remember. I was upset and just wanted out of there."

"What was it about him you remember?"

I drank from my glass and mulled over the question. "It was the way he looked at me. And there was something vaguely familiar about him, the shape of his eyes, I think. But the beard? I'd have remembered if I met a man with a beard like that."

"It was a fake."

My heart raced.

"Look closer," Den said. "Look right there." He pointed to a tiny mark on the man's lower face.

I gasped. "Was he the same man from Layla's?"

"We can't be certain," he said. "But that mark could lead to the scar. It's in the exact right position on his face."

My fist pounded on the table. "I can't believe he was there and I missed him!" I remembered the feeling the man gave me when our eyes met. When would I ever learn to trust my instincts?

"Calm down," Den said, and then laughed. "We all missed him, until the idiot left his beard in the trash can in the men's room. Now we have his DNA."

"What good is that going to do if he's never been in your system?" My stomach churned. The man who'd killed Justine had been right there at the memorial service. I saw him. We'd made eye contact.

"First, we don't know that he hasn't. Second, when and if we find him, it will just be more evidence against him. Police work is not like you see on TV where everything happens in a nice orderly puzzle to be solved at the end. Sometimes it's more like…gathering a hodgepodge of ideas, facts, incidents, and hunches. Sometimes you never know how one relates to the other. If it ever does."

I bit the inside of my cheek. *My, my.* Not only was Den a looker, but he was astute as well. Someone I could carry on a conversation with, which hadn't been my experience. Much.

My phone dinged, alerting me to a text message from Kate, who planned to join me for the will reading. The law office happened to be two blocks away from me. I texted her back and told her where I was.

"WHAT?"

"Calm down. We're going over Justine's case."

"I'm coming RIGHT NOW."

I laughed.

66

"What's so funny?" Den asked.

"My friend Kate is going to meet me here. I hope you don't mind. She's joining me for the reading of Justine's will."

"I think I've gone over everything I wanted to talk with you about. For the case, that is." Den's eyebrows lifted. Then he exhaled. "I don't date women involved with cases I'm working. But I like you. What do you think? Maybe after we get this guy, you and I go out for dinner or something?"

Or something.

I hesitated. I didn't want him to perceive that I'd been entertaining thoughts of my own. Thoughts not necessarily including dinner. But it could be a nice change. To actually date.

"Sure," I said. "I'd like that."

Just then, Kate came sauntering over. She must have been close when she texted. She leaned over and kissed me.

Den tilted his head slightly as he looked at Kate. He was a trained observer.

"Please sit down, Kate. Let me get you a drink." He stood. "What'll you have?"

"Just a diet coke for me, thanks," she said. As he walked off, she turned to me, wide-eyed. "Damn, he's hot."

"Indeed," I said, laughing.

"Kate to the rescue then," she said and winked. She wore a bright red blazer with a huge rhinestone pin on it, focusing the attention right smack on her gorgeous pert breasts. She glittered and popped, as usual. "Or you may have been out five hundred dollars." She wriggled her eyebrows.

Almost as soon as Den came back, his phone buzzed. "I'm sorry," he said. "I have to take this." He rose from the table and walked into the lobby area.

"Listen, Charlotte, I'm so sorry," he said when he came back. "I've got to run. A case I'm working is breaking. I need to be there."

"You said you were off duty."

"I was, but this case is important. I'm hoping it's going to mean a promotion for me. Why don't you two stay here and have another drink? I'll tell them to put it on my tab."

Kate's eyebrows lifted and she smiled. "I like this guy. Do you think he'd spring for a facial? How about a boob job? "

Den shot her a grin. "How many more do you need?"

Kate exploded into laughter as he walked off.

Twelve

fter finishing our drinks, Kate and I took off to find the law office. Typical official building, kind of nondescript until we reached the fifteenth floor, which had marble floors, deep wood-paneled walls, and leather chairs and sofas placed strategically around the large spaces. People gathered in some of those areas.

I walked up to the receptionist and told her who I was, and she nodded. "Someone will be here to show you to the meeting room momentarily. Please have a seat."

Kate, who had already found a spot perched on a high-backed leather chair, fooled with her chiffon scarf. She was accustomed to these offices. Since I worked for Justine from home, I rarely had reason to be somewhere like this. The places I frequented were libraries and…cop bars. I sat down on a couch and sank in, my feet barely reaching the floor, and I couldn't imagine getting up gracefully from this position. Never mind. This was just a formality. I'd never see these people again.

We waited longer than I'd expected, which gave me plenty of time to dwell on the fact that yesterday, I had looked into the eyes of a murderer. It had been such an emotional day—draining—but that was no excuse. Why hadn't I recognized him, despite his disguise?

Then Chad Walters' eyes flashed into my mind. I could have been gazing into a madman's eyes today. No, he wasn't the killer of Justine, but I'd not be surprised if he had a hand in it.

What had my life turned into? I'd gone from living the quiet life on Cloister Island, researching movie stars and assisting Justine wherever she needed me, to a person whose mind was filled with death and murder. I didn't like it. But still I owed it to Justine to help bring justice in her untimely death.

"What's going on in that little pea brain of yours?" Kate asked.

"You don't want to know," I said.

"We've been waiting fifteen minutes," she added. "I wonder what's going on? These lawyers live by the billable hour."

Just then, a woman dressed in a cream pantsuit came from behind the door and called us. We stood and followed her back through a long gray hallway, past closed doors, until we happened on an open door where several people sat around a shiny rectangular table.

Greetings and introductions were exchanged. Judith Turner barely acknowledged me—nor did her lawyer. Lawyer? Why did she have a lawyer? Odd.

Susan Strohmeyer, Justine's attorney, handed each of us folders. A stack of official papers were piled inside. But I couldn't spot the will.

"First, I need to apologize to you. Justine made some changes to her will several days before her death. The changes have been misplaced so we can't discuss them right now," she said.

"Jesus Christ," Judith Turner muttered.

I glanced at the clock. Perhaps I'd be home within the hour. Maybe things would be wrapped up quickly. But Susan's face gave no indication that she would give up the search.

"As I said, I'm sorry. But we do have other matters to take care of. There were some addenda to Justine's previous will still in place."

"Can I get anybody water? Coffee?" the assistant in the cream suit said.

"Just get on with it." Judith waved her bejeweled hand.

I despised her. I could see why she and Justine were not close. "I'll take some water," I said. I'd make her wait. Yes, I would. Judith briefly glanced at me with the gaze that said, "Oh look, the help would like some water."

"Me too," Kate said, smiling politely, following my lead. Which she rarely did.

"Thank you, Sarah," Susan said as she watched her assistant walk out of the room.

"Since you both knew Justine so well, you'll not be surprised to know some of her wishes about probate and so on are out of the ordinary," Susan continued, smiling with a twitch. Her assistant walked back into the room with water, placed our crystal glasses in front us, and poured. She sat down next to Susan, where larger files full of papers sat on the mahogany table.

I suddenly wondered what I was doing there. I had assumed I'd be helping to disburse the funds because I worked for Justine. But it dawned on me that her lawyers had been hired to do this very thing. So why was I here?

"Justine was very concerned that her clothing be properly taken care of," Susan said. "By that I mean, she wanted her clothes to go to a charity where homeless women are seeking employment... Second Chances?"

"How lovely of her," Kate said.

"But she would like for Charlotte to pick out a few things for herself. Whatever she wants," Susan said. "She has asked for Charlotte to be the person who sees to her wishes and thought it only fair that she select a few items."

Of course. That's what I was doing there. Justine was giving me more work to do. Along with the book on Jean Harlow, I was now in charge of Justine's clothes. I pictured her wardrobe—mostly suits, including several Chanel suits, and garish scarves and hats, like something out of another century.

"The estate will pay you for your efforts," Susan continued. "As well as your efforts to clean the apartment."

My face reddened. Clean? When had I ever cleaned for Justine? What would make her think I would clean her place?

"Oh, for God's sake, why don't you just hire a professional to do it? Why would Justine want her assistant to clean her apartment?" Judith said with venom.

Kate cleared her throat. "I've got to agree." She laughed nervously. "Charlotte is not a cleaner."

"Charlotte is the only person Justine trusted enough to be alone in her apartment."

My heart went from pounding to bursting.

"She's left an allowance for large items you might want to take care of. Carpet cleaning and so on."

The dusty carpets and drapes would need professionals. "But I thought she had a maid," I said.

"No, she let her go months ago," Susan said.

Judith Turner sighed. "What am I doing here?" It was hard to believe she and Justine were related. I couldn't find a family resemblance at all.

"I had thought we'd be reading the will, but since we've been unable to locate the changes …" Susan said and shrugged. "I'm sorry. As soon as we find them, we'll inform you."

"How does that happen?" Judith's lawyer spoke up. "How do you misplace something like that?"

Susan stood, gathering her papers and folders. "As I said, it was changed just days before her death. Her holdings were extensive. We think it may have been misfiled. You have my word that finding her will is a priority. In the meantime, Ms. Donovan, here's the key to her place and the instructions on what to do with her clothing." She walked over to the door. "Good day."

The keys sat on the table reflecting in my glass of water. A bubble of emptiness or grief welled up from deep in my chest, as a sob escaped and my head dropped into my hand. *Justine.* Judith Turner *tsked* and slammed her hand down.

Kate stood, grabbing her purse and my arm.

"Let's go," she said.

Thirteen

*K*ate and I hopped on the next train and were lucky enough to snag two seats next to each other. "I can't wait to dig in. I'd love to check out her wardrobe. Do you want to start tonight?"

The man sitting on the other side of me had an extreme case of manspread and smelled of old cheese.

"I need a few days. First I need to get some actual writing in. I have to finish this book. The deadline is unforgiving. So the cleaning will have to wait." I shifted my leg a little more to the side of the manspreader. *Move over, bucko, you only get one seat.*

"Just let me know when you're ready," Kate said as the train was halting.

"How about Saturday?"

She stood. "This is my stop. I'll check my calendar and get back with you."

I watched her waltz off the train.

A man took her seat and turned to me. "Miss Donovan?" A whiskey-gravel voice said.

Was it me he was asking about or another Miss Donovan? I wasn't acquainted with him.

"Charlotte Donovan?" His eyes caught mine and I couldn't turn away. I was trapped between him and the cheese-smelling manspreader. The train started back up.

My face must have shown my shock and concern.

"I'm sorry. My name is Severn Hartwell. I'm sure Justine must have mentioned me," he said.

Hartwell. What was he doing here? Didn't he live in California? Had he come to town for Justine's memorial?

"Yes, Mr. Hartwell," I said.

"I'm so glad I ran into you."

How did he know who I was? How did he recognize me? Was he at Justine's service? My heart raced and a wave of nausea nearly overcame me.

He went on. "I may be hiring an assistant in a few months and was wondering if you'd be interested."

This man was Justine's biggest competitor. I sat there remembering all of the dirty tricks he'd tried to use against her to attempt to ruin her career. There was the time he'd sent fake documents to her, hoping to fool her into writing the biography of Norma Shearer on a completely false note. There was also the time he'd hacked her social media accounts. Oh, I could go on. The train car lurched and rumbled.

Justine had been dead a week and he was already scoping me out.

"I don't think so," I said, attempting to smile politely.

"I'm sure you don't have a very good impression of me," he said. "I'm sorry about that. But I do need help, and Justine used to say you were the best assistant she'd ever had."

A chill moved along my spine. I doubted Justine had ever even spoken with him. What was he about? Did he just happen to find me on this subway train? Or had he been following me?

My heart thudded against my ribs. My breath was shallow. My hands balled into fists in my lap.

"I'm making a bid to finish the Harlow book, you see. My agent is in negotiations with Justine's publisher," he said with his thin lips glazing over perfect teeth. "By all rights I should be writing that book."

Wasn't there any air in this train? Sweat pricked at me as I wondered how anybody still breathed.

I drew in what oxygen I could find. "I'm sorry, Mr. Hartwell. I'm finishing the Harlow book. I think you've been misinformed." I smiled a stiff smile at him. I stood as the train came to a stop. It wasn't where I would usually exit, but I needed to get some air—and shed this man.

"Pleasure meeting you," he said as I walked off. The words didn't match his menacing tone. I never turned back. A wall of ice felt as if it were sliding up and down my back. Why was he making a bid on the book? The contracts were all signed and ready to go.

Unless Justine's agent had it wrong?

I moved with the crowd and slipped into a coffee shop as soon as possible. I searched in my purse for my cell phone and lifted it, surprised by my trembling hands.

"Natalie, this is Charlotte Donovan," I said, not even giving her a chance to say hello. "I ran into Severn Hartwell on the train and he said he's bidding to finish the Harlow book."

"What? Calm down, Charlotte. Okay?"

I drew in air. "I think he must have followed me from Justine's lawyer's office. That's the only thing I can think of."

"He followed you?"

"I think so, and he offered me a job," I said.

Natalie laughed. "What makes him think you'd work for him? Listen, the last I heard of him is that he's writing another Harlow book. He's been trying to sell it. Nobody will publish it." She quieted. "Did he threaten you?"

"Not in so many words," I said. "But he must have followed me." "I'm slapping an injunction on his ass. He has no business anywhere near you."

No wonder Justine thought so highly of her agent.

"If he wants to publish a book on Harlow, he's going to have to indie publish. Justine was very highly thought of. Believe me. No publisher will touch his project," Natalie said. "Now, how much have you gotten done?"

Damn. I didn't think she'd ask me that question. "Not much."

The silence on the other end of the phone spoke of disapproval. Then, "You need to get cracking. I know it's hard on you, with Justine's death and all. But get those words on the page."

Of course I would. I could. I'd been way too busy with mundane details like memorial services and meetings with lawyers. Plus spotting a Jean Harlow twin around the city.

A sigh escaped me. "Yes," I said. "I hear you."

I was fine. I was going to write this book. No matter what Hartwell said. Or thought. I owed it to Justine to finish it and do the best I could do. I needed to focus on writing. But first, in the spirit of cooperating with the police on Justine's murder investigation, I called Den. He needed to know about this "impromptu" meeting.

Fourteen

The next two days I worked on the book, camping out in Justine's office-library on the couch. I succeeded in my attempt to not go online and investigate the Jean Harlow look-alike or dig deeper into Justine's records. Nor did I check my email. I just had to get words on the page, as Natalie said.

I started each day with a cup of coffee and a walk in Central Park. When my sickness wasn't flaring, it was the way I started every day. Walking. I missed Cloister Island the most in the mornings, when I would walk along the beach, no matter the weather, and watch the sunrise. The reservoir in the park was lovely but it wasn't a beach, with its driftwood and seashells, rocks, and pounding, rushing surf.

I had spotted the Jean Harlow look-alike more than once during my morning walks. I decided not to chase her. Not yet. I didn't want her to know I was aware of her existence. I hoped this would throw her off a bit so that, eventually, I could confront her.

Saturday morning, after my shower in the bathroom off of the library, I launched into writing even though I was expecting Kate. I reached the end of a chapter and took a breather. I itched to make a search of more of Justine's files, even though the Harlow files seemed to be missing. What the hell?

I made my way to the filing cabinet and grabbed a stack. I knew it would come to this. I wasn't going to rest until I examined every file. Had she misplaced the Harlow files? Filed them under some weird system?

I sat down in the leather chair next to the bookcase and sorted, glancing over each file.

An hour later, my cell phone chimed and continued to chime. I was surrounded by papers and files and hated to move in order to answer. But I did. It was Kate. She had arrived to help me clean.

"C'mon up," I said into the phone.

"The doorman," Kate said. "He won't let me."

"Let me talk to him," I said.

A scuffling, echoing noise came over the phone "Yes," he said. "I see no permission here to let this woman in."

"Permission? She's a guest of mine. Do I need to fill out a form?" I said, half kidding.

"Yes, you do," he said, then let out a gravelly breath. "But for now, I'll approve her. But if you're going to be here, you'll need to familiarize yourself with our policies."

"Okay," I said. Duly scolded.

I didn't know how long I was going to be here—long enough to justify learning all the rules? Hard to believe Justine had lived someplace with so many rules. But then again, she was extremely security conscious.

I glanced around the library and it filled me with awe and delight. I still hadn't explored the rest of the place, but I was falling for this room. The spread-out files and papers seemed to fit right in.

A knock came at the door. I made my way there and opened it to a slightly bedraggled Kate.

"I thought your doorman was going to frisk me. Seriously," she said, and then hugged me.

"C'mon in," I said. With Kate's arrival I was forced out of my head-space and into reality.

"Holy shit!" she said as she entered the apartment. "I've never seen anything like this."

"It's gorgeous," I said. "I don't know where to start."

"First of all, we're going to clean it," Kate said. "It's so dusty."

"Yeah, dusting and vacuuming will help," I said, suddenly realizing how stale the air was. Why hadn't I noticed before?

"Can we open windows?" she asked.

We went around the front room and tried to open windows—all but one was sealed shut. We pulled back the heavy curtains and cracked that one open. Light and air streamed into the place.

I caught a sudden whiff of something. What was it? Justine's perfume.

"You okay?" Kate said. "You just paled."

"It's nothing," I said. Of course pockets of the scent would be strewn about the place. It made sense. Justine only ever wore one kind of perfume: Cotillion, by Avon. I had always found it odd—and endearing, frankly. Here was this very wealthy woman who insisted on wearing Avon perfume. *"I have a sensitive nose. I like Cotillion. It's the only one I like."*

Kate sneezed. "I brought you more clothes." She handed me a bag. She'd been shopping for me again.

Dust particles scattered in the light and landed all around us. "Bless you," I said. "And thanks for the clothes."

"Thanks. I need all the blessings I can get. I think you're right. We need to get the dust under control before, you know, before we start to sort through her things. Where's the bathroom?"

"The small one I've been using is right over there, but I wonder where the master bathroom is," I said, walking through the hallway. "It might be back through here." I opened a door to a closet. "Nope."

Kate opened another door and gasped. "Now that's a bathroom!" she said and entered the room.

I peeked in. A sunken marble bath tub, a huge shower, and a sink to match, surrounded by candles and silk flowers. The tile work was breathtaking; the original art deco tile and patterns were worked in with the newer marble, and so on. It was an amazing space.

I left the room to give Kate privacy and headed back to the library. I gathered up the files and piled them on the edge of Justine's desk, right next to the second set of keys I now possessed. Then I turned my attention from those files to vacuuming and dusting.

A little while later, I dragged Kate out onto the balcony for some fresh air.

"Would you look at that?" she said as we stepped outside. The view was astonishing. The balcony overlooked Central Park and the southernmost part of the Jacqueline Kennedy Onassis Reservoir. Beyond that, the West Side of the city. It was almost as if we weren't a part of the city at all while we stood here.

Separate from the city. Quiet. Undisturbed. This is where Justine lived and worked. As much as she was a social animal, the work she did required solitude. Did she ever sit on this balcony and take in one of the most beautiful views of the city? Or did she spend all of her time behind her computer, between our lunch and dinner meetings?

"We better get busy," Kate said. "I've got a dinner engagement later with clients and can't miss it."

Justine's bedroom was bigger than two of the largest rooms put together in my family's Cloister Island home. Floor-to-ceiling windows and a settee draped by a silky turquoise shawl gave the room a pop of color. Otherwise the room was austere white and cream. Even the furniture was blonde. The bed was a king-size platform bed and was flanked on either side by low, built-in wall tables, which might have been original to the apartment.

"Holy shit," Kate said. "Look at those lamps. Do you think those are original?"

"Yes, they look art deco-ish, though I'm no expert. Very boxy and modern," I said.

Above each lamp were huge inlays into the wall—each held a huge, sleek, matching tall vase. Hanging lights added even more elegance to the room.

"I think it's cold," Kate said. "I mean, it doesn't seem comfortable at all."

"I disagree," I said. "I love this room."

In the center, between the two huge inlays, was another one, exactly above the bed, which held a painting—an art deco version of a goddess? Nymph? Painted in tones of pink and flesh. Very feminine.

"There's something comforting about simplicity," I said.

"And easy to clean," Kate replied as she flung open the closet door.

"Now that's a closet," I said and grinned.

"And not so easy to clean." Kate whistled.

Not only were there clothes, and purses and scarves and so on, but there were boxes of who-knew-what stacked under the clothes, and, on the shelves, big mounds of stuff. The stuff of life.

Kate flapped open a garbage bag. "This is going to take longer than I expected."

"Days," I said, with my chest squeezing. I recognized so much of the clothing. All of it too small for me, as Justine was a tiny bird of a woman. Her Chanel suits and handbags were not Kate's size or style, but she adored the scarves and hats.

After filling two huge trash bags with her clothes, with still more to go, I slid the boxes on the floor out and lined them up against the wall.

"Good idea. We need to move some of this stuff out of the way so we can get further in," Kate said.

"I don't think I've ever seen such a deep closet," I said.

"A few of the designers I know have similar closets, but not quite this big," she said.

As Kate pulled out the last box, I spotted a faint line in the wall. And another one. I blinked. "Is that a door?"

I pointed to the seam in the wall. Kate and I ran our fingers along the edge of it. She pushed—and it opened.

Kate's eyes widened. "What the hell?"

My heart flickered. "Another room."

Fifteen

"After you," Kate said.

I stepped through the door, half expecting to find Narnia or Wonderland, but what I found was a storage room full of more boxes, along with draped-over paintings and furniture. An odd, stale, but dark, soft, and powdery scent filled my nose.

"Perfume," Kate said as she followed close behind me.

"I don't know, maybe," I said. "Not Justine's perfume. She wore Cotillion." Cotillion also bore a soft scent, but not like the one in this room.

Even though there was absolutely nothing interesting about the room itself, it had an energy about it. I couldn't quite describe it. Maybe it was because it was secret.

"It looks like our workload may have just doubled," Kate said, eyeballing the windowless walls. Was this a closet? A closet behind the closet?

A bare light bulb lit the secret closet-room, which I noted because the rest of the apartment had gorgeous light fixtures. But this space?

One light bulb. Crammed with oddly shaped boxes, the room barely had enough room to walk in.

"I wonder what she had to go through to get this stuff in here. I mean, she would have had to almost tear apart her closet," I said.

"Yeah. I mean, she could have paid for a storage facility. Why bother with this?" Kate said and shrugged.

One of those odd déjà vu feelings came over me, even though I'd never been in this space. But it was the only way I could describe the feeling. Maybe déjà vu was the wrong term. Maybe it was just that something about the space held an emotional resonance. If I dwelled on the feeling, I felt as if I were teetering on the edge of something, some unnameable thing of great importance, and it became overwhelming. *It's just a bunch of junk in a secret closet.*

"We'll have to leave this to another day," I said, turning to go. But a chill came over me and I dizzied. Probably all the damned dust, I told myself.

Kate caught my sway. "This has been quite a day. Let's rest a bit and decide what to do next. Are you taking your meds?"

"Of course I am," I said. It wasn't just me who found my Lyme disease a force to be reckoned with. I'd lost friends, boyfriends, and even one fiancé who couldn't deal with my bouts of it. *"You dodged a bullet, if you ask me, sugar."*

We shut the door behind us and made our way to the kitchen. A wave of exhaustion came over me. Maybe I really had overdone it. Lyme was an odd disease. I could push myself some days and be fine. Other days, if I did anything above and beyond the ordinary, I had to take a nap. Maybe I needed my meds adjusted. Maybe I was just tired because anybody would be. We'd been cleaning most of the day.

Even though it frustrated me to hear people talk about Lyme disease as if it were fake, sometimes even I didn't believe in it. But when I was down with it, I had no choice. I'm stubborn that way.

"Let's get something to eat," Kate said.

"Okay. I need to make a list of contractors to get in here and clean the drapes and carpets after we get her clothes out of here. I don't know what else there is to go through."

We sat and ate the chicken salad sandwiches Kate had gotten on her way over.

"Any word about scar face?" Kate asked.

"Nothing," I said. "Den called yesterday and left a message."

"Den," Kate said and wriggled her eyebrows.

I ignored her. But I told her what Den said to me that night in Charley's. She chuckled and said, "I don't care if you go out with him. But sleeping with him is a no-no until you've made it a month, right?"

In the meantime, my usual casual-cop-lovers were still pinging me on Tinder. I wasn't sure how much longer I could keep putting them off.

Too much mayo in the chicken salad. But the bread was good. I took another bite.

"How about that person you keep claiming to see? Aren't there any famous Jean Harlow impersonators out there?" Kate asked, then popped a chip into her mouth.

"None that I could find. It seems she was born looking like Jean Harlow," I said.

"Poor girl," Kate said with sarcasm, then laughed. "Though I have to say, Harlow was not my idea of pretty."

I took a swig of my drink and set it down on the table. "I'd say 'pretty' is not the word."

"What would you call her?"

"Sexy," I replied. "Stunning. But not pretty."

"Was it the hair?" Kate asked. "I mean, what was it about her?'

I'd had some time to think about the question. I sucked in air. "No," I said, "it wasn't her hair. When she was discovered, she was blonde but not platinum. Howard Hughes gave her that platinum blonde color. I mean, yeah, it was one of the things she was famous for, but she was so much more."

"So, famous for the hair."

"I know, right? But she had a great body, an interesting face, and the camera loved her," I said. "Plus she was very comfortable in her skin and wasn't afraid to use her body."

Kate snorted. "Must be nice."

"Indeed," I quipped. "But remember, this was the thirties. Women weren't supposed to feel comfortable in their own skin. They weren't supposed to like sex or even think about it. So Jean's open sexy nature was unusual, in a way."

"Well, there were other sexy movie stars."

"Yes, but she was a kind of enigma because she didn't seem to be anything at all like what Hollywood portrayed. She was down to earth and kind of, I don't know, a tomboy. She couldn't understand the fuss," I said.

"I find that hard to believe," Kate said. "She was a sex symbol."

"Yes, but that was the image Hollywood gave her. It wasn't who she was. She didn't believe her press," I said. The reality of the statement sunk in for a moment. I needed to write it down and follow through on this thread of a concept. "When I think about all these young celebs now, with the drugs and legal problems and so on, I often think, there goes someone who believes he or she is what the press tells them they are. They don't have a backbone. Moral fiber. I think Jean knew who she was long before she came to Hollywood—and she never forgot it."

Sixteen

*K*ate and I cleaned up from our meal.

She held up the kitchen trash bag. "It's so full already I can't believe it. I'll run the trash out. Where did you say the chute was again?"

"I'll show you," I said, leading her to the back door of the apartment. We each clutched a bag of trash in our hands as we walked through the building's dim hallway.

The sound of heels clicking in the stairwell was not a normal sound here. Most people took the elevator. So, as the noise erupted, Kate gaped my way and shrugged. But when the stairwell door opened, it was the blonde Jean Harlow look-alike who appeared, wearing a shimmering pink dress and silver heels. She was out of breath and gasping for air.

"Hey!" I said. "Stay right there, please!"

She was surprised to see me. Her hands flew up as she shook her head and glanced around me before she turned back down the stairwell. What was she seeking? Was she searching for someone or something? Her lilac scent trailed after her.

"I'll take the stairs," I said to Kate. "You take the elevator."

Kate nodded.

"I think we've got her," I said, pushing open the door.

Kate rushed down the hallway to the elevator. She was muttering terms of disbelief as she went.

I nearly flew down the stairs. Fourteen floors. What was fourteen floors?

I stopped momentarily to see if I could hear the look-alike's heels clicking. But it was silent. Had she slipped out onto another floor? How could she have gotten into the building?

But then again, I'd gotten into the building for several days with no questions asked.

But I had a key.

Did she know someone in the building?

Was she living here herself?

I tried to listen.

Deadly silent. She was gone. There was no way to find her.

But maybe Kate had better luck?

I continued down the stairs, alert to sound, smell, anything pointing me in the look-alike's direction.

I was convinced she was stalking me. But why?

And how did this all add up? Were there connections I wasn't making? What had Justine been trying to tell me about the Jean Harlow kooks? I'd assumed she meant collectors like Chad Walters, and maybe some Hollywood types and even Severn Hartwell. It never entered my mind that she might have been talking about someone like my beautiful stalker.

My thighs and calves were burning by the time I reached the small landing on the bottom floor. There was an open door leading outside, a different one than the back door I'd used. I poked my head out and strained my eyes. No blonde bombshell-types to be found.

I walked around the building to the front entry way, where Kate stood chatting with the doorman. Her arms were flailing wildly as the man slowly shook his head. From this tableau, I gathered she hadn't had any luck either.

"What kind of a place is this, that someone could sneak in through the back door?" Kate said.

"We don't know that's what happened," I said as I approached her. "She could still be in the building. She could live here."

The doorman, nonplussed, shook his head. "I think I'd know if someone looking like Jean Harlow lived here."

"Let's check with management. Maybe they can give us a list of names of people who live here," I said.

"Against policy," the doorman said.

"I should think it's against policy to allow people to wander the stairwells in the middle of the day. The stairwell's outside door was propped open. That's a security breach," I said.

"Please," the doorman said, "calm down." He glanced behind me at a stiff-faced management-looking person. The irony of my situation was not lost on me even as I pursued this.

"What seems to be the problem?" the manager asked, eyeballing us. Our clothes powdered in dust from cleaning.

I explained what happened.

"She most certainly must be a resident, or was here visiting," he replied.

"But the back door, you know, near the stairwell was open," I said.

He tilted his head. "Let me check into this further and get back to you. We sometimes have vendors who enter through that door. But they should be closing it behind them."

"Thank you," I said.

Kate and I turned toward the elevator. She pushed the button. We stood out in the beautiful lobby. But it wasn't as if the residents all walked around in evening gowns, especially not on a Saturday afternoon. A few women walked by us wearing sundresses. Another group of women wore nice jeans and flowy shirts. But Kate and I wore old jeans and T-shirts—not Kate's usual style at all. At least not since she'd made the change.

I'd been staying here a week now and was beginning to get a feel for the general population—most of whom were like Justine, coming from old money and not interested in showing off.

The elevator dinged when we reached the fourteenth floor. It opened to a foyer that was a part of Justine's apartment, but there was another door to open to actually get inside.

That door was wide open.

"Did we leave the door open?" Kate asked.

"We didn't leave from this door."

"No, I mean earlier. Did we?" Her voice quivered.

I'm sure she knew the answer. No. We'd not left the door open. Either someone was inside, or had been.

I started to forge ahead to see what was going on, but Kate pulled me back. "Someone might be in there. I think we should call security. Or Den. Or both."

"And say what? The door is open and we think someone may be inside?" I asked. It sounded ridiculous. I walked forward, but Kate's strong arms held me back.

"I can't let you do that, my friend." She pulled out her cell phone from her back pocket. "Call security."

Seventeen

The intruder was gone.

But so was Justine's computer and most of her files.

"Now let me get this straight," Den said, as he paced the floor of the library, with the head of L'Ombragé security standing at the corner of the desk, pale, bereft, embarrassed. "You two are cleaning. You went down the hall to empty trash and saw a suspicious person coming up the stairwell. You"—he lifted his chin toward Kate—"decided to go down the elevator to try to catch her. And Charlotte ran down the stairs. After chatting with the doorman and security officer, you both came back up, planning to come in through the front door, and it was open. Open," he repeated. He turned to face the head of security.

"This has never happened before. I don't know how this happened." The man had said this several times.

"And the only thing missing is Justine's computer and file folders."

"As far as I can tell," I said. "I've not done a complete inventory of the place. So I have no idea if anything else is missing. But the boxes and bags of clothes we've been packing are still there. Everything in the bedroom and kitchen looks untouched."

"We're going to need to get forensics in here," Den said. "I understand you're staying here?"

"Yes, in this room," I replied.

"You'll need to find another place to stay for a day or so."

I'd not been back to Cloister Island since Justine's death, and it seemed like a world away, not just a ferry ride. A simple world, where some days I'd take a break from my work and walk down to Sol's for lunch, stopping in to see my grandmother at her antique shop. Those images poked at me. That was then; this was now.

"You could stay with me," Kate said. "I've cancelled my dinner engagement."

"Let me think about it." Logically, I knew I should feel unsafe and frightened and want to get out. But instead, I was pissed. Someone was messing with me. Worse, I was certain this all linked back to Justine's killer. What was going on?

"I think it would be best," Den said. Then his phone buzzed. He answered and said, "Send them up."

I gathered that forensics was here. I drew in air. "Can I get my laptop?"

"Sorry," Den said. "You'll get access to it in a day or so."

A crew of about three people entered the apartment. They wore matching uniforms.

"Get your things and come with me," Kate said.

"I really don't want to leave," I said.

"Aren't you afraid to stay here?" she asked.

Right then, I couldn't feel anything but anger. Moving out of Justine's apartment felt like giving up. Maybe it was stupid. "I think the intruder got what they came for. They probably won't be back."

"If they come back, we'll be ready for them," the security guy said. "We'll watch this place. Believe me. We don't wish to inconvenience you, Miss Donovan. Please stay here at L'Ombragé. We have a few apartments available for guests. One studio you might find convenient."

"Thank you," I said. "I'll take you up on that."

"Still, we've not caught the woman … you know … the Harlow look-alike," Kate said. "This is starting to creep me out. I don't feel right about you being alone." She scrutinized me. "But I can see you've made up your mind. I suppose I can stay with you."

Den was otherwise engaged, speaking with the forensics team, which appeared incongruous with the decor. Suddenly the elegant library, my hideaway from the world, had been invaded by cops and shiny-shoed security people and management. My eyes traveled to the stained glass window. The rose.

I needed a strategy. I needed to figure out what was going on. I had no idea where to begin. My words swirled incomprehensibly. I longed for clarity, but I sensed the foggy mind of my Lyme-diseased self taking over. Or was it just the stress of the moment? I tried to will it off. Instead, I found my way to the kitchen, poured myself some water, and sat down.

I reached for the pen and paper Justine had kept on the counter and doodled. Something solid for my fingers to do while my brain attempted to make sense of things.

"There's nothing on that computer," I said to Kate as she came up alongside me. "I mean, I read everything. There's nothing that could possibly be of any value to anybody."

"What about in her file cabinets?"

"No Harlow folders. I tried to make sense of what was there. But Justine had her own filing system. I'd just started going through each folder again before you came today. I figured it was the only way."

"Do you think it all has to do with her murder?" Kate asked after sitting down across the desk from me.

"Yes," I said. "The Harlow look-alike ... what was she doing here?"

"A distraction. Obviously she's working with someone. The person who took Justine's computer."

I nodded. "Yes, but she looked as if she was looking for something or someone. And how did she know we were going to be in the hallway then? It doesn't seem as if she was merely a distraction for us. There's something more going on there."

"We need to find her," Den said from the doorway. "I agree. Something more is going on with the look-alike. She might be the key to the whole case."

I doodled. Fingers pushed the pen. Roses. Leaves. Jagged little thorns.

Eighteen

After several hours of questions, Kate and I pulled our things together and settled into a guest studio in L'Ombragé, which I would have been more than content to live in. The apartment building offered these apartments for their out-of-town board members and other business types.

After pouring herself a glass of champagne from the fully stocked refrigerator, Kate plopped down on the couch. "Well, I guess I can slum it here with you for a few days."

I grunted in acknowledgement. I'd barely taken in the surroundings. My nose was in my phone, screen still cracked. I'd texted Natalie, and also Lucille, Justine's editor, to inform them that my laptop had been confiscated by the police. I had no idea when I'd get it back, let alone be able to work on the Harlow manuscript. Another setback.

Thank the universe, I still had my cell phone and could field emails on it. I also had my briefcase.

"Here's another email from a medium," I snorted. "She has a message for me from Jean."

Delete.

"Do you want champagne? It's so good," Kate said, as if she'd just had the best chocolate ever. "Let me get you some."

"Okay," I said with my nose still in the cell phone.

I read the note from a woman whose grandfather was a photographer and had "special" photos of Jean Harlow. Would I like to see them?

Delete.

Kate sauntered back into the room with a glass of bubbly for me. I sipped it. Not bad.

"Good, right?"

I nodded. "Shit, here's an email from Chad Walters."

"Charlotte,

I'm so sorry things went the way they did during our meeting. Please forgive me. You must understand I've been searching for the Harlow ring most of my life. I spoke to Justine about it and I know it's in her possession. When things settle, maybe you'll find it and keep me in mind should you wish to sell.

I know you have a better appreciation of these matters since antiques is your family business. Is it not?"

I shot up out of the chair, knocking it over.

"What the hell?" Kate said, sitting up and sending the latest issue of *Vogue* from her lap to the floor.

"He knows about Cloister Antiques!" I said, my voice a harsh whisper, air pressing down on my throat.

"Who? What?" She rushed over to help me lift the chair.

"That bastard Chad Walters knows about my family's business." I showed Kate the email. Her mouth dropped. "What do you think? Is he threatening me?" I didn't recognize my own voice, which was almost shrill now.

She read it over carefully again.

"He seems nice. He's apologizing. But you said he was combative in person, right? Then he's letting you know he knows about your family. Maybe it is a threat."

"I think I should let Gram know." My voice was still quivering.

"You need to calm down first," Kate said.

I nodded, then started pacing. "You know, this is crazy. Ever since we made the announcement that I'm writing the book, it's been nuts. I knew it was a mistake."

"You had no choice," Kate said. "You want to finish it, right?"

Did I ever. But now I didn't even have my laptop. And Justine's had vanished. Plus her desktop computer was stolen, right out from under our noses.

"Yes, of course. But how can I with all these distractions, let alone now that my laptop is gone."

"You'll have that back in a few days. Is there anything you can do to move forward on the project without your computer? I think maybe it would help keep your mind off things."

"First there was the Harlow look-alike, then Walters, then Hartwell. Now Justine's place has been broken into. Does this really all have to do with the book? I have to know, because my name is going to be on the cover of it right next to Justine's."

Kate handed me back the phone.

"Drink your champagne, darling," she said. "Then I'm going to call for a pizza. We're having a PJ party, right?"

She was trying to get my mind off my situation, but it's not what I needed. I needed to focus on it. Figure it out.

But I also needed to warn my grandmother.

I pressed the button to call her.

"Charlotte!" she said. "We've be been worried. How is it going?"

"I'm fine. I'm just busy. I'm sorry I haven't called." I sat down on the white velvet sofa near Kate. Images of Gram's dusty old antique shop played in my mind and comforted me.

"I read about Justine. Someone killed her?"

"It looks that way."

Kate handed me my champagne, which I'd left near the chair. Cool in my hand. I sipped from it.

"I'm surprised someone didn't kill her years ago," my grandmother said.

"Gram! I know you didn't like her."

"I don't like how she treated you. I didn't like how she paid you under the table. Crooked. The way you had to do all the grunt work for her. I'm sorry, you just don't treat people who work for you like that."

It was true, of course. Justine and I had our tense moments. And she insisted on paying me under the table, which is why I had problems with health insurance. But she'd been good to me in her own way.

"Okay," I said. "I'm not calling you to talk about her."

"When are you coming home?"

"I don't know. I still have things here to do."

"Are you still staying in her place?"

"Sort of," I replied.

She paused. "What the hell is that supposed to mean?"

"I'm staying in the same building, but not her apartment. Listen, have you ever heard of Harlow's sapphire ring?"

"Yes," Gram said after a minute. "Why?"

"There's a collector who's hounding me for it. Said that Justine had it."

"Did she?"

"Not that I know of," I said. "I'd think she would have told me."

Gram guffawed. "I don't know about that. She was dishonest."

I didn't have the energy to go there. True, Justine had her own brand of honesty. It was her "code."

"The thing is, the guy appears to be scouring the city seeking the ring. I was thinking he may head your way. Just keep an eye out and let me know," I said, maybe with a somewhat lighter and softer tone than usual. I didn't want to frighten my grandmother, though she was no shrinking violet.

"Is he the guy that killed Justine?" Gram said. She was too sharp for her own good.

"No. He's a collector. You know how they are."

After I gave her his name and a description, she hemmed and hawed. "I may have seen him the other day."

My stomach clenched.

"Let me think on this."

Walters had been to Cloister Island. Already. He was trying to scare me. And it was working. My knees quivered and sweat pricked at my forehead.

Kate looked up at me from *Vogue*, which hardly ever happened. *Vogue* was her Bible, like the dictionary was mine.

"I'm just not sure, but it may have been him," Gram went on. "And he did seem to have a particular interest in my jewelry."

"Okay, Gram, if he comes again, call me. Okay? No. Wait. Call the police. He's got no business on Cloister Island."

Kate sat the magazine down on the sofa next to her and her mouth dropped open.

"He's a free man and can go where he wants to," Gram said. "The cops won't care. That's why I have Bessie." Bessie was the nickname she'd given her hand gun, which she kept behind the counter. As if that should make me feel any better.

"You know," I said, after breathing in and out a few times, "you're right. I'm probably making a mountain out of a mole hill, but just in case, I thought you should be on the lookout for him."

After hanging up, I called Den and left a message for him to call me back. I needed his voice of logic right now. Did I need to be worried about my grandmother? Should I head back to Cloister? Then I called the police on the island. Couldn't hurt.

Kate listened intently to my conversation.

"Maybe a trip home is in order," she said.

Maybe. But maybe that was exactly what Walters wanted me to do. Get out of his way so he could ransack through Justine's apartment or find a lockbox. Was he trying to divert my attention by going to Cloister Island?

"I'm second-guessing myself. That's so unlike me," I said. "I'm not sure what to do. I want to talk with Den first." I yawned, then sipped my sparkling beverage.

"Looks like you're ready for bed," Kate said.

She was right. The meds I'd taken earlier were starting to kick in, and, right at that moment, the only thing I could do was close my eyes and fall into a deep, dreamless sleep.

Nineteen

One of the first tasks for me whenever Justine began a new book was to create a timeline, which is nothing more than a straight line with marks off to the sides indicating major events in the subject's life, and also historical happenings. What was going on in the world when Jean Harlow was born? That would go on the timeline across from the mark where "Jean Harlow's Birthday" resides. What songs and movies were popular? Books? It's a simplistic exercise that can get complicated and often resembles a complex diagramed sentence. It can be time-consuming and mind-numbing, but it helps when actually plotting out the book. It's the framework I helped Justine build the biographies on. A solid visual.

Thank goodness I'd placed it in my briefcase and had it with me. I placed the printed-out Jean Harlow/Harlean Carpenter timeline on the floor. The floor being one of my favorite spots to spread out and think. I propped myself on my elbows.

Kate leaned over me. She was working today from our cozy guest studio apartment. "'Indian Love Call,' hey?"

"Yes, it was popular in 1936. It was Jean's favorite song, sung at her funeral by Jeannette MacDonald," I replied as I studied the timeline more. There were just a few gaps in Harlow's twenty-six years of life. After she became a star, almost every minute was accounted for.

Kate pulled up the song on her laptop and the lyrics came spilling out of the speakers. "Kind of spooky. I don't know why," she said.

"If you think that's spooky, check out 'Sweet Mystery of Life.' Nelson Eddy sang it at her funeral. It's so depressing," I said.

"Nah, I think I'll skip it," she said.

I continued studying the timeline. There were branches of the timeline written in purple. Those represented her mother. We'd investigated Mama Jean as well, since their lives were so entwined. Mama Jean married Marino Bello years after divorcing Mont Clair Carpenter, Harlean's biological father. To say Marino was no good would be an understatement. He scammed his famous stepdaughter on more than one occasion, bilking her out of thousands.

"Prick," I said aloud.

"Thanks," Kate said and burped.

"I wasn't talking to you. I'm sorry. I was talking about Marino Bello, Harlean's mother's second husband."

I was so glad Kate hadn't wanted to leave me alone today. Such friends are hard to come by in this life. I glanced up at her. "I love you, Kate."

"Why wouldn't you?" she said with a broad smile.

I couldn't imagine my life without Kate. It didn't matter to me if she was Karl or Kate—the essence of her remained the same, no matter the gender. But her offer to take a trip to Cloister Island with me was fraught with difficulty. Even though it was a healing place for me, she really couldn't go back, no matter how much she wanted to. Her family was unforgiving and unaccepting—it was a wound she still suffered. No matter the brave face.

After studying the chart a bit more, I phoned Den. "I need my laptop."

"I know. I'm trying hard to get the ball rolling," he said. "You might have it tomorrow. In the meantime, we recovered Justine's stolen computer. Found it in the alley behind the apartment building. Thought you'd want to know."

"So you've got her computer, but I can't have mine back yet?" Kate glanced up from her laptop and rolled her eyes.

"Two different units," he said, breathing into the phone. I pictured his mouth next to his cell phone. "So anyway, the cybercrimes unit has made a few inroads with Justine's computer. You available to answer some questions?"

"Well, since I'm not working because you have my laptop, yeah," I said. "Why don't you come over. You know where I am."

Kate shot me a glare.

Did that sound more flirtatious than I meant it?

"How could I resist an invitation like that?"

After we hung up, Kate asked how it was going now that I was abstaining from my habit of sleeping with cops.

"Fine," I said, trying not to snap at her. I'd gotten pinged several times by some of my favorite guys. What would the harm be? What was the harm, anyway?

"Maybe I was wrong to think you couldn't do this," she said.

I snorted.

"But maybe not. There's still time. Can you honestly say you're not just itching for a cop in the sack?"

I couldn't lie to Kate. "I wouldn't say itching, but I've thought about it." I paused. "But you make it sound like I'd just screw any cop because he's a cop. That's just not the case." I rolled the timeline into a tube. "He's got to be hot."

Her eyebrows shot up. "There's plenty of hot cops in the city. I know. But can't you date someone else? Hey, how about a firefighter?"

I chewed it over for a few seconds and shrugged. "Sure, find me one and I'll date him. I've nothing against hot firefighters."

"I've heard they do amazing things with their hoses," Kate said and laughed.

When I opened the door to Den, he nearly took my breath away. As he stood there in his uniform, sex emanated from him. Tendrils of excitement raced through my lower regions. *Calm down, woman.*

His eyes smoldered and relayed he was feeling those same impulses. We stood, taking one another in for a few beats. Kate angled her way in between us.

"Sergeant Brophy, how lovely to see you," she said. I could have smacked her, with her big boobs flaunting in his face. But he seemed unmoved.

"Ah, yeah," he said. "Nice to see you too." He smiled politely.

He was draped with several briefcases and bags. But in his arms, he held my laptop. When my eyes went to it, his mouth curled into a grin. "I had to pull a few strings." He handed it to me.

"Well, Sergeant Brophy, aren't you something," Kate said and lead us both into the apartment.

"Thanks, Den. I could hug you for that," I said.

"Hold that thought," he said under his breath.

Twenty

"Can you at least send me the first few chapters of the book?" Natalie asked over the phone as Den, Kate, and I set up Den's laptop and a printer.

"Justine never would have sent them to you until she was further into the book," I told her. "You're asking me to do something she would not have liked."

"Right," Natalie said and paused. "But I need pages to show the publisher that you're working on it. It's extenuating circumstances."

Justine hated the practice of sending the first few chapters along while the book was still in progress. So many times things changed. And then she'd have too many versions, which became confusing for her. But Natalie was right. The situation was odd. Justine had written the first half of the book. I'd yet to go over it. But delivering the first couple chapters couldn't hurt. It would get Natalie off my case for a while.

"Okay, since I've just gotten my laptop back, I can send you the first few chapters," I said, glad Justine had emailed me her latest version of the manuscript. "Justine wrote them, of course, and I've yet to fact-check or proofread them."

"Oh, that's fine. I just need to see words on the page."

Den sat at the kitchen table, with Kate on one side of him and me on the other. "I don't understand the techno speak and all that," he said, "but here's the gist. The cybercrimes unit loves having the computer, because before, they'd just copied all the files onto a jump drive. But until they got their hands on the computer, they didn't see the other stuff."

"Other stuff? What do you mean?"

"Well, they say nothing is ever deleted. I guess it's not, and Justine had a lot of trashed files. Most of it *was* trash; you know, spam emails. But the unit was able to recover some very interesting emails she'd deleted." His lean fingers clicked over his keyboard. "I'm going to print these out to make notes on actual paper. I'm hoping you'll recognize some of these folks and we can find something. I don't know…a pattern. Maybe you can help make sense of all this."

"I'll do my best," I said.

As the printer spit out the paper, Kate cleared her throat. "Can I get you coffee? Water?"

"I'd love some coffee," he said. "Thank you." His attention turned back to me, his chin angled up. "We need to talk about that ring."

"Ring? Jean Harlow's sapphire ring?"

He nodded. "It seems like a lot of the emails are about a valuable star sapphire ring."

Adrenaline zoomed up my spine. "Like I told you at Charley's, that ring was lost years ago. Most people assume she was buried with it."

"Evidently it's resurfaced, and your boss did know something about it."

"What?" My heart thrummed. So Chad Walters was correct? "No way," I said out loud. "Justine would have told me. We discussed the ring. We talked to someone who knew her jeweler. We interviewed a sapphire specialist who said it really wasn't worth anything as far as gems go."

Den shrugged. The printer spit out emails. He stood and sorted through the papers. "Sometimes people surprise you. Maybe she learned more than what you think and she never got a chance to tell you."

Kate walked back into the room with a cup of coffee. "Cream? Sugar?"

"No thanks, Kate," he said.

"So this Chad Walters might be on to something?"

"I don't know," Den said. "Let's not rule it out. There are several lines of inquiry here. The ring is just one of them. I looked into Chad Walters," he went on. "Let's just say he's not a person you want to mess with." He handed me a file.

I read through it while he splayed papers out on the table.

"Rape charges? Murder charges?" I gasped as I read over the information. My heart thudded as I considered my grandmother. A man like that wouldn't think twice about killing someone.

"Yeah, he got out of those, barely. Hired a kick-ass expensive lawyer both times," Den said. "But look at these newspaper clippings."

There was an article about the underground Hollywood collector group called Hollywood Cartel Collections. Chad Walters' name popped up in the story as a source, not as a member. Another passage mentioned Chad and his art collection—most of which was illegal. He'd been busted twice for owning illegal antiquities.

"Jesus," I said.

"Yeah," Den said. "No wonder he said money's no object. He's like something out of a movie. I didn't know guys like this actually exist."

I set the file down and looked at the papers on the table.

"I've taken the liberty of choosing the emails I found most relevant. If you want to examine them later to see if anything else jumps out at you, that's fine. But to start, check these out."

I hovered over the papers and picked up the first one. My hands slightly trembled.

"J.
If such a ring were to exist, the bidding would open at 1.7 million.
So, my offer of 2 million is more than generous.
C.W."

Chad Walters.
He'd been telling the truth. He had been in contact with her.

"Dear C.W.
I told you once before that I don't know anything about the whereabouts of the ring.
J."

"Okay," I said. "Walters contacted her, and she claimed she knew nothing about it." My stomach settled. Thinking of Justine keeping such a huge secret from me rankled me.

Then:

"J.
My sources say you have the ring. They are never wrong.
C.W."

"C.W.
Screw your sources. You are wasting my time. Bugger off.
J."

I smiled. Justine.

"*J.*

Make no mistake, Justine, I'm not going anywhere. And will do anything for that ring.

C. W."

"Sounds like him, " I muttered. "He's a serious collector."

"Here's more," Den said, handing me a few other emails from Hollywood collectors. Some of them I recognized. Some were more threatening than others.

Gregory Horvath, a member of Hollywood Cartel Collections, that mysterious group of Hollywood types seeking authentic memorabilia, was a bit threatening in his notes as well. He too assumed Justine possessed the ring. Why?

"He's one of the people who was on my list, remember?" I said to Den.

He nodded. "But he has a solid alibi. His mother passed away and he was at her funeral."

I crossed Horvath off my list of possible killers.

"So all of these people believed she had the ring?" I said.

"And where there's smoke there's fire," Den said.

I took him in. The tilting of his chin, the crooked pursing of his lips, the knowing look in his eyes. "You think she hid the ring somewhere."

Kate harrumphed. "I'd not put it past her, Charlotte."

"Why wouldn't she tell me?" I was trying to tamp down the feeling of betrayal. "Justine told me everything. I'm the only person she trusted to clean her house. I'm her assistant. Um. Was."

I mentally sorted through the weirdness of the circumstances of Justine's death and all that had happened afterward. All the people contacting me. But only one had approached me about the ring, even though several collectors had connected with Justine.

"If she had the ring and didn't tell you, she may have been trying to protect you," Den said.

A cool breeze brushed across my skin. I shivered. A soft and powdery scent tickled my nose. Was it a real whiff, or a memory?

Was it Cotillion, or just a smell reminding me of it? Was Kate wearing something similar? Was Den?

"I'm not sure I accept any of it," Kate popped off. "If I had a jewel like that, one the love of my life gave me, I'd be buried in it."

"But she didn't have any say about her burial," I found myself saying. "That would have been left to her mother."

Mulling over the horrible last days of Harlow's life, I recalled she was swollen to at least twice her size. If she'd had the ring on her finger when she was sick, it would have had to come off at some point. Otherwise it would have dug into her finger. So maybe she wasn't buried in it. Perhaps either her mom or someone at the hospital took the ring.

Pure conjecture.

"There's no way of knowing if she's buried with it unless we have her body exhumed," I said.

Den guffawed. "You wouldn't believe the paperwork. Two states. And Hollywood? Jesus. What a field day. Exhumation is the last resort. Trust me."

I sat down on a kitchen chair. Still chilled. Could it be Justine knew something about this ring? That she was killed because of it?

"I don't know where Justine was the last few weeks of her life," I said, more to myself than to Den or Kate. "It was obvious she hadn't been living in her apartment for a while. Was she hiding? She wasn't easily frightened. I can't imagine her hiding from someone. But then again, she really wasn't herself. She was more on edge." I drew in a breath. "But I knew Justine. Maybe better than anybody else. She wasn't interested in money—not so much that she'd be running for her life. She was well off. Old money. She had quite enough. If she did have the ring and was keeping it a secret, there was good reason for it. And it had nothing to do with money. So these collectors were barking up the wrong tree."

A look of respect came over Den's face. Or newfound admiration. He liked the way I thought, which was a whole new experience for me. Most men didn't appreciate it when I used my mind.

"Okay," he said. "But listen. The ring and all that goes with it is just one possibility."

"What? What else can there be?"

"That's what I'm hoping you can help me with."

He handed me more printed-out emails. My hands trembled as the papers slid into them.

"More?" My voice was a throaty whisper.

Twenty-One

*A*fter taking a few gulps of water, which Kate brought me as I studied the next batch of emails, my hands stopped trembling. But my heart still raced and my stomach jumbled.

"Who is this person?" I asked as I read.

"Please, please help me. You have to understand. Once the Harlow book comes out, my life will never be the same. I'll need to go into hiding." It was dated six weeks ago, way before Justine died.

"There's two people," Den said as he directed me to the next email—which I'd seen before.

"I swear if you go public with this I'll kill you," it said.

I nodded. "I've read that one. Are these two related? Did they come from the same place?"

"They're from two different individuals. That much we can tell. The cybercrimes unit is working hard to get a lead on where they came from. Who these people are. But it looks like some emails were sent from the New York Public Library. So," he said and shrugged, "it's easy for people to sign it with fake names and such. It could be the same person using different aliases. I've got guys checking into it.

But we've been down this road before, with other cases. It probably won't go anywhere."

"That tells me that whoever sent it wants to be anonymous," Kate said. She was now standing next to me, looking over my shoulder.

"Yet asking for help."

"And look at this email," Den said.

"I can't stay with you without placing your life in jeopardy. I gave you my story. If he identifies you, he will kill you. I need to leave the country. I am certain he knows I'm here. If he finds out I've been working with you, he'll kill me as well."

Stunned into silence, Kate and I looked at one another. Her eyebrows were drawn into a V. "What the hell?" she said.

"This doesn't seem to have anything to do with the ring," Den said after a moment. "So do you have any idea what this is about?"

Dumbfounded, I shook my head. The room silenced once again.

"Did Justine run all of her sources by you?" Kate asked.

"Usually," I managed to say. "And I fact-checked them. It doesn't make any sense. I don't think this person is a source. This is something different."

"But it says 'Harlow book' right there. It does have a link with the book," Den said.

I bit my lip. The Jean Harlow tale was straightforward. Nothing new had resurfaced in recent years, unless you were counting her medical records, eventually released because the appropriate amount of time had passed. Was there a secret in her records? I'd reviewed them myself. Did I overlook something?

But even so, it still made no sense. There was nothing earth shattering, no juicy story, in the working manuscript. At all.

"I don't understand," I said. "I have no idea what this person is talking about. I'm sorry. I wish I could be more helpful."

Den placed his hand on my shoulder. It heated where his hand lay. "I get the feeling this is hard on you, and I'm sorry." He paused a few beats. "Remember how you said Justine called you to that meeting at Layla's, saying she had something important to tell you? Could it be that she had some new scoop about Harlow's life?"

I drew in a breath. "It's possible. But the Harlow story is not complicated. I have no idea what this person is talking about. I've looked over Justine's files. I've read almost everything on her computer. I haven't seen anything leading me to conclude there was a new twist to the story."

No Loretta Young–Clark Gable secret love child story lurked. Nor even a *Mommie Dearest* tale. The only whiff of scandal in Harlow's life was the suicide of her second husband. Which, when all was said and done, did not have much to do with Jean.

"But what about Justine's laptop?" Kate said. "You said you haven't been able to find it."

"Yes," I said, "she had a laptop. It might be wherever she was staying the last few weeks of her life. I have no idea where that was. I wasn't even aware she wasn't living in her apartment."

"Okay," Den said, removing his hand from my shoulder, leaving the spot tingling with faded heat. "We can pull financials. She had to pay for wherever she was staying, right? Hotel? B and B? Food?"

He reached into his pocket for his cell phone and then, standing, walked to the other side of the room.

Kate sighed. "What the hell do you imagine Justine had gotten herself into?"

I shrugged. "I have no idea. Nothing like this has happened before. I mean we've had lawsuits, threats of lawsuits. But never death threats or desperate pleas for help."

"Let's hope the cops can locate Justine's laptop. It might have just what you need."

"It's not that simple," I said. "I'm supposed to deliver the completed manuscript to the publisher in six weeks. Usually it wouldn't be a problem, but if the story is changing, it's going to be a huge dilemma. But how do I know? How do I finish the book knowing there may be more to the Harlow story?"

"Can you get an extension?"

"I already did."

"Damn," Kate said.

We sat for a few minutes, each in our own reflections. "I can't imagine anything about the Harlow story that could get Justine killed. If anything, the murder must have to do with the ring. It must have resurfaced. That's all I can think."

"If it did, where would it be?" Kate said in a low voice. "I mean, if Justine had the ring."

"I've no idea if she had a safe, or a safe deposit box or lockbox, like Chad Walters said, or a secret...place..." My eyes met Kate's. One of her well-drawn eyebrows lifted.

The secret room.

"Okay," Den said as he walked back into the room. "We'll start looking into her financials. Maybe it'll lead us to her laptop. Thanks. That might be a great lead."

"I'll need the laptop when you find it," I said.

"You can certainly have it when we're done with it."

"I have a book to finish."

"But first we have a killer to catch."

Den's voice was full of confidence and authority. And who was I to argue? As if I could, with the molten heat forming in my lower regions.

One thing at a time.

Twenty-Two

I was itching to return to the book, but Den stayed longer. I confess, I couldn't have written a word if I wanted to—not with all that maleness in my space.

"Hey, ah, I got your message about your grandmother," he said, spreading his arms across the back of the couch. I want to slip right in there between his arm and chest. But not under the watchful eye of Kate. He caught me checking out his arms and his eyes lit up.

"And?" Kate said, interrupting the silent exchange.

"Well, I called the chief of police on Cloister Island and talked with him a while. They'll be on the alert for Walters and it's not necessary for you to go back to the island. Besides, you've got work to do here, right?" His eyebrow lifted.

"I can do my job most anywhere," I said. "My mom sent me most of my stuff, so I'm set. And there's this ongoing murder investigation..."

"All that and we're still waiting for the actual will reading," Kate said. "Do you believe it?" Her mouth puckered and twisted. "Some people."

"A little problem with Justine's relatives?"

"No, the law firm lost the updates to her will." I sat on the chair next to the couch.

"That's a first," Den said. "Losing a will?"

I nodded. Just then my phone buzzed. "Excuse me," I said, looking at the number. Damn, it was Lucille. I allowed it to go to my voicemail. Did I need another call from her checking on the manuscript? I'd just spoken with her yesterday about the extension. What was the problem? Did she not trust me? Did she not know I'd done a lot of Justine's work before she passed away?

"I can let it go," I said waving my fingers.

"Listen, I'm about ready to head back down to Layla's," he said.

"What for?"

"I'm checking in there with the staff I haven't gotten a chance to interview before. I keep feeling there's something we overlooked. It might help if you come with me. We can walk you through what you saw and heard."

"That's a great idea," Kate said. "I'll come too. Let me get my purse." She walked to the dining table, where her purse was flung across a chair.

Den grinned and shrugged. "It's fine with me." Then he twisted his hand around and gestured as if to say, *What gives?*

I shot him my best *Who cares?* smile.

∞

It had been a full week since I'd been at the scene of Justine's murder. From the minute I walked in, I tried to tamp down the darkness creeping into my chest. The scent of jasmine, orange, and saffron would forever remind me of death. And of losing Justine.

"Are you okay?" Den asked.

I nodded. "I'll be fine." But my voice came out as a strangled whisper. Who was I trying to convince—him or me?

"Sergeant Brophy, we've been expecting you," Alfredo said. "Madam Donovan."

"Nice to see you."

He led us to Justine's private booth, where a pot of mint tea and honey cakes awaited.

"This is lovely," Kate said. "Thank you."

I stood dumbfounded, strange emotions pulling at me. This was the table, and that was the tea and that was the cake. The same thing served to me on the day Justine was murdered.

"I need to interview a few of the staff and I'll be right back to talk with you," Den said, then turned to Alfredo and said, "Thanks for the list of members who were here. I appreciate it."

The two of them walked into the back room, and I flashed to a memory of waking up there.

"Sit down, girl," Kate said. "You look as if you've seen a ghost." She was sitting in the exact same spot Justine had sat.

"This is the exact table we sat at. Where she died." Where I'd held her until the paramedics pulled her from me. Where, I swear, I'd felt the cold like never before.

Kate grimaced. "I didn't know that. But look. They've laid such a lovely table for us. I'm sorry. The memory of this place and this table must be awful."

I sat down, wilting into myself. "Yes, it is. I wasn't prepared for this."

Kate poured the tea. Steam curled upward as she slid the cup to me. "Drink your tea. It will do you good."

She reached for a honey cake, which I usually ate with abandon, but my stomach was doing its own thing and I wasn't going to push it. I held the drink to my lips and drew in the scent of the tea.

"The tea is tasty," Kate said. "Peppermint is good for you, or so I hear. Good for your stomach, your sinuses."

We sat there for what seemed like forever, drinking tea. The murmurs of the other tea drinkers were present, but in the distance in my mind. The servers bee-bopping around with trays. Music playing softly in the background, which allowed customers to talk.

"Hey," Den said as he came up beside me, along with Alfredo.

I gazed in his direction.

"You're in the same exact spot, right?"

"Yes." My throat squeezed as I poured more tea.

"Okay, now you're here, can you remember anything else odd about the day Justine was killed?"

After a few moments, I closed my eyes. "It was packed that day. I don't think I've ever seen it that crowded. As I came through the crowd, I thought someone grabbed my purse. Then told myself it caught on something."

Why hadn't I recalled that before?

"Fascinating. Do you remember exactly where that was in the tea room?"

"Yes." I nodded in the direction. "It was almost right in the center. You see where the lady dressed in purple and black is? Right there."

"Good," Den said, turning to Alfredo. "Can I get more security footage from you, ones focused on that area?"

"Absolutely. Shall I send them to your email?"

Den nodded. "Yeah. The same email address."

"Success?" Kate said and lifted her tea cup.

"Yeah, I hoped this exercise would lead us somewhere," he said. "Are you okay?"

I checked myself. My queasiness had disappeared. I reached for a honey cake. My heart raced, but in a good way. "I'm fine. I'm not getting my hopes up. But I feel great about helping out."

Twenty-Three

*D*en drove us back to L'Ombragé and we said our goodbyes. "Are you thinking what I'm thinking?" Kate asked me after he left.

"That you'd like to get Den in the sack?" I replied with a twisted grin.

Kate laughed. "No. Not my type." She sauntered onto the elevator.

"Okay, okay," I said. "You want to get into Justine's secret room. But how can we? The front door to her apartment has been bolted by the cops."

"What about the back door?"

"I assume it's bolted as well."

Kate grabbed the keys out of my hands. "Let's go check."

"It's probably an exercise in folly, but I'm game."

We exited the elevator and went down a hallway to Justine's kitchen door, which had no crime-scene tape across it like her front door. Kate slipped the key in and, voila, we were back inside the apartment.

"I hope there's no silent alarm on that thing," I muttered, out of breath, as we sauntered toward the master bedroom, where the boxes and bags of clothing still sat awaiting their new lives.

"We were so smart to close up the closet door," Kate said. "Nobody else knows it's there." She walked in the direction of the closet-with-a-closet.

I grabbed her arm. "Wait. What happens if we find the ring? Then what? What will we do with it?"

"I say let's worry about it when the time comes." Kate forged ahead and I followed.

We clambered through the first closet, and then she stretched out and pushed open the hidden door, which opened with a long creak and moan. We stepped inside the crowded space and once again, a strange feeling came over me. It wasn't déjà vu—more like a buzzing or humming beneath my skin. I pulled the string to turn on the light. A covered couch sat under a full shelf. A sheet draped over a group of paintings. Boxes of all sizes were scattered through the room.

"Where to start?" I said, reaching for a box, opening it to find a collection of old gloves. Some were long, others short. Some had gems on them.

Kate gasped. "Holly Golightly!" She reached into the box and pulled out long black gloves and a tiara.

"Surely not," I said.

"I'd recognize this tiara anywhere, and look, here's the cigarette holder."

For a moment, beneath her makeup, Kate looked exactly like she had as a kid, her face full of wander and awe. I flashed back to her prancing around my room playing dress-up. It was her favorite thing to do—well, that and play pirate. None of the other kids on the island wanted to play with either one of us——"Karl" and his "sissy" ways, and me and my bookish ways. We didn't care. We were fine in our own little world.

"So maybe this is all Hollywood stuff," I said. "Looks like Justine was a collector." I tried to let that sink in, but it didn't make sense. Justine despised collectors. My grandmother was going to love this— Justine had been hoarding valuable Hollywood collectibles in a secret room! Which made me wonder what else she'd been hiding from me. I'd believed I knew almost everything about her. This threw me.

"What's wrong?"

"This is just very weird. Justine claimed she hated collectors."

"Because she wanted what they had, evidently." Aspersion seeped from Kate's voice.

"I don't know. It doesn't sit right with me. Something's not right here." I pulled another box toward me as Kate inspected the smaller boxes on the shelves.

The haunting scent I'd smelled the first time we were here caught my attention as I opened the box, which held several scarves and a bottle of perfume. I picked it up—the deep orange liquid was long past its prime, but the bottle was elegant and artsy looking. Its lid was an upside-down heart, and a gold silky sash wrapped around the bottle. I read the label: *Mitsouko*. A rush of excitement tore through me. Jean Harlow wore this fragrance. I opened it and sniffed—even as old as it was, the scent was murky with oak moss and citrus, maybe patchouli? It spoke of Eastern mysteries and sensuality.

"Close that lid please." Kate's nose crunch up. "What an odd scent. What is it?"

"Mitsouko. Very popular in the thirties and forties. It was Jean's signature scent." I capped the bottle.

"Do you think that bottle may have been hers?"

I shrugged. "There's no label. But she was the only actress known to wear it. So it would stand to reason." The scarves in the box were saturated in the scent. Silky and delicate, I ran my fingers through them.

"The creepy thing about Mitsouko was that Paul Bern's body was found drenched in it," I said.

"He was her second husband, right?" Kate set a box aside. "The one who killed himself."

"Yes, even though there was a lot of mystery surrounding it. The first people called to the site were not the police, but the studios, who spun the story how they wanted it. The cops were as corrupt as the studios."

Something bobbled around in the box beneath the scarves. I wrapped my fingers around it and untangled it from the silky strands of cloth.

It was beautiful. And familiar. "Christ!" I said. "This is Harlow's hand mirror!" I held it up and admired myself in it.

"What?"

"I've seen photos with her and this. How the hell did Justine get her hands on this?"

"Looks like there was a lot more to Justine than we appreciated," Kate said.

I pulled the scarves from the box. "I wondered if this all was Harlow's?"

Kate's mouth dropped open as she looked at a pink silky scarf. "Uh."

What?"

She pointed to the scarf. "I think there's a piece of jewelry attached to it."

My pulse escalated and my fingers sought purchase. And there it was.

It resembled a milky-blue marble attached to a ring. And that's what it was, except that it was a blue star sapphire—and may have been the very thing we'd been seeking.

"I've never seen a stone so huge," Kate said after she gathered herself.

"It's not even that pretty," I said.

Turns out that Chad Walters knew what he was talking about. Justine had the ring. Disappointment reeled through me. Why hadn't she told me? Was Den right when he said she'd been protecting me? Or had she been getting ready to tell me the day she died?

Even though I'd been completely ignorant that she had the ring, one thing I understood was that if Justine had wanted Chad to have it, she'd have sold it to him already. There was more to this ring than anybody comprehended. Which is what made it so dangerous. Was this bauble what Justine was killed over? What Chad was threatening me about? The ring Justine had gotten countless emails about—some not so friendly? Was this also what the look-alike was after? Why she was stalking me?

"What do we do with the thing?" Kate asked.

"I'm already being followed and harassed. Is this why? Can this be the reason Justine died? We need to hide it." *Should I tell Den?*

"You mean like in a secret room?" Kate grinned.

I considered. "No. Someone is bound to discover this room. We need another place."

A noise erupted from the front of the apartment. Kate quickly closed the hidden door. I shut off the light. Someone was inside the apartment. We could only hope it was the police.

Twenty-Four

*M*uffled voices and shifting sounds filled the apartment outside of the tiny room where Kate and I stood, arm in arm, breathing. I wished I could make out what the voices were saying. But all I heard was my blood rushing and my racing heartbeat.

Were they cops? Management? Criminals revisiting the scene of the crime? In any case, Kate and I were not supposed to be here.

Kate's eyes glistened in the dark, wide and frightened. I was no mind reader, but I could guess her thoughts.

There we stood in a secret room in an apartment we'd been given strict orders to stay out of because it was a crime scene, holding a ring some people would kill for.

We remained still. Breathing as shallowly as possible while the noise in the other rooms escalated. Then nothing. No sound. A door closing. Were they gone?

We stood a few more beats, listening. Finally, feeling it was safe, I switched on the light.

"Christ," Kate whispered. "We need to get out of here. We've got what we came for."

"But what are we going to do with it? If we're right about this, people are getting killed over this thing."

"Take it to the cops," Kate said, opening the door.

"Are you kidding? Some lackey cop gets their hands on it and we never see it again. Den is too busy to be watching over a priceless ring for me." The NYPD was the worst at keeping track of valuables.

"What do you care?"

We were standing in Justine's bedroom now. What did I care?

I mulled over everything I understood about the ring. "There's something more to this ring than what we know. Justine was keeping it for a reason—or else she'd have sold it to Chad Walters. I need to figure out why."

"Why? It's not your concern. Like, just get rid of it. Then it's out of your life, along with all of this crazy shit."

Kate had a point.

But then again, I was writing the definitive biography of Jean Harlow.

The ring was an item that held meaning for Harlow. And it had taken on almost mythic qualities over the years. Who could I trust with it? Who could I trust to even *tell* about it?

Den, of course, seemed to be the person. And yet I didn't feel like I could burden him with it. Shit was going to hit the fan if this news came out. Den needed to stay focused.

If I was going to include the ring in the biography—and I should— I needed to figure some stuff out about it before I turned it over to the authorities. Once I gave the ring to them, I'd probably never see it again. And who knew what would happen to it? The ring had been so important to Justine that she'd kept it hidden, even from me. What secrets was it keeping, or pointing me toward? If only I could see.

"I'm going to have to write about the ring in the biography," I said, almost to myself, as we made our way through the kitchen.

"You don't need it on your person to write about it," Kate pointed out.

"I just have a feeling about it. Like there's an important reason Justine kept it. Something very important, yet to be revealed."

"She was going to sell it and make a shit-ton of money."

I gestured to the apartment we were standing in. "Nah. Money wasn't a huge motivator for her. I mean, she liked money, but she wasn't going to do anything risky or illegal for it. She didn't need to."

We walked into the library-office and surmised it was the cops who'd been in the apartment because all the crime scene tape was now taken down.

"Thank God," Kate said. "It wasn't your beautiful stalker. Just the cops."

"Wonder what would happen if they caught us here."

Kate shrugged. "We better get going. We don't want to find out, do we?"

As we walked out the door and stood at the elevator, my attention focused on the ring. The fact that it had been found was big news and most assuredly would need to be in the book. It was a new development in the Harlow story. She hadn't been buried with it. Justine and I had been certain she was.

But evidently Mama Jean's word was the last.

Mama Jean's word was the final command on most decisions regarding her daughter. You could say what you wanted about Jean's mother, but she rightfully swindled William Powell into buying the crypt in Forest Lawn where her daughter's remains still lie. Jean's elaborate marble crypt in the Sanctuary of Benediction, inside the Great Mausoleum, Forest Lawn, Glendale, cost William Powell a reported $25,000. Jean's mother sent him the bill. Jean was buried in the gown she wore in *Libeled Lady* with a single gardenia in her hands, and a note from William Powell: *"Good night my dearest darling."*

The gesture seemed really sweet until you grasped what a prick he'd been to her—a flower and a note was the least the man could do. Powell probably wouldn't have paid for Harlow's crypt, either, had Mama Jean not seized the opportunity.

What was $25,000 to Powell?

Nobody ever knew for sure whether Harlow and Powell were officially engaged—their relationship had been on again, off again for a few years. She'd worn the huge star sapphire ring on different fingers at various times. She wanted to be married to Powell—but his failed marriage to Carole Lombard prevented him from going into the relationship full force. He'd been called "Mr. Lombard" one too many times. And, after all, he was a star in his own right.

Ah, men. Such fragile creatures, I mused. *"He could screw her, but he couldn't marry her. Imagine that,"* Justine had said with a snort. And back then, marriage was everything for most women. I wondered about Jean—was it everything for her?

I'd read about other women divorcing in the 1930s, and it was a big deal. Women were often shunned in small communities. Children sometimes were given to orphanages and mothers shuffled to the poorhouse. Even if the results were not quite so dramatic, a divorced woman in the 1930s dealt with a whole other set of problems—things like women not even being allowed to have their own bank accounts, let alone their own property. Even a married woman would have to get her husband's permission to do anything official. Yet Jean Harlow, at the age of twenty-six, had been married three times and divorced twice. All accounts agree she was an old-fashioned woman who wanted to settle down with a man and "be happy."

Could something as deceptively simple as a good relationship have been all Harlow desired, even as she strutted around on camera?

But then again, why couldn't she have had both? Was it possible in the '30s? I grunted.

Was it possible today?

Hunger pangs brought my mind back to the present. "Let's get something to eat," I said to Kate as we entered our guest studio.

"Sounds good to me," she said.

While she slipped into the bathroom, I slipped the ring in my purse.

This was a bit chancy, I admit. But then again, who'd think to look for a valuable ring in an ordinary handbag?

Twenty-Five

The next day, I was able to move back into Justine's apartment. We'd boxed up most of her clothes and were just waiting for the charity to come and get them. Kate was back at her Chelsea townhouse, checking in with me what seemed like every hour on the hour. My Jean Harlow look-alike was still at large, which made her nervous.

I remained ever-watchful when I took my daily walks in Central Park. Once I thought I saw her near Strawberry Fields, the section of the park dedicated to John Lennon. But it turned out to be another platinum blonde, of which you don't see many these days.

Maybe the look-alike was gone. Maybe she'd finally stopped stalking me.

I wished I could say the same for my cyber-stalkers.

What information was I missing? Along with the psychics, Hollywood strangeness, and collectors, there was a thread of dark angst running through the newer emails I was seeing, but they seemingly had nothing to do with the ring. Or maybe they did and I just wasn't understanding how. A family secret?

I forged ahead, diving into genealogy records of the Carpenters, examining newspaper accounts and probate records, poring over the timeline again. Nothing had stood out. Perhaps the craziness only surrounded the ring and the superfans, who oddly enough were worse than any fans we'd previously run across. And I hadn't been prepared for this. It was astounding how so many people were still so interested in Jean Harlow.

One thing was clear in the middle of all of this murk: I needed to get the book finished and turned in. Then my life would get back to normal. Well, semi-normal. I'd need to find a job.

I nodded to Gerald as I entered L'Ombragé's glittery lobby. I knew is name now, as well as his wife's. He nodded back. "Miss Donovan," he said. All the staff were familiar with me and had been alerted to the break-in, as security had been taken up a notch.

I still couldn't make my mind up about what to do with the ring. And the book wouldn't get finished until I decided. I could write an afterword covering the ring…but without provenance and proof, I couldn't be certain the bauble was the real thing. If I took it to a jeweler, it would only be a matter of days before the news was out. And my life would be hell.

A crushing sensation filled my chest. I was certain the ring was why Justine was killed.

I focused on the story in front of me, willing away monkey-mind notions of another deeper narrative here. It was just my imagination. I had no real proof of anything. *Stick to the facts.* Stick to what I knew.

After several hours of writing, my cell phone brought me out of my reverie. Den.

"Sergeant Brophy," I said.

"Charlotte," he replied. "How's it going? Any news?"

A stab of guilt tore through me. How could I keep this secret from Den? He was working so hard to find Justine's killer.

"No news," I said. "I'm still getting emails. So is Justine. I have stacks of them. I've been printing them out and organizing them. There's a psychic pile. A collector pile. A Hollywood pile. And then the mysterious pile from someone pleading for help, but those stopped a while ago."

"Have you seen your look-alike?"

"Not at all," I said. "How's the case going?"

"We've got a bit of a lead. Can you meet me at Bryant Park in about an hour? I hate the phone."

I glanced at the clock, then back at my computer. I was on a roll. But Den might have news. And, well, Den. "Sure. See you there."

The only time I didn't like Bryant Park was during fashion week. I tried to steer clear of long, lanky, beautiful women wearing outfits that would cost me a year's salary.

I found a seat at a metal bench and took in the view. It was a nearly perfect late spring day. People were strewn over the middle lawn, which in the winter was an ice rink. Metal tables and chairs were scattered along the sidewalks. A young mom pushed a stroller holding her daughter, dressed in pink. The girl held her doll and giggled while the mom talked into her cell phone.

I glanced around for Den. So far, I hadn't spotted him.

A maintenance guy walked by me pushing a rolling trash can with one hand and eating a huge soft pretzel with the other. I wasn't the cleanest person in the world, but that nearly made me gag.

The scent of spicy food, greasy and peppery, suddenly distracted me. Where was it coming from?

Tourists snapped photos with their phones, couples hunched together drinking coffee, and the carousel spun forward.

Still no Den, and no spicy food. Soon the scent was replaced by a strong perfume. In the crowd, a sign poked up. Was someone protesting? What this time?

He moved forward, dressed in a wrinkled suit and tie. The sign said, *Jesus is my boss*.

"There you are," Den's voice came from behind me.

I shifted my gaze to him. My breath caught in my throat. I'd been trying not to think about him, since we couldn't date as long as he was on this case. And we couldn't sleep together because of my bet with Kate. It was best not to fantasize about him. But a hot rush moved through me as he took a seat next to me. Our thighs touched, barely.

"What's up, Den?"

"I've got some news. A lead."

"Ah, yes."

"The tox reports are back on Justine. And she did in fact have a heart attack, but it was brought on by a mix of Valium with some other drug we've not been able to pinpoint yet. The guys are working on it. Said something about chemical reactions eliminating traces of the other drug."

The news hit me like a brick wall. Proof. We had proof Justine was murdered—as if the security footage wasn't enough.

"We can't be certain, but all the clues we have lead us to the ring as the motive. Someone wanted that ring and determined that by getting rid of her, they'd get access to it."

A rush of fear shot through me as I sat there with the ring in my purse. "What would make them think they'd get access to it?" I asked. "If Justine had it, it would be hidden away somewhere," I managed to say. The maintenance guy strolled by us with another trash can, still eating his large pretzel.

"Still, maybe if we find the ring, it will lead us to her killer."

Not likely. My heart skipped a few fluttery beats. *Here I am, lying to Den.*

134

Well, not exactly lying, but not telling him the truth, either. Nevertheless, I resolved to go with my gut on this. The ring would stay in my purse.

"How would it help?" I said.

"If we found it, we could make a big splash about it, luring the killer out of hiding."

Not bloody likely.

"Sounds dangerous," I said, breathy.

Den nodded. "It would be."

We watched a few children walk toward the carousel.

"But since we don't have it, the point is moot." He paused. "But we do have a lead. At least I think it's a lead."

"What? What do you have?"

"One of those emails stood out. It was one that was asking for help. Came from the Dream Girl agency, according to the guys in the cyber crimes unit. Do you recognize the name?"

"No."

"It's an entertainment operation that specializes in impersonators. You know—the actors work through this agency, get jobs. It runs a club where some of them work."

"Is my stalker in show business?"

"I don't know. It's possible." He paused. "I think if we find your Jean Harlow impersonator, she can shed some light on what's going on, where the emails are coming from, and so on. At least she can tell us why she's been following you."

It made sense. Where else would a Jean Harlow look-alike work? The entertainment industry. My heart sped up in excitement. Maybe we were getting close. Maybe she could tell us everything we needed to learn to bring Justine's killer to justice.

"Let's go," I said. "What are we waiting for?"

Twenty-Six

"I'm sorry. We don't represent a Jean Harlow impersonator. Truth is, the younger crowd doesn't even know who she is," Sal Mendo said from behind his too-neat desk. Shelves lined with gleaming awards, and a few plants, served as decor.

You wanna bet, I wanted to respond, but didn't. Den had only agreed to allow me to come along if I promised to be quiet. As in: not one word.

"As I say, Mr. Mendo, this is a murder investigation, so it compels you to think about it. Someone sent an email from here."

Mendo flung his hands up. "What can I say? Jean Harlow is not on the program here. Do you think she's a killer?" His double chin jiggled as he spoke. I tried not to stare.

"I can't comment on the specifics of an ongoing investigation. But it's imperative we find her."

Mendo fussed with his tie. "Understood."

I'd been in enough talent agencies to realize there was more to the place than the official office where they greeted potential clients and other business-sorts.

Den stood, with the exacting confidence I more than admired in him. He moved like an Adonis. "Here's my card. If you remember otherwise, please call me."

I followed Den's lead, but I wasn't ready to give up. Why was he? Didn't he know people clam up in front of cops? Why didn't he press the guy more?

"Excuse me," I said. Den shot me a glare. "May I use your ladies' room?"

"Certainly," Mendo said as he opened his office door. "Down those stairs and off to the right."

"Thanks." Was I really going to do this? Damned straight.

I made my way down the stairs. Show posters lined the walls. All impersonators: Cher. Beyoncé. Britney Spears. If this was any indication of the Dream Girl agency's audience, maybe Mendo was correct—they may not appreciate Harlow. A winsome note of regret moved through me; it was too bad. But as I rounded a corner, more posters hung on the walls, and I followed them. Off to the left: Marilyn Monroe. Audrey Hepburn. Mae West. Several doors lined the hall.

"May I help you?" a voice from behind me said. I turned to find a Madonna look-alike, dressed the part.

"I've gotten lost. I was looking for the ladies room."

"The other way," she said, pointing. "Busy day here. You don't want to get run over."

"Oh?"

"Publicity shots." She smiled and posed, hands on hips in a very Madonna-like stance.

I chuckled. She curtsied. Very un-Madonna like.

I gathered my courage. "I was wondering if you'd answer a question for me."

"You a cop?" She slanted her eyes at me.

"No, no, no," I said, smiling and shaking my head. "I'm a writer working on a Jean Harlow biography."

A door opened from behind me. Madonna glanced and nodded at the person.

"And?" she said.

"Have you ever seen a Harlow impersonator here?"

She crossed her arms and leaned on the wall, appearing to be thinking it over.

"Hey, Madonna, get your ass in there. The photographer ain't got all day," the person behind us said.

"Hold your horses," Madonna said, standing her ground. "Sorry, hon, I can't think of anybody. Hey, Marilyn! C'mere a minute."

The next thing I noticed was a Marilyn Monroe impersonator standing next to my Madonna. "She's a writer," Madonna said, nodding her head in my direction. "Working on a Jean Harlow book."

"Really? How cool," the impersonator said, breathy like Marilyn.

"You've been at this a lot longer than me. Have you ever seen a Harlow act?"

Marilyn stiffened. "Why?"

Madonna blinked.

"Hey lady," Sal Mendo's voice came down the hallway. "Don't you know your left from your right?"

"Sorry, Mr. Mendo," I said. I reached into my bag and handed both of them a card, turning my back on Mendo and as I whispered, "She may be in trouble. I need to talk with her."

They each took my card and scattered into the rooms.

∞

"Why did you do that?" Den asked once we were far enough away from the agency. We were walking along the busy sidewalk, the sky darkening and the wind picking up. A spring storm fizzled at the edges of the late afternoon. "We have a protocol," he said.

"Look, Den, I know these entertainment types, and they don't care for the cops. I thought if I could get past Mr. Slick I'd get a scoop. That's all."

"He wasn't too thrilled to find you snooping around downstairs. You may have jeopardized this line of the investigation."

Curls of disappointment moved through me. I hadn't wanted to do that. "But I also made what might be an in-road."

Den didn't realize how I could be. Giving up was not in me. After all, this was research—a different kind than I usually did, huddled behind my laptop or between stacks of books at the library. But still. I didn't take no for an answer. Especially from a slick talent agent.

"And?"

"I'm not certain, but I think Marilyn Monroe may know something."

He grimaced. "Did you get her real name?"

"No, but I gave her my card and told her our Jean Harlow might be in trouble."

Den tilted his head, raised his eyebrows, and snapped his fingers. "Appealing to a possible friend like that might work. Did she say she knew her?"

"No, Mendo interrupted our conversation. But she seemed interested, like she was ready to talk about it before he interrupted."

"Let's hope it works. Let's say she does know the impersonator. If she mentions you, it could either send Jean Harlow to you or force her deeper into hiding. And what are you going to do if she reaches out to you? She's been stalking you. Do you think she has your best interest at heart?"

I had to admit I had no idea what to expect. But for the first time since Justine died, I was in control. Nobody was chasing me. I'd turned the tables. The undeniable spark of inspiration energized me.

Twenty-Seven

When I sat down at Justine's computer, I had every intention of writing an email. But as I read over the threatening words of that first email again, uncertainty crept in.

"I'll kill you. I swear if you go public with this I'll kill you," it said.

What could be so important and secretive about Jean Harlow's life that someone had threatened to kill Justine to keep it private? I'd convinced myself the murder had something to do with the sapphire ring, but as I read the email this time, my theory made no sense. Going public with the fact that the ring had resurfaced wasn't enough to kill someone, was it?

I could just ask, couldn't I? After all, that was why I'd sat down here. I would email back, explaining that I had taken over writing the book and requesting that he or she fill me in.

Why not?

The person could be a nut job. But their beef was with Justine, not me. Although perhaps their problem would be with anyone writing the Harlow book.

Another notion caught my mind. One of those nagging ethical dilemmas placed into my brain years ago by a journalism professor. What would you do for a story? For the truth? Do you owe it to your readers to deliver it without hesitation? Why write biographies if they are just going to perpetuate the same stories repeatedly?

There was nothing new in this book. It was Jean Harlow's biography, written in a fresher style, repackaged, with the famous Justine Turner's byline. But connecting this tale with the importance of the ring, along with the existence of my beautiful stalker and the fact of Justine's murder, would give me a real story. Meaty.

I had no proof of connections anywhere, though. Not yet. And I had to wonder if telling Harlow's story was worth dealing with a potential threat because of the ring—or because of some rumor of a deep, dark family secret?

I typed the words: *"To whom it may concern."*

Okay, that was a good start. What to say now? *Excuse me, why did you threaten Justine?*

I paused. How to handle this? I heard Justine's words: *"I always say sleep on it."*

Okay, I was going to table this until the morning.

But the next day my mind was even more murky. I would just focus on getting words on the page.

A few more days of writing, secluded in Justine's place, and I'd not heard a word from either Madonna or Marilyn Monroe. Nor did I see the Jean Harlow look-alike during any of my Central Park jaunts. Perhaps my strategy had failed.

I read over the last chapter I'd completed, adding a few commas and fixing spelling errors.

I was feeling very familiar with Jean Harlow. Or, Harlean Carpenter. This happened with every subject during the writing of the book. I'd refer to them in present tense as they became a part of my thought process—it was as if they were still alive. For example, I'd run across a certain style of a dress and think, "Oh, Clara would adore this." Seriously. It was like living in a strange time warp. Just me and my imaginary friends.

After we finished the books—or at least, up until that point—I would go into my ritualistic hibernation mode for a few days. A cleansing. Sometimes I started pre-researching the next biography during that phase. I didn't know if this would be the case for the Harlow book, since it differed from the get go. And now, with Justine gone, I wasn't certain where any of this left my career.

For all of my talk of selling out to be her lackey, Justine had been a good mentor, guiding me through the difficult, almost impenetrable publishing world. All I wanted to do was write—but writers no longer had that luxury. We needed to market, do social media, and blog.

Justine's agent and publisher tended to most of those details. She was a force in the publishing business. But I was not. I didn't expect the publisher to work as hard for me.

But I was carrying on Justine's legacy with this book. Wasn't I?

My cell phone buzzed.

I recognized the number. It was Lucille, the editor. Calling to check on the manuscript. I'd gotten a lot of work done. But what to say about the revelations nagging at me? Again, I let the phone go to voicemail.

I stood and stretched and walked out onto the apartment balcony. The day had warmed, shifting to more summer than spring. The sky was as blue as I'd ever seen, with big puffy white clouds floating by. Maybe I should finish the book, hang onto the ring until I could hand it over to the proper person, and then put all this behind me. After all, I needed to find a job.

My cell beckoned me back inside the apartment.

Den's number blinked onto my screen.

"Hello, Den," I said. "Any news?"

A long pause. Then, "Yes, I'm sorry. I've got bad news for you."

A rushing, sinking feeling came over me. What could be that bad? Here I was with a ring in my purse that people were killing for, a woman resembling Jean Harlow had been stalking me, and death threats were appearing on the computer screen. Not to mention my boss had been murdered.

How could it possibly get worse?

Twenty-Eight

"Come by the medical examiner's office," he said with an edge in his voice. "We'll talk in person."

"What?"

"I need you to come here as soon as you can."

My pulse quickened. His voice commanded me, and I had no choice. This was Den. Sergeant Den Brophy. Tendrils of fear, tinged with lust for him, circled through me as I readied to go to the morgue.

Nothing could prepare me for what I saw when I arrived.

Shimmering platinum-blonde hair curled on the metal table. A dainty upturned nose sprang from the pretty face. My gaze traveled along a bisque-white, perfectly proportioned body: breasts, flat stomach—and a slight scar on the pubic mound.

"So, what do you think, Charlotte?" Den said "Is this your Jean Harlow?

He obviously believed it was her. How many could there be? He'd warned me it would be bad, asking if I would be okay viewing the body. I said sure. And now here I stood, unable to speak. Finally, words formed in my mouth.

"It certainly looks like her. And like the real Jean Harlow," I said. "Right down to the fake mole on her face."

"Fake?"

"Yeah. Jean's mole changed locations a few times." I hovered my finger over the mole. "Can I?"

"Yep," he said.

I lifted it. Sure enough, it was fake.

"That's kinda strange."

"This impersonator was trying to be really authentic, even down to the fake mole," I said. "Interesting."

I snapped a few photos with my phone, feeling sick but thinking that I might need them someday.

"I think this scar means, well, that we're looking at a transgender individual," Den said.

I took another picture, for future reference, and swallowed another wave of nausea. There was a further tale here. Between the already written lines of Harlow's life story, here was this person, this beautiful person who'd been following me. Had she wanted the ring? If so, how did she know Justine had it? Or was there something else she'd wanted?

I breathed in deeply. No, I refused to let the sickening formaldehyde stench make me heave.

I remembered an old journalism professor of mine. He used to say it was fine to throw up because of being sickened by a corpse or gruesome crime scene—but *never* in front of a cop.

But then again, I was no journalist. I didn't even harbor those inclinations anymore. I was a lackey and a hack—and I was feeling every bit of it in that moment. Had my meeting with the other impersonators placed Jean Harlow in danger?

"Do you have an ID on her?" I asked, my voice a whisper.

"Nothing. Has anything in your research led you to other impersonators of Harlow?"

"I looked up impersonators online and found little. And the agency gave us nothing, remember?"

If I'd had more time, it might have been interesting to explore impersonators to the stars. But as Justine used to say, *"We don't have time for deep thought and years of research. We're writing pop biography. Our readers want the drama."* There'd been no point in deviating from this approach, especially because Justine was one of only a few writers who made a living with writing. She'd developed a system—a formula, if you will—and readers responded to it. They adored her.

I'd often wanted to go a little deeper into our subjects, particularly Clara Bow. But Justine had thwarted me by giving me even more research on clothing, makeup, and Clara's many affairs. So I hadn't had the chance to go into depth, given publishing deadlines. The deadlines always pressed, one right after the other.

"Probably a waste of time anyway," Den said, shrugging, tucking his chin slightly in.

I loved that gesture. He was the cutest damn cop I'd ever seen. When he smiled at me, I tingled. I figured it wouldn't last. It never did. But then again, I hadn't even slept with him yet.

"I want to point out this may have nothing to do with Justine's murder," he added.

"Of course it does. Why would you say that?"

"Transgender people as a group are one of the highest in murder rates."

Weight pressed on me. I had no idea. I immediately thought of Kate.

"It may be a hate crime."

"Or my talking with Marilyn Monroe and Madonna set something off," I could barely say.

146

"A possibility—but remote." Den spoke with empathy, reminding me again of the day Justine passed away and how he'd soothed me, his voice reaching out and wrapping itself around me. His arm went around me, rubbing my shoulder. "It will be okay."

I wanted to believe him. But things appeared worse now than they were when I walked in the door. Now there was another dead body. She was linked to the Harlow story. But exactly how? And was she associated with Justine's murder? Den must have considered these same facts.

"Okay," I said, taking one last look at the corpse on the table in front of me. She resembled Jean Harlow so much that it chilled me. And she must have had a hell of a plastic surgeon. It looked as if she would open her eyes and lift herself from the table at any moment. This creature was more beautiful in death than most of us ever are in life.

"Please tell me what you find out. Cause of death and so on," I said. "I'm curious."

"We all are, " Den said as he opened the door. I walked through, brushing up against him, enjoying his breath on my neck.

As we moved into the main office, a group of cops gathered around a desk. They were watching us. I wondered what Den had told them about me and hoped none of them were my Tinder friends.

"You okay? Where you off to?" he said, pulling me into him in a warm rush after we exited the building. "I have about half an hour. There's a great coffee shop around the corner. Old school. Ya know what I mean? What do you say?"

I say my work can wait.

Twenty-Nine

Two more weeks until I'd make my move. Or allow him to make his. As long as it was made. Though I had to say, the way this was unfolding was interesting. It had been a few years since a man was interested in learning about me, asking my opinion and advice, caring about my mind. I'd been focused on the rush of need and burn. The warm simmering broth of a relationship had been beyond me.

Was Kate right? Did I have a problem?

I did like cops. Hell, I loved them. Lusted after them. But they weren't the only men I lusted after, were they?

Before I became even more distracted, I forced myself to get back to work. I clicked away at the keyboard. One word after the next.

My cell phone rang. It was Den.

"Hey," I said.

"Hey yourself," he said in a breathy voice.

"What's up?" I stood and walked around the library glancing over the floor to ceiling built in bookcases. The kind my dreams were made of. I could live in this room, just this room, and be happy among the books.

"Other than the fact that I had coffee with the most amazing woman?"

"Den! You didn't call to tell me that, did you." I ran my fingers along Justine's collection of first editions—Hemingway, Fitzgerald, Faulkner. "But thanks for the compliment," I said with a laugh.

"Are you in Justine's apartment?" he asked.

"Yes, in her library. It's still so … amazing."

"I was calling to let you know we've got a name on our Jane Doe, and you're not going to freaking believe this."

"Okay," I said with an inflection in my voice. "Get to it, Den."

"She's Jean Harlow."

"She is not Jean Harlow," I said.

"No, I mean that all of her ID and everything says she's Jean Harlow," Den replied.

"But even Jean Harlow wasn't Jean Harlow. She was Harlean Carpenter. Jean Harlow was a stage name," I said. "Actually it was her mother's name."

"I figured that. I remember you saying something about it," Den said. "But I'm telling you, all the records say she's Jean Harlow."

"Well, obviously, she changed her name."

"But there's no record of it," Den said. "Name changes are documented."

"What about family? Does she have any family? Someone must know why she was walking around looking like a movie star and taking her name."

"So far, we've found no family," he said. "She was alone here in the city."

The idea of that beautiful person alone in New York City overwhelmed me with some unnameable emotion, forcing a tear to spring to my eye. Hard to believe the look-alike hadn't had men, at least, clamoring around her. If she hadn't, there must have been a reason.

Jean Harlow herself always had men flitting around her. She enjoyed the attention. But she never quite found happiness in the arms of a man. There was nothing unusual about that, I mused. The big irony in her life was that she found love with her last lover—William Powell. But he was a raging alcoholic, which strained their relationship. And then she died. At twenty-six.

"How could the impersonator be alone? You saw her," I said. I walked into the room off the library, a formal dining room with a huge chandelier hanging from the ceiling. I switched on the light and watched the crystal reflect onto the ceiling. Marvelous.

"Yeah, man, I don't know," Den said. "But it looks like she just moved here."

"From Hollywood?" I said, joking.

He laughed. "How did you know?"

My mouth dropped. "Seriously?"

"Yep," he said. "But she's been everywhere. Paris. Munich. Vegas."

"Was she an entertainer?" I asked. She must have made a living as a Jean Harlow impersonator, even though the agency claimed otherwise. Of course, there were other agencies.

"We have no record of her working at all," Den said.

"Have you checked with the IRS?"

"We're in the process. Once I hear, I'll call you. But the mystery of our Jane Doe slash Jean Harlow deepens. Wouldn't you say?"

How could a world traveler, looking like Jean Harlow and using her name, not attract attention? Why hadn't she come up on our radar before now?

I made my way back into the library, sat down at Justine's desk, and opened my laptop. I was hoping to get another extension on the biography from Lucille. The story of Harlow's life might have just deepened, warranting a tangent. Perhaps it would lead me nowhere. But it was worth at least two hours of research.

Truth be told, Jean Harlow's life was not that interesting to me at first. But as with all of my subjects, as I moved forward in the research and writing, she grabbed hold of my imagination. There were nuggets about the actress that I chewed on and found inspiring—which was just sufficient to keep me going—and they made her feel alive to me. But the Jean Harlow look-alike? She'd already reached out to me in a way that the real Jean Harlow never had.

"Any idea how she was killed?"

"No yet," Den replied. "We're rushing on the tox reports. So far, heart attack is the cause of death. She was in her mid-thirties, so I'm thinking a heart attack's not quite right."

Shards of excitement zoomed through me. "Heart attack? Like Justine's? Is it possible she was poisoned?"

"I'm trying not to project on this situation, but I'd say it's possible. If that's the case, we have a very valuable connection." Den paused and sighed. "A connection leading nowhere at this point."

I didn't accept it. I wouldn't. If they were connected, there had to be a reason. I'd find that reason. Or die trying.

Thirty

I plotted out Justine's life, as I did for any biography, on a timeline. It took several hours. There were gaping holes in it. For example, her apartment—when did she get it? This line of thinking reminded me I needed to check in with the lawyer again about Justine's will. Surely they'd found the updates by now? Surely her cousin Judith had gone back to Florida?

I now plotted out the Jean Harlow look-alike's life. Not much there. She was in her mid-thirties, so she'd been born in the 1980s. She'd lived in New York for the past few weeks, coming here from Hollywood. That's all we understood. How long had she been here?

I listed my questions, which, once the police investigated further, might be easy to answer:

Had she connected with Justine while she was here?

When, exactly, did she come here from Hollywood?

Where was she before she lived in Hollywood?

What did she do to make a living?

Family?

Boyfriends?

Girlfriends?

Where had Justine and the look-alike crossed paths? They must have. What did they have in common? The ring? Or was it something else?

I almost didn't hear my cell phone beep. It jarred me back into the real world.

"The IRS has no recent Jean Harlow on record," Den said when I answered the phone.

"If the IRS doesn't know about her, who would?" I stared at the computer screen. I'd just written a few chapters. I wanted to write at least one more before the day was over.

"I don't see where the investigation is heading. We're meeting about it today. Justine's case may go cold," Den said.

"Why?" I asked.

"We've not gotten any real leads yet. We have the killer's DNA. A grainy picture. But nothing after that. You realize we don't have those kinda resources."

"Yeah, but the look-alike? Her case is new, right? Perhaps the two of them link? Have you gotten the result of the tox tests for her? "

"No, not yet," Den said. "But yeah, the woman in the morgue, she freaks me out. I was looking at some pictures of Harlow, and I gotta say I don't think I could tell 'em apart."

"I hear you." The image of the perfect corpse etched in my mind, I shivered. "What's going to happen to her if nobody claims her?"

"Do you really want to know?'

"Yes," I said.

"The city will take care of her body. She'll be buried over on Hart Island. You know about that place?"

"Sort of," I said. It was where the indigents and other unclaimed people were buried. The notion of the Jean Harlow look-alike over there set my teeth on edge. Not right. Somebody had to claim her.

"It's all respectfully done," he said. "Sometimes they even have funerals."

"Why would they do that?"

"I'm not sure, but I've been to a few of them. It's not required, but a lot of us go to pay respects," he explained. "Just seems like the right thing to do, especially if it's a body you found or something. Pay your respects. Every person's life matters. They deserve a little respect when they die."

A growing twinge of awe for this guy settled in my center. There was so much more to Den than his looks. Longing tugged at me.

I struggled with how to react.

Den broke the silence. "I can't imagine our Jean Harlow there."

Our Jean Harlow.

When the real Jean Harlow died, it was more of a spectacle than Justine's star-studded memorial service had been. I'd read in detail how Harlow's funeral had all the trappings of a Hollywood movie. At nine that morning—June 9, 1937—all the Hollywood studios observed a moment of silence. Louis B. Mayer made sure the service, held in the Wee Kirk o' the Heather Chapel at Forest Lawn, Glendale, was a grand event. Fans clamored at the gates of the cemetery and photographers scaled fences. Flowers overflowed onto the lawn from inside the chapel. None other than Clark Gable served as a pallbearer and usher, with Carole Lombard saving him a seat in a pew. All of Hollywood turned out to say goodbye to Jean, two hundred and fifty mourners packing into the small chapel. Jeanette MacDonald sang Jean's favorite song, "Indian Love Call," and then joined Nelson Eddy in a duet, "Ah, Sweet Mystery of Life." Afterward, hordes of fans swarmed in and stripped away every flower and personal memento.

One of the real mysteries in Jean's life, of course, was the death of her second husband, Paul Bern. Rumors ran amuck.

The most interesting rumor was that Jean herself had killed him after finding out about a woman who claimed to be his common-law wife. Could sweet-faced, well-loved, newly married Jean Harlow have taken a gun and, in a fit of mad jealousy, shot her husband? Call me crass, but I liked to think so.

But his death was just one of the unsolved mysteries of the day. One challenge in writing about any star of this period was that the studios spun their actors' life stories, making it difficult to get at the root of any star's personality. Also, it made it possible for many of them to get away with many things—yes, even murder.

It's not so easy these days to get away with murder, kidnappings, and so on. Cameras are all around us. Big Brother is watching. If you run a red light, the cops trace it and send you a ticket. Tracing people online is easy. Which is why thoughts of the Jean Harlow look-alike held firm in my mind. There were so few traces of her life—at least, none that we could find. That had to be deliberate.

∞

My cell phone buzzing awakened me at three a.m. Who the hell would be calling? I blinked away the blur. No number. I rolled over and let it ring.

The damn thing buzzed again.

"Hello!"

Heavy breathing.

"Hello? Who is this?" I sat up on the chaise. It wasn't as if I'd never had a heavy breather on the other end of the line. But things in my life had gotten so strange that this call freaked me out.

A sob. Female.

"Can I help you?"

"She's dead," the voice said between sobs.

"Who?"

"Harlow," the garbled voice said.

"Yes," I replied. *Keep her on the phone.* Didn't they always say that on TV? Why? "Do you know anything that could help us find who killed her?"

Silence. Then muffled sobs. "I should never have called."

Which one was this? Marilyn? Madonna? Her voice was too soft and muffled, like an old-fashioned radio losing its signal.

"It's okay. We'll protect you." I somehow found words between the thoughts circling in my brain. "We'll do everything we can."

"Her father," the voice whispered. "Her father."

"What's his name?"

"I don't know." She hung up.

"Wait!" But it was too late.

I examined my phone like it held the secrets of the universe. But the number was "unrecognized." Still, maybe the police could trace it and we could compel the person to tell us more. If she knew more.

Wide awake, skin prickling, I stood and paced around the library. *Her father. Her father.* Why would a father kill his child? How naïve was that question? It probably happened a lot.

But wait. Was I going to believe an anonymous caller in the middle of the night? It could have been someone wanting to throw me off the trail. We didn't know the look-alike's real name—let alone her dad's.

And, what's more, we were uncertain if her murder had anything to do with Justine's. We needed hard evidence.

Evidence. Den's face sprang in mind.

It was three fifteen a.m. Could I call him? He was a cop, used to getting calls in the wee hours.

My phone was burning in my hand. I pressed Den's name.

Ring. Ring. Ring. Pick up Den.

"Yeah." A gravelly, sleepy voice came over the phone.

"It's me, Charlotte."

"Yeah. What's up?" A smoky image of him in bed swirled around in my mind. I shoved it out.

"I just got a call from someone about our Jean Harlow."

"And?" He yawned.

"She said her father killed her."

"Yeah? Did she give you a name?"

"No."

Disappointment vibrated in the air between us.

"Will you be able to trace the call?"

"We can try. Let's hope she's not using a burner phone. Then there's not much we can do."

"Sorry to call you in the middle of the night."

"Come down to the station tomorrow and I'll have the guys look at your phone. Around ten."

"Okay. See you then. Good night."

I lay back down, tossed and turned. I couldn't find peace. Who was I kidding? I lifted myself from the chaise and padded into the kitchen, where I brewed a big pot of coffee. I expected this to be a break in the case and not just some Jean Harlow fan fruitcake. I hoped the phone call would lead us down the path to answers.

When I walked into the station, a kind of buzz was happening. Something electric and untouchable, but exciting.

Den met me at the front desk with a grin. "We've got a break. C'mon. C'mon back."

I followed him through the snaking hallways and cubicles.

"This is Joe Delvechio. He'll take your phone and get it back to you before you leave."

I smiled at Joe and handed him my phone.

"Please sit down," Den said, gesturing at a chair across from a small, plain desk.

"What's up?"

"We've found out exactly how Justine was killed." His cheeks were flushed and the veins in his neck throbbed. "All we have to do is uncover a trace of it in Harlow to link these two murders."

As I couldn't seem to locate any words in my brain, Den continued. "He injected her with potassium chloride. That was the other drug, the lethal one."

"What? We witnessed him slip something into her tea."

"That was the Valium. But on closer examination of the security footage, we could see him quickly inject her right after he dropped the pill in her tea. The ME confirms it."

I remembered viewing that on the recording—the quick pat on Justine's shoulder. That must have been when he did it.

"So, how it works is an overdose of potassium causes severe heart arrhythmias and mimics a heart attack. In a matter of minutes, the heart spasms and then stops. The ME says huge amounts of potassium goes into the blood whenever any muscle tissue is damaged. The heart is a muscle, right? So it would look like a fatal heart attack. Unless there were more tests."

I felt a loosening in my lungs. An unraveling. A release of tensions, as if I'd been holding my breath for all this time. My hands glommed onto my burning face. Unwanted tears splashed over my cheeks in a waterfall of emotions. Was I crying in front of Den?

He leaned over. "Are you okay?" Placed his hands on my shoulder. "Take a deep breath for me?"

I tried. Breath came in heaving stutters.

"I assumed you'd be thrilled about this," he said softly. That voice. That soothing voice of his spread through the center of me. I nodded.

Sorting my emotions was beyond me. *Conclusive evidence.* A half-resolution sat in my chest as I attempted to gain composure, but it ripped and tore at me. This wasn't the closure I'd anticipated. It was empty. Justine was still gone, and we still had no idea who killed her. The same with the Jean Harlow look-alike.

Joe came back into the room. "Sorry to interrupt."

"What do you have for us?" Den stiffened, now alert, sounding official and not sympathetic at all.

"Nothing. Not one damn thing." He handed Den my phone.

Thirty-One

Such is life. One door opens, another closes. Or so they say.

We knew what killed Justine. But we still didn't know who.

We didn't know who called me or why.

Nor did we learn who killed the Harlow look-alike—or if she had been injected with the same substance. Den assured me they were rushing as fast as they could. He sounded dejected, almost as if he were ready to give up.

But I wasn't finished. Not by a long shot. Whether Den liked it or not, I was heading back to the Dream Girl agency. One of the emails sent to Justine had come from there. My gut told me that both Madonna and Marilyn were acquainted with Jean.

"Hey, Kate, are you up for a show?" I said into the phone.

"What kind of show?"

"An impersonator show. I'm guessing there may be drag queens."

"I'm in," she said.

The anticipation and energy in Jezebel, the Dream Girl club, was almost palpable. The host sat us at a table with a candle votive glowing in the center. From our vantage point, we could see the stage, but not completely.

"I'll have a martini," Kate said. "What else? This place calls for it."

"I'll have the same," I said to the server, a woman dressed in a tuxedo who reminded me of the usher at Justine's memorial service.

"Nice establishment," Kate said, fingers tapping on the pink tablecloth.

Though it was dim, my eyes were adjusting and taking in the other audience members. An older man and woman sat catty-corner from us, holding hands. On the other side of us was a gay couple, also holding hands.

"Maybe we should hold hands," I joked.

"What?" Kate said, then realized the surrounding couples were all doing so. "No thanks," she said, waving me off.

But still, it was the kind of place that made me feel a bit wild. Like I could do anything here, be anybody here.

Music played softly over the speakers. Heads were bobbing in front of the stage; I wasn't sure we'd be able to view much. But it wasn't important. What I wanted to do was approach Madonna and Marilyn after the show. Madonna was on the bill, headlining. The rest of the cast? A surprise billing. But I was hoping to meet Marilyn from the agency again.

The server brought our martinis and placed the glasses on the table. "Enjoy the show," she said, smiling.

The lights blinked out and we sat in the dark, all eyes on the stage. "Like a Virgin" came over the speaker and the spotlight shone on to a Madonna impersonator, who pranced around and lip-synched to the song. I was certain this was my Madonna.

I suddenly wondered whether she was transgender, too, but that didn't matter. What mattered was finding her after the show to ask if she was the one who'd called me. If it wasn't her, then I would need to find Marilyn—whether or not Marilyn was here tonight.

I glanced at Kate, who was enthralled by Madonna and clapping her hands in time with the beat.

I had to admit, the Madonna impersonator rocked. You'd swear you were looking at a young Madonna, tarted up in a wedding dress that was gradually being pulled away from her and tossed aside. A bump. A grind. Body sways. Pouty lips. Brazen, raw sexuality.

Almost like Jean Harlow's. In fact, I'd read somewhere that Madonna credited both Jean Harlow and Marilyn Monroe as inspirations.

Soon she was down to a sexy white chemise and body suit, slinking around the stage.

The song suddenly changed rhythm and another person pranced out—a Beyoncé impersonator.

Kate caught my eye. She was a devotee of all things Beyoncé. Her eyebrows rose. "Nobody can even come close to the real thing."

But as Beyoncé gyrated her performance, a grin spread across Kate's face. Madonna exited the stage.

"I'm going backstage," I said into Kate's ear.

"Wait. What?" She grabbed me. "They will not let you backstage."

I flashed Justine's press pass. "Be back soon."

Kate hesitated. "I should come with you."

"No, that would be suspicious," I said into her ear, above the music.

"Okay," she said after a few beats, then looked at her watch. "Thirty minutes and I'm coming after you."

I nodded. A part of me hated to leave Beyoncé.

But I headed out to find the backstage door, which I did without a problem. A security guard lifted his eyes from his magazine.

"Hold up," he said. "Where are you going?"

"Press," I said, and flashed Justine's pass. Given the way most people felt about the press these days, I wasn't certain this would work. But I had to try.

"I see nothing on the schedule," he said, unsure.

My eyebrows knitted. "Are you sure? They're expecting me."

He sized me up. A shortish woman, dressed casually in nice jeans, a shirt, and a blazer. I looked harmless.

He nodded. "Okay. Go ahead."

The knot in my stomach relaxed. I wasn't aware it was there until it eased. I walked down the narrow brown corridor, with its stench of stale perfume mingled with jaded dreams, and found a dressing room. I rapped on the door. No answer. I moved down the hall toward a sign that read *Stage door—Quiet*.

A group of performers stood there. It was as if I'd just wandered into Hollywood. In that clutch of people, I found the Marilyn impersonator. I was certain it was the same one I'd met at the agency.

"Excuse me," I said. All eyes on me.

Marilyn flashed me an uneasy look. "Say, you're that writer from the other day."

"Yes. Can I talk to you?"

"Quickly. I'm going on in ten." She fluffed her hair as she came forward. We grouped together off to the other side of the hallway.

"So, how can I help you?" She leaned on the wall, crossing her arms.

The resemblance remained startling. Disturbing. I reminded myself she was not Marilyn Monroe.

"I guess I need to know if you called me."

Her eyebrows gathered. "No, I didn't call you." Her eyes traveled to someone else. She looked behind me.

Sal Mendo ambled up the hallway.

"Hey! How did you get back here?" He grabbed my shoulder. I squinted at him and his hand. He removed it. "You're bothering the girls. You need to go."

"I'm working on a story." I flashed Justine's press pass.

He reached for it and examined it. "I don't know who you think you're kidding. You're not Justine."

Crap. Shards of fear moved through the center of me.

"No. I'm her assistant," I found the voice to say.

Mendo paused. "Look, I had the utmost respect for Justine Turner, but you don't have any business here."

"You knew her?"

He nodded. "I didn't know her well. But I knew her."

"Did you realize she was working on a Harlow biography?"

The man's face changed. "Yeah, everybody knew, but like I told you, I know nothing about any Harlow impersonator. And you need to go."

I glared at him, then looked at Marilyn, who would not make eye contact. Okay, if she hadn't called me, it must have been Madonna. If she was telling the truth, it was Madonna I needed to speak with.

"Okay," I said. "Sorry to trouble you."

As I turned to leave, cold pressed into my back and I shuddered.

Thirty-Two

*B*ack at the apartment, Kate and I discussed what went down. "I couldn't stay because the guy was watching me like a hawk," I said. "But I need to get to Madonna."

Kate laughed. "Don't we all."

"I'll look for her tomorrow."

"Don't you have a book to write?"

"Yes, but this has something to do with the story. I feel like there's a strange connection here."

Kate leaned forward after fussing with her scarf. "I'm not following."

"Den and I suspect the person who killed the Harlow impersonator is the same one who killed Justine."

"You said that earlier. But I don't understand why. It could be two very unrelated cases. First, you said the look-alike's body was found where?"

"In the back of an abandoned car down by the East River."

"I don't guess the tea room killer could be the backseat killer. Do you? It doesn't seem to fit."

I mulled that over. "I doubt where the bodies were discovered counts. What matters is Justine was working on the biography. I was being stalked by a person who looks like the subject of the biography, and now she shows up dead. Of a heart attack, no less. Maybe caused by poison."

"Hmm, I see your point. But why? Why would someone murder them? Is there something about Harlow? The ring? Surely he or she didn't kill them for the ring. They're dead. If they had the ring, the killer just eliminated their chances of getting it. Right?"

"You're right. On the face of things, it makes no sense. And yet, there's more here to chew on."

Kate sighed, a long, drawn-out, yawn-type of sigh. "Girl, you are borderline OCD. I swear. You always have been. You never know when to quit."

"Is that bad?" I said, grinning.

Kate waved me off, shaking her head. "I guess it's served you well," she said after a few beats.

"And then there's the phone call," I said.

"Yeah, that's weird and creepy. How would she know anything about the look-alike's father?"

"Well, it sounded like she'd met him, or maybe the look-alike told her about him." My stomach knotted. I hated speaking with Kate about fathers.

"I see why you need to find that person and ask what it's all about."

"So I'll check into the Madonna impersonator. If Marilyn was being honest about not calling me, then it must be Madonna."

"You know what's funny? You're chatting about Harlow on the one hand, and two celebrities who've said she was their inspiration on the other."

"An odd coincidence, but you're right." I was chilled. The slight scent of Cotillion hung in the air. "Did it get cold in here?"

Kate nodded.

"I've not been able to figure out the thermostat."

"That felt like someone opened a window, not anything to do with the thermostat. Odd. These old apartments are so sturdy. But they can also be drafty and dilapidated."

"That must be it." I didn't mention Justine's perfume. "I can't wait for the tox reports to come back on Harlow."

"Yeah, that'll tell us everything, right? If she was poisoned by the same thing. Man, how freaky would that be?"

Freaky, indeed.

As Kate filed her nails, my eyes moved to my laptop and I reflected on the story. I always felt I should write instead of doing anything else. But then, after hours of writing, I suspected I should get out, away from the computer and the story. The constant push and pull between these things was a part of my life, and I wondered if it was the same for every writer.

"The writer's life is a bitch, believe me, kid."

Still, it was the only thing I'd ever wanted to do. Was I sadistic? Were we all?

I never wished to be anything else, like a computer programmer or a teacher or, God forbid, a police officer. But here I was, investigating two murders. The daughter of a cop who left his family; the woman who craved cops in her bed. Sometimes I worried Kate was right. Sometimes I wondered if I had a problem with the men in blue. I mean, who wouldn't, after it all. But I wouldn't give her satisfaction over that revelation. Not at all.

The startling fact I'd found out about myself over the past few weeks was that I didn't need sex as much as I believed. Or maybe I'd just been distracted by the murders and my work. But that had never happened before. Another surprising revelation was that Den, an incredibly hot cop, liked me without sleeping with me. But what would happen after?

My heart fluttered. I didn't know what would transpire with Den, but he seemed different. *"Proceed with caution, dear girl."*

Thirty-Three

Kate and I decided to attend the impersonator show once again. This time, I vowed to have a conversation with the Madonna entertainer. I figured she was my caller, and I needed to learn what she meant by implying that the Harlow look-alike's father was responsible for her death.

We stopped in a nearby bar for a few drinks before the show. Kate plopped herself onto a bar stool and I stood next to her, leaning on the bar. She wore a crimson pantsuit with lips to match, and thick gold chains and drooping earrings.

The bartender took her in. "What can I do for you?" he asked, hands on the bar.

"I'd like a diet coke and JD." Kate flipped her hair back.

"I'll take a Guinness. Do you have some on tap?"

He nodded in my direction, but his eyes never left Kate. "Sure thing."

"So, do you expect this woman to know anything at all about Harlow?"

"If she's the one who called me, she definitely knows something. Any little piece at this point would help."

The bartender set our drinks in front of us. Two more people sauntered up to the bar and he moved in their direction.

Kate grunted. She probably was remembering her own father and the beating she took when she told him she was getting the operation. She'd showed up at my door, half dead. It sickened me to remember it. Even now. Even after all these years. He was enraged so much about his son's gender that he beat the living shit out of him.

"I think about my father sometimes," she said. This surprised me, because Kate didn't like to talk about him. "I wonder if he ever regrets his actions."

"I'm sure he does." I lifted the Guinness to my lips, downing the thick, bitter liquid as the foam kissed my mouth. Our families had assumed Kate and I would get married, even when we both knew that wasn't the case—we were simply best friends of different genders. Why was that so hard for people to understand?

She shrugged and sipped from her drink. "I'm not considering him tonight. Let's think about getting answers from Madonna."

I lifted my glass. "Damn straight!"

As I drank, a weird sensation crept up my back, as if someone was behind me. I set my drink down and turned to see Severn Hartwell—Justine's biggest competitor, the man who'd followed me onto the subway. He sneered. "Fancy meeting you here."

The hair on the back of my neck stood at attention. My body tensed.

Kate was looking in the other direction. But the bartender headed our way.

"Hey, what can I get you?"

Hartwell paused. "Nothing now. I didn't realize you let scum like this broad in the place."

"What?" I turned toward him. "Get lost, Hartwell."

Kate's attention zoomed in on him.

"What gives, mister?" the bartender said.

Hartwell grabbed me by the shoulders—so hard I swear every vertebrae in my neck jammed. A rush of focused anger moved through me and, without planning it, my knee jabbed into his groin and he yowled, crouching into a ball.

A large man headed our way. Must be the bouncer. Kate grabbed Hartwell and shoved him into the large man. "This guy attacked my friend!"

"What a bitch!" Hartwell said between labored breaths as the bouncer dragged him off.

The air buzzed around us for a few minutes, and then a calm came over the place. The bartender set two more drinks in front us. "On the house, ladies." He grinned one of the widest I'd ever seen.

"Who the hell was that?" Kate asked, after thanking the bartender.

"That was Severn Hartwell. Another biographer. He wanted to write the definitive biography of Jean Harlow. Justine got the exclusive book deal. No other publisher would touch him. So he's throwing a hissy fit. Followed me onto the train one day."

"Oh," Kate said. "I remember." She shrugged again. "So why doesn't he write about someone else? Greta Garbo? Chaplin? Seems like there's a lot of stars to pick from."

"A few months ago, I would've agreed. But like Justine said, this biography brought out all the Harlow kooks."

Kate laughed. "Who knew?"

"Right?" The absurdity of the situation grabbed hold of me as I finished my first stout and moved on to the second. I found myself laughing too.

"This is not funny," Kate said with a sobering quality. "You've been chased, threatened, and stalked."

"Yeah. It's not funny at all." I took a sip from the new glass of Guinness, my hands trembling.

"Hey, where'd you learn to kick like that, anyway?" Kate smiled.

She knew perfectly well where I'd learned to kick. My gram taught all the girls on the island how to defend ourselves.

Adrenaline coursed through me and my hand still trembled as I lifted the glass to my mouth again. I'd never put into practice any of my gram's self-defense moves. I always theorized that if I were attacked, I wouldn't have the presence of mind to remember to kick a man in the groin. But damn, it was a reflex I didn't know I possessed.

"A lady never divulges her secrets." I licked the foam from my mouth.

Later, Kate and I sat at our table at the club. The atmosphere, once again, bristled with energy and excitement. Fifteen minutes until show time. Last time I'd waited until about halfway through the performance. But tonight I couldn't wait. I excused myself and headed for the backstage door once again.

The guard stopped me. It was a different guard, which was a good thing. I didn't want to cause any trouble. I wanted a smooth entry and exit.

I showed him my press pass and he motioned me through. I walked down the long gray halls to the doors with names painted on them. I tapped on the door that read "Madonna."

"Okay!" she yelled. "I'm almost ready."

I knocked again.

"Jesus!" She opened the door in a huff. For a brief flick of a moment, I swore Madonna herself was standing in front of me. "You again? Does Sal realize you're here?"

"No. Can I come in?" I looked both ways and didn't see Sal Mendo coming. I moved forward.

She pressed her hand on my chest, stopping me. "Look, I don't know what you're doing here. But I've got nothing to add to what I've already said, okay?"

"Did you call me the other night?" I asked. Madonna's eyebrows gathered; her arms folded. "Because the Jean Harlow impersonator is dead. Probably was murdered. If you knew her and have any information—"

The Madonna impersonator pushed me hard, and I landed on my ass with an embarrassing, painful thud. Then she slammed the door and locked it.

"Go away!" she yelled. "Just leave me alone or I'll call the cops!"

Fuck. Every instinct within me told me Madonna might know something, and that she was the one who'd called. But it was obvious she wasn't interested in talking. And if I pressed it, it might spark more attention.

I reached into my jacket pocket, pulled out another card, and slid it beneath her door.

Thirty-Four

"Well?" Kate said as we left the place. "Any luck?"

"She shoved me and slammed the door."

Kate laughed. "I wish I could have seen that."

"Well, you missed it," I replied.

We walked along the lively street. It was dark, but well-lit by businesses up and down the pavement. We were moving at quite a clip when an arm reached out and grabbed me.

"What the—"

Kate turned and followed as the person, wrapped in a long overcoat, pulled me into an alley.

"Hey!" Kate said just as the person revealed herself to us.

"Shhhh," she replied.

Madonna.

"What's this about?" I said. My shoulder ached where she'd snagged me.

"It's a warning," she said, breathless. "Don't come back to the club. Sal has your photos, and the bouncer won't let you in."

Was that it? She pulled me off the street for this? There had to be more to this.

"Okay. I wasn't planning to return. You pushed me. I don't need that. I'm just trying to bring justice to the Jean Harlow impersonator."

Kate stood with her chest sort of puffed, crossing her arms. Her eyes narrowed. She sensed danger. And so did I. What was going on here?

"About that…" Madonna said. "I did know her, but not well. She tried to get work with us and Sal was unimpressed." She shrugged her shoulders. "I'm not sure of his reasoning. She was a beauty." She paused. "But she might have sent an email from the agency, if that's why you keep asking us about her. We all use the agency's computers from time to time."

That was interesting. And so far, it all rang true. But there had to be more to it. Or else why was Madonna being so secretive?

"I spotted her at the computer and she was frightened," the impersonator added.

"Of what?"

"Well, at first I assumed it was because I'd caught her and she wasn't supposed to be there. She hadn't been hired." Madonna twisted her head and looked both directions, lowered her voice. "But she said her father had located her and would kill her." The impersonator's face drained of color. She herself was frightened. "I don't think I've ever seen anybody so scared."

Kate's eyes were now wide with excitement—or was it fear? Sweat beads formed on my forehead. If the Jean Harlow look-alike's father had found her, and killed her, her murder had nothing to do with Justine's. It didn't figure. I wasn't sure why, but I couldn't let go of the idea that the murders were connected.

"So do you suspect her father killed her?" I asked in a whisper.

"I'm almost certain of it." Madonna cracked her gum, a habit I despised.

"Do you have a name for her dad?" Kate asked.

Good question. I should have thought to ask that.

"No," she said. "So many trans people have such a rough time with family. It's very... sensitive. We're not all Caitlyn Jenner, you know."

Kate grunted.

I felt queasy when I considered it. "Did you learn her real name?"

"Jean's?"

I nodded.

"Oh, no. We never use our real names," Madonna replied. "The only person who'd know would be Sal, for paycheck purposes, and he never hired her, so..."

A pedicab driver whizzed by me, cutting it close.

"Those bastards," Madonna said. Chew. Chew. Chew. "A menace to the streets."

"So the only information you can offer is that she was frightened of her father and maybe he killed her. But you're uncertain," I said.

"That's right. And please tell nobody where you've gotten that information from. I don't need cops poking around in my business, if you know what I mean." She blew a large pink bubble, and I thought once again how she was so Madonna-like.

It was interesting to get confirmation for our theory. But I doubted it would help without names. We needed names, the one thing these impersonators didn't seem to want to give.

"Why so secretive?" Kate asked. "Is that Sal guy a prick or what?"

"Yeah, he's a piece of work. I don't need him to learn I've talked to you, okay?"

We both nodded.

"I'm also afraid that Sal might know Jean's father. Or Jean's father is around somewhere watching us? I might be paranoid. But I'd like to live a while longer, such as it is." She rolled her eyes. "Gotta get home to the kids. The sitter hates when I'm late. But promise me you won't come back. It could be dangerous for you."

I didn't expect to return. Besides, Madonna might be right. "Okay, I promise. Take care of yourself."

A softness came over her face, as if nobody had ever said that to her before. "Thank you." And she was off.

"What do you think?" Kate said after she left.

"She's genuine. But we need details."

"Interesting to learn about the Jean Harlow impersonator's father."

"Yes, but we don't know her real name, let alone his," I said, exasperated.

"How much longer can these people remain unnamed? I'm certain a name will turn up soon."

I hoped Kate was right. I wanted justice for both murdered women. But the eccentric way both of them lived their lives was making it difficult. Nobody ever suspects they'll be murdered and people will try to track down their killer.

Then again, it sounded like the Jean Harlow look-alike might have suspected it. Perhaps she'd left a trail of bread crumbs somewhere—or was that too much to hope for?

Thirty-Five

The next afternoon, Den called with news. "Breast implants," he said.

"She was transgender, so I figured." I turned away from the keyboard. "So, what does it tell us? Anything?"

Now that I was drawn away from my words on the screen, images of her body played in my mind. Would I ever forget that heartbreaking corpse on the metal table?

"Evidently there are traceable numbers on the implants, which should be able to tell us where she had the reassignment surgery, at least," he replied.

"That's a start," I said. Thank goodness for implant manufacturers. Never thought I'd be thinking any such thing.

"Have you had further luck finding information?" he asked. Papers crinkled in the background.

"No. I've been writing. Haven't been online at all," I said. "I might do some research later tonight." I wanted to tell him what I'd found out from the impersonators, but I needed to do that in person.

"Speaking of later tonight," he said, "I thought I'd stop by with a pizza and some wine. What do you think?"

I blinked. The real world beckoned. And I had to eat, didn't I?

"But I thought we'd agreed not to see one another until after we solve the case..." I wasn't sure I could handle the temptation.

"This isn't a date. This is a brainstorming session," Den said, but his voice spoke of a different kind of session.

I paused. I really wasn't sure I could contain myself and it hadn't quite been a month yet. I couldn't lie to Kate, but it was tempting.

"Well, sure then." A girl had to eat. And drink wine.

Sometimes I lived too much inside my head. The realm of ideas and words was my comfort zone. When I'd been in the zone for days, the world I created in my writing seemed more real than the physical one. I appreciated people like Kate and Den in my life, who pulled me out of my reverie from time to time. Human contact was necessary.

"Okay," Den said. "See you soon."

Curls of excitement rippled through me.

I straightened up the place a bit. I was still hunkered down in the library, so I gathered my papers there, folded the blanket I was using while sleeping on the chaise, and took a few dishes into the kitchen and rinsed them off. The gleaming faucet curled around in a curlicue, hovering over the porcelain sink.

In my mind's eye, Justine stood next to me, running her fingers through the warm water. Every inch of this place spoke of her. It still carried her scent within the walls, carpets, and draperies.

I hadn't been back to the secret room. The book deadline was pressing and I was in the zone, words were flowing. Besides, it freaked me out a little. A secret room filled with Hollywood memorabilia. Maybe some of it was priceless. A secret that Justine kept hidden from me all these years. It stung.

But she'd also kept her apartment a private haven, never allowing the "help" to enter. Yet here I was. Struggling to unravel the mystery of who killed her, and who killed my stalker, and trying to figure out if there was a link.

The Jean Harlow look-alike knew Justine lived here, of course. Had she been stalking her? Did she know about the secret room?

Just how many apartments in the building might have such a room? The L'Ombragé had an interesting history. Known as one of the city's finest art deco buildings, its apartments had been gutted and updated so many times that the floor plans were sometimes inaccurate. The apartment in its spire intrigued me. Who lived there? Why would you live in a tiny circular abode?

The buzzer buzzed. "Ms. Donovan?"

"Yes," I said, pushing my little black button.

"A Den Brophy is here to see you."

"Send him up."

Excitement spun through me. No greater aphrodisiac than temptation existed. Could I resist if he made a pass? Would he? He seemed determined to not date someone involved with a case. But how far was he willing to stretch it?

"I'm coming up too. Surprise!" Kate's unmistakable voice came over the intercom.

Oh boy.

Thirty-Six

"Any more clues?" Kate asked, wide-eyed, then bit into her slice of pizza. It wasn't bad. The wine made it even better.

I glared at her. Kate didn't trust me to be alone with Den. Hell, I didn't trust myself—but no matter.

"Just the numbers on her implants, which we're still working on. Nothing new," Den said. "But I wondered if maybe we're overlooking something." He drank from his wine glass, his eyes never leaving mine. Smoldering. Wanting. I was starting not to care about the five hundred dollar bet.

Kate cleared her throat. "Like what?"

"I should tell you that Kate and I went to the Dream Girl show a few times," I said quickly. "I talked with the Madonna impersonator before you-know-who caught me."

"You did what?" Den laid his pizza down on the plate.

"I figured that call I got had to be from one of the impersonators I'd met, right? So I wanted to ask them about it. But I got nowhere with that."

"Too much interference on your part. This is an ongoing police investigation." Serious tone. Blank expression.

"Yes, but—"

"Besides, these people are dangerous. The look-alike was killed, and Justine was killed. Do you want to be next?"

A chill came over me. He'd verbalized how I felt. As if I might be next on the kill-list of people connected by Harlow. But how and why?

"Leave this kind of in-person questioning up to us. Research on the computer, that's one thing."

Kate spoke up. "But you're a cop. These people won't tell you anything. They might trust Charlotte more."

Her words hung in the air, and we all went back to our pizza and wine. Touchy subject these days, cops and trust.

"We did learn that the Jean Harlow impersonator was at the Dream Girl agency using their computer," I said.

"We knew that, right? The computer guys told us that. We knew Sal was lying."

"The Madonna impersonator said Harlow's dad probably killed her," Kate said. "But she had no names at all."

Den's mouth puckered to the side. "So here's what we have. We're sure of the method for Justine's murder and we've got DNA of the person who killed her. We still don't know who the Harlow character is, how she was murdered, or if the two murders have anything to do with one another."

"But the Harlow look-alike was following me, which leads me to believe she was after me for a reason. Why me? Because I'm now working on the book?"

"That's when most of the stuff happened to you. After the announcement at Justine's service," Kate said.

"Which all begs the question, why?" Den said. "I mean, Christ, is there a secret baby or something in Harlow's past?"

"Nah. Even if there was, what would be the big deal about that at this point in time?" I asked. "I mean, yes, it would be big news if there was a living blood relative of hers. But at this point, who would have a stake in it? Who would care enough to try to keep it a secret?"

Den shrugged.

"There must be some kind of secret," Kate said. "A secret someone will kill for."

Once again, chills came over me and I shivered.

"Are you cold?" Den asked.

"No, just felt a chill."

My phone beeped. It was the New York Public Library. "Oh! Excuse me, I have to take this." I answered it and walked back into the library. "Charlotte Donovan."

"Hi Charlotte, it's me, Lizzie. You won't believe what I've found."

Lizzie Hill was a digital archivist at the New York Public Library of the Performing Arts. I adored her. She was one of the sources for my biography research who never failed me—and she was lovely to boot.

"What?"

"Do you remember the famous reel of film of Jean Harlow that we all thought was lost?"

"I'm not following." Maybe I'd already had too much wine. Or perhaps I was just too tired and scared with all this talk of murder.

"The outtake of her in the bath scene!"

"Oh!"

"I've already sent you a copy. Check your email."

"Thank you so much, Lizzie, for contacting me about this."

"Any time," she said. "This is a major find, but I'm keeping it to myself for a little while longer. Call it the librarian's quiet revenge."

I laughed. "Okay. Mum's the word."

"But check it out. It's amazing. She was so comfortable in her skin. I've seen nothing like it."

My stomach fluttered. How lovely it would be to be that way.

"I'll watch it tonight."

"Great, get back to me soon," she said, signing off.

I called Den and Kate into the library and turned on my computer. "I've got something to show you. This is a rare clip."

"Cool," Kate said.

"Let's turn off the lights. We'll be able to see it better."

Kate complied, and I pressed play on my laptop.

Red Dust. I recognized the scene. Jean in an old-fashioned wash tub, giving herself a bubble bath. A famous scene.

Jean's voice was not crisp and clear. Muffled, as if through a tunnel from a distance.

"This is for the boys in the editing room!" she said and stood, revealing her naked self.

A valuable outtake. Not public. Only collectors had ever seen it—and the lucky folks who'd been there.

The black-white-gray lights stopped flicking and the film came to a standstill. There was Harlean Carpenter, Jean Harlow, standing naked, arms lifted, reveling in a joyous, fun moment. "Lighthearted" was the word that came to mind. Who could stand there naked like that, in front of all those people, and be so comfortable and have fun? There was something innocent and natural about it—childlike, even though she certainly wasn't a child.

My heart exploded with some unnameable longing, twisted with another emotion. Admiration? Envy?

"Stunning," Kate whispered.

Den breathed out. "Yeah. Wow."

Thirty-Seven

That night, I dreamed of the nude Harlow, secret rooms, and running for my life from some strange person on the streets. Maybe it was the combination of the wine and pizza. Maybe it was just the weird twist my life had taken since Justine's death. I sucked as a murder investigator. But the researcher in me refused to let this go.

After emerging from my cocoon of blankets, I drank coffee, ate a bagel, and dialed my grandmother.

"Charlotte? You okay?"

"Yes, Gram. I'm just calling to check on you." I rinsed off my plate and opened the dishwasher.

"I'm fine."

I placed the plate in the dishwasher and shut the door. "How's Mom?"

"She hasn't taken a drink since you left."

A brief pang of something like hope sprang up in me. But I'd hoped before, hadn't I?

"Fantastic."

"How's the book going?"

"I've made progress." I walked over to the balcony door and opened it to the view of Central Park and its soft sloping hills, green tree tops, and curving paths. It called to me—but not like the beach on the island where I grew up. "Have you seen that man again?"

"No, and I've been looking for him. Me and Bessie," she said and chuckled.

"I'm glad you haven't seen him." But it didn't ease my fear. "So, Gram, about this Harlow ring."

"Yes?"

"How much would it be worth?" I leaned on the kitchen counter.

"As much as someone will pay for it," she said and cackled. "But seriously, somewhere in the neighborhood of millions, with provenance."

"What would you do if someone brought the ring to you?"

"First I'd lock it away and make inquiries."

"To whom?"

"Charlotte, why are you asking me these questions? You never cared about this stuff before."

I paused. "The ring may have surfaced, and perhaps Justine learned about it, and maybe someone else did too." I hated lying to my grandmother, but the exact truth was dangerous.

"Why did you come to that conclusion?"

"I can't think of another reason for any of it—Justine's death, the death of the Harlow look-alike." I sat down and turned on my computer.

"It makes little sense, Charlotte. Killing Justine would not give someone the ring—even if she had it."

"Unless they thought that by getting her out of the way, they'd get their hands on it." That had to be it.

"You may have something there. But she didn't mention finding the ring to you, did she?"

I walked back into the library. "No."

"Humph."

"Maybe she was protecting me."

"I doubt it. She was self-serving. "

"Of course she was," I said. "She was alone, with no family. Other than that cousin in Florida." Where was Judith Turner, anyway? Why hadn't I heard from the lawyer about rescheduling the will meeting?

"When are you coming home?"

"I don't know." I pictured our rundown beach house, with its creaky floors and chipped paint, my quilt-covered bed in the room I'd had almost my whole life. A winsome pang centered in my chest. "I haven't heard from the lawyer about the will. Kate and I have almost everything boxed up in Justine's apartment, but there's still more left to do. Between taking care of Justine's things and trying to write the book..." I didn't say and "investigating murders."

"Okay. Well, we miss you," Gram said with a crack in her voice.

"I'll get home as soon as I can."

I wrote most of the day, even though I may have been missing a part of Harlow's story. I didn't know if I'd ever find it.

Later, I stopped writing and checked my Tinder account. A habit. A nervous habit. When I was jittery, my first inclination to soothe myself was sex. And I'd made a stupid bet with my best friend.

A message from Zach. He was one of my favorites. If I had to, I couldn't choose between Zach and Juan. Thank goodness I didn't have to.

"Hey, sexy, where've you been?"

Should I answer? Or leave him hanging? It wasn't as if we were having a relationship. I didn't owe him any explanation. But still, just the thought of him, and his gorgeous thighs, sparked something deep inside of me. He was tempting. How would Kate find out if I slept with him once?

I hovered there for a moment, imagining his thigh muscles moving beneath his skin.

Nah, I couldn't lie to her. I never had and I never would. But what to do about Zach and his thighs?

I should at least be polite.

"Sorry, my boss passed away and I've been very busy. Touch base soon."

Although, would I? When I thought about Den, my Tinder friends didn't hold my attention. But Den wanted to date me, which meant a relationship. Was I ready for that?

After John, I'd promised myself never again. We'd planned to marry, then I'd gotten very sick and was hospitalized. And although he professed his love for me every day when he visited, at the same time he was screwing his best friend's wife. Yeah. It used to make me furious to think about it. It still did, but it was tempered by a few years and thoughts of gratitude. Thank God I hadn't married him.

If John couldn't handle my illness, I had no business with him. It wasn't as if I was sick all the time. But I hadn't learned to manage it at the point. To pay attention to its tiny warning signs, like exhaustion over nothing at all, confusion, and lack of clarity in my mind. Those were the days Justine said to walk away from my work. She understood. Many bosses would not have.

It was that trait of hers that held me to her. I loved her for it.

But now she was gone, and I wondered what I'd do with myself after I finished this book. Who would hire me now? It wasn't as if there were rich writers around the city searching for an assistant, especially one with chronic Lyme disease. I'd dedicated eleven years of my life to Justine. And while she'd taken care of me by giving me this job and I would always feel grateful for it, I now wasn't qualified to do anything but assist her. Sure, I'd ghostwritten many chapters in her biographies. But who would believe that? How could I prove that? I owed thousands in medical bills. My mom and gram still needed my paycheck to help at home.

I stacked papers on the desk, turned away from the words on the computer screen, and tabled ideas about getting another job. I had too much to do right now. I needed to write this book—and I needed to find Justine's killer.

Thirty-Eight

"*Divorce in the 1930s decreased due to the Depression. In the preceding years, it had been continuing upward,*" an online article declared. So while Jean Harlow and other Hollywood stars were getting divorces, the rest of America was not. Apparently because of the Depression. Divorce was unaffordable for regular folks.

Even though Jean Harlow's mother divorced her father, and Jean became a child of divorce, I wondered what she believed about herself. Did she consider herself a failure because of her unsuccessful marriages? Was it the one thing her heart desired, and it eluded her?

Maude had told me that it was a real possibility that Jean's work ethic came from her parents' divorce and her feelings of unworthiness. She wanted to prove herself. But didn't everybody? Even today? Was it so different in the 1930s?

I'd read about divorce and single mothers. It was the number one predictor for poverty. Yet Jean Harlow's mother had flourished. Couldn't it be construed that her mother, by choosing to divorce Mont Clair Carpenter, was a good role model—an example of why to *not* stay in a bad marriage? If so, where did that leave Maude's theory?

My head hurt. I turned away from the computer, stood, and stretched.

I needed to get out of the apartment. A beautiful spring afternoon beckoned. I slipped on my running shoes, shorts, a sports bra, and T-shirt and headed for Central Park. I hoped to take a run but maybe it would end up being a walk. Who knew? My body was in charge.

Before leaving, I checked my cell phone out of habit. Most of my cop lovers seemed to have given up on me—and it had only been, what? Three weeks?

I pushed the button for the elevator, hoping the run would give me what I needed. A physical distraction. Fresh air.

My mind latched on to the five hundred dollars I would collect from Kate. I had a million different places for it. My past-due credit card. Helping my mom with the mortgage. Or paying on my hefty medical bill. None of it was fun. How I longed for a chance to splurge, just once, on myself. Simply buying a few secondhand outfits while I was staying at Justine's had made me suffer pangs of guilt.

As I crossed the street, I contemplated Harlow and wondered again about her feelings. Did she feel guilty or empowered by her divorces? American culture was far from supportive of divorced women, even now.

I entered the park and welcomed the shift of awareness and atmosphere. The shade, the green, the blossoming flowers. The fountains and water. It was easier to breathe in the park—at least so it seemed. I stretched, warmed up, the warm breeze caressing my skin. Making me enjoy the promise of spring and feeling I could do almost anything. A trick of the mind, I'm aware. I started off with a slow jog, tuning in to my thighs, hips, and legs.

I ran toward the middle of the park, which was always more crowded, but I loved its dips and sways and bends. Gratitude welled up inside of me. Thrilled that I could run. Sometimes I found it hard to even walk. But today was a good day.

Running was like a meditation for me. It worked wonders when I needed ideas or needed to calm my mind. I kept trying to understand Harlow's mindset about her divorces. Maybe I couldn't. Maybe it was best to be honest and write that nobody knew her inner experience. Jean never opened up about her marriages or divorces, which was unlike today's celebrities, who latch on to the media and reveal way too much about themselves. The difference between the stars of the Golden Age of Hollywood and today were immense.

Maybe someone should write a book about that. Maybe someone had?

The park was crowded. Children playing. Couples on benches, having picnics, posing for the camera in front of fountains. I rounded the corner into the underpass of the Bethesda Terrace. I'd read about its restoration. Created in the 1860s, the original panels had been removed in the 1980s and it reopened in 2004. It was like running through a jewel box. I marveled at its electric blue and gold painted tiles and anticipated the street music in the echoing chamber. Stepping through it was like moving through a colorful, dreamy tunnel of sound.

The scent of falafel teased my nose, along with the horse shit I spotted and leaped over.

As I ran, the beauty of the park lulled me even further. The budding trees and flowers were a perfect distraction for a near-perfect day. Not a cloud in sight.

A man with a dog passed by me. A German Shepherd who didn't even look my way. A group of tourists clamored by in a horse-drawn carriage. The black horse wore dazzling red headgear, including a huge red feather. I ran by the fountain everybody claimed was in the opening of the popular TV show *Friends*. It wasn't, though it bore a striking resemblance to it.

I had reached the runner's high, and confidence sprouted from my center. I might be able to finish my run this time.

But an abrupt awareness of eerie doom came over me.

A shock of intuition flared. Even among this happy park crowd, a sudden sense of foreboding crept through me, a darkness encroaching. Someone was following me, running closely behind me. Too closely. Right on my heels. What the hell? *I left my pepper spray at the apartment.*

A hard knock on my back sent my body slamming against the paved path, my head hitting the edge of a bench.

As I landed with a stupid, clumsy thud, I heard someone say, "Hey, get away from her!"

Thirty-Nine

My eyes felt as if someone were pressing the ball of their hands into them, preventing me from lifting them. Muffled voices sounded between the pulses of pain in my head. Flashes of light and my body in motion.

When I finally opened my eyes, the room I was lying in was unfamiliar and white. Sterile. I closed my eyes again because the brightness hurt them.

Voices said words like *concussion, stitches, bruising.* Then another voice. *Lyme disease. Not thinking clearly.*

Maybe whoever said those words was correct. I remembered going for a run. Remembered the sudden attack and not having my pepper spray. Maybe I hadn't been thinking clearly before that moment.

"Hey." A whisper of a voice came from the side of my bed. "Are you going to wake up?"

I struggled to open my eyes and saw Kate leaning over and peering at me, her concerned face turning into a smiling one.

"What happened?" I said, even though my mouth seemed sand-paper dry.

"You were attacked at the park."

"I remember running... and someone hitting me."

"I'll tell you, New Yorkers have a bad rap. But several came to your rescue. One man almost caught the guy."

"Really?" A pain shot through the center of my forehead. I winced.

"Hurt?"

"Yes," I said. "Kate, you need to go. I know you're busy. You don't need to be here."

"That's a bunch of crap. You were with me for every one of my procedures, bestie, and I'm not going anywhere. Can we get her something more for the pain?" Kate said as she turned away from me.

I closed my eyes and didn't open them again until later into the evening.

"He had a scar on his face," someone said.

"The same place?" I recognized that voice, for it had reached out and comforted me once before—when Justine died. Smooth, deep, strong yet commanding. Den must be right outside my door.

But another man came into view.

"I'm Doctor Pearson," he said. Gray hair, tiny round glasses framing droopy blue eyes. "How are you feeling?"

"Like shit."

He smiled with compassion. "Can you be more specific?"

"My head is still throbbing. I'm nauseated and my whole body just hurts."

"It sounds about right for what you went through earlier today. Had you been keeping up with your meds?"

"Yes. I was taking care of myself."

"But you've been under a lot of stress?"

"I guess you could say that." Justine's murder, then the look-alike's murder, with the stalking in between, and having to write the book—plus finding the ring, still buried in my purse somewhere at the apartment. The ring so priceless that it was worth killing for.

The doctor drew in a breath. He wasn't my regular physician, but I saw the lecture coming. "Lyme disease is one thing you must learn to manage. Maybe you should take a break."

Maybe I should. A mad man running through the park had attacked me. A beautiful Jean Harlow look-alike had followed me. Sal Mendo scared me away from the Dream Girl show. Severn Hartwell had tried to attack me at the bar. I'd received emails and phones calls from all sorts of crazy people. Why? What was I doing to myself? Would any of it bring Justine back? I needed to finish the book and get it out of my life. How could I do that lying in the hospital bed?

And what to do with the ring?

That still required some mulling over.

"Now you have no choice," the doctor was saying. "You're just going to need to take it easy for a few days. Maybe longer. Listen to your body."

Listen to my body? I'd been listening to it for years. Lyme disease had taught me the necessity. But I didn't have time to lie around counting sheep. And Justine wasn't around to pick up the slack.

"Concussions, even mild ones, can be very serious if you don't take care of them," he said. "I'll need to keep you until tomorrow, and then you need to be on bed rest for at least two days."

When I imagined a bed, I thought of my home on Cloister Island. I'd be damned if I was going back to stay at Justine's place now. The sorting and pitching of her belongings would wait—as would the book. There was no choice now.

"Preferably somewhere you'll have people around to watch over you."

I needed to go home. This was the kind of thing my mom and gram lived for. Taking care of somebody. Kate was too busy. She'd missed too much work already for me. And I hated that. And Den, well, Den was a busy cop. No. I needed to go home.

Den now entered the room, dressed in uniform, which lifted my spirits more than just a tad. "How you doing?"

"About how I look, I imagine." I was embarrassed that he saw me with a huge knot on my head and God knows what else.

"Did you see the man who pushed you?"

"Not at all," I said. "Sorry."

"I need to get a statement from you."

"Tomorrow," the doctor said in a clipped tone, pointing his finger at the door.

Forty

ailure.

The word bobbed around in my brain, but it seemed housed in a tight knot in my guts. I'd failed Justine and my beautiful stalker. I'd let my guard down and left the apartment without my pepper spray.

Fool. Fool with a black bruise on her head and scabs on her knees and hands. With every bone in her body on fire with pain. Sitting in a hospital room with the best cop I'd ever known. Maybe the best man.

I closed my eyes, trying to wish away the throbbing, and Jean Harlow's image emblazoned itself in my brain. The weird image of a nude, carefree woman reveling in herself and joking around about being naked. Imagine.

There was a space between sleep and awake in which I was quite happy. That's where I was, floating, thinking of Jean, when I was yanked back into reality.

"Okay," Den said. "The wheelchair is here. Let's get you up and out of here."

Den helped me as I slid in, dizzy, nauseated, a little in shock. Nothing like this had ever happened to me before. I'd spent a lot of time in the Big Apple. The scariest part was not even the attack, but how my brain was moving in slow motion. It was so hard to think. It was scary how one slip, one accident, and you could almost become a completely different person. My case wasn't exactly that dramatic— but I still felt as if a piece of myself had been stolen.

"Any word on our Harlow impersonator's case?" I asked.

"Not yet," he said. "We know where she had her implants done in London. But with the time differences, we're having problems connecting."

Made sense.

"I wish we could rush the tox screen, but they tell me they're doing their best."

He was quiet on the drive to the harbor. I figured he'd drop the breakup bombshell on me any minute, although it wasn't technically a breakup since we'd never even gone on a date. It's been my experience that most men don't want to be bothered with a woman who isn't healthy, let alone one with Lyme disease. Den understood all that now. I figured he might have the class to wait for a few days, though. Again, we'd never dated. He owed me nothing. Nothing at all.

A police escort wasn't a bad thing in this city. When we got to the harbor, another police escort waited in a boat to take me home to Cloister Island—yet again broken and bruised. Like the last time I'd had a police escort in a boat. I wasn't living right.

Kate apologized for not coming with me. If anybody had reason not to go to Cloister, it was her, shunned by her family and other islanders when she'd transitioned into a woman. She was welcome at my home, but being on the island still brought up too many painful memories for her.

I tried not to examine Den too closely. But when I glimpsed his face, an odd, almost sick-looking bearing had fallen across it.

Den and the other officer help me into the boat, along with my bag, my laptop, and my purse. The choppy and gray river carried me away from the city, its famous skyline fading. Den stood on the edge of the dock until I couldn't see him anymore. I wondered if I would ever see him again.

If the murder cases went nowhere, which apparently was where they were going, there'd be no reason for us to see one another again. And I doubted his attraction to me after this.

The journey across the river out to the sound and sea was tortuous. Every rough wave echoed in pain in my head.

Thirty minutes later, my island came into view. St. Peter's steeple came into sight first, as it always did, then each shop and restaurant along the boardwalk. Houses perched along the mountainside. Some of those houses were incredible.

My mother and gram stood at the dock waiting for me, along with Ed, a family friend who was also a nurse. He'd tended to me before, taking no money, only asking for Gram's oyster soup as payment.

The officer in the boat helped me to solid ground. My sea legs took a moment to adjust.

Gram stepped forward and wrapped her arms around me. "Charlotte, what happened to you?"

Mom stood shaking her head as she took me in, as if she couldn't believe her eyes, and finally moved to hug me.

Ed nodded at me. "Here we are again, Charlotte." Long and lean, with a bad complexion, he studied me.

"I suppose," I said.

It always took more than a few moments to adjust from the city to Cloister Island, with its wide-open spaces of the sky and sea. In Manhattan, buildings hovered over me, providing a barrier to real air and space.

Cloister Island is one of the many smaller islands off the coast of New York. It was founded by a group of Irish nuns, and next to arrive were the Irish fisherman and oystermen with their families. My family had been here for four generations, its root in deep.

We rode in Mom's car to our house. As it came closer into view— its fading turquoise blue color, its sagging front porch with the empty swing—warmth came over me. Underneath, a deep sense of regret and foreboding. Here I was again. A failure. Hurt. Sick. And coming home to heal.

∞

I dreamed of boxes.

I was searching through them for something important, and almost frantic about it.

Where is it? Where is it? I kept saying.

I shoved aside a big box, peeking inside at the piles of linen inside. Another box brimming with scrapbooks and photos. But I wasn't interested in those. What was I seeking? I'd know it when I saw it. Not the wine boxes, not the cigarette boxes. No.

A soft floral scent wafted through the air as I searched, and I got distracted by it for a moment or two.

Finally I spotted it. It was the box I was looking for—an old hat box with a sweet vintage floral pattern and *Paris* stamped on it. My heart raced. What was inside? I was certain I'd find what I sought.

A bell sound jarred me awake.

"What the—" I grabbed my chest.

I was at home, in my bed, and someone was ringing the front doorbell. I struggled to get out of bed, still deep in the clutches of sleep and my dream.

"I've got it," Mom said.

Discombobulated, I wondered about the time of day. When I spotted the clock, I realized I'd been sleeping for hours.

Mom opened the door.

"Did I wake you up?" she asked. She'd colored her hair red, a sort of plum color. And it spiked up in tufts on her head. She held a glass of water in her hands.

I nodded.

"I'm sorry," she said. "But you should get up. Don't you think?"

My head was pounding. I should take more pain pills.

"I need more medicine," I said, more to myself than to her, but she brought my pills along with the water. "Thanks. It's past time for me to take one, and I'm feeling it."

"How about some soup?"

Food still made me queasy. But I needed to eat to keep my strength. Whatever I had left.

"Maybe a little," I said. I laid back down, my head in my pillow.

"I had the weirdest dream," I said.

"Yeah, you look a little spacey for someone who hasn't had their pain meds," she said, sitting at the edge of my bed.

"I was in such a deep sleep," I said. "I dreamed of boxes and searching through them."

"Well, you've been cleaning Justine's place, right? Makes sense," Mom said.

Every time I was away from her and came back to her, she aged. Or maybe it was the booze taking its toll. The lines in her face were deeper than my grandmother's.

"Yes, but this was different. I was on a mission to find something. I'm not sure what."

"You hardly ever dream," Mom said. "But when you dream, it's always interesting. It's that imagination of yours."

It was true. We'd talked about it once when one of the neighbor's kids was having nightmares. I used to have them too. Not exactly nightmares, but strange dreams that frightened me. Yet when I tried to tell my mom about them, the dreams didn't sound frightening at all. After all, it wasn't monsters and goblins I'd dreamed of; it was more the eerie feeling I'd gotten from the dreams. In fact, I recognized nobody or anything in my dreams. But I'd always come away from them in sorrow and fear.

"Maybe it's the medicine or the bump on the head," I said.

"Could be," she said standing. "I'm glad you're here. I'll heat up some soup. Ed will be here tomorrow to check on you."

Was Gram right? Had Mom stopped drinking? Hoping seemed liked the worst kind of self-hatred. I shoved it aside for now. With everything else going on, I didn't want to lead myself down the path of hope. The path I'd been down so many times before.

I situated myself with several pillows, and just when I got comfortable, my cell phone rang. It was Maude.

"Hello, doll," she said. "Where have you been? What's going on?"

I explained to her what had happened.

"How dreadful!"

"I was getting too close to whatever the mystery is on this Harlow thing," I said, almost more to myself than her.

The sound of her inhaling smoke from her cigarette and shuffling papers around came over the phone. "What Harlow thing?"

I explained to Maude what had been happening. "They wanted me out of the way," I said. "And that's what they've got. I'm just going to finish the damn book and not worry about the rest of it."

Justine's image popped into my mind's eye as Mom came into the room with a tray holding chicken soup and a few pieces of buttered bread. She set the tray on the bed in front of me. I breathed in the scent and steam of the soup.

"Smart," Maude said to me. "How are you feeling?"

"Like hell," I said. "My head hurts. I'm having weird dreams. This concussion stuff ain't for sissies."

She blew out air. "No."

"I'd like to know more about those dreams," Maude said. "That's the psychoanalyst in me. You've been through a lot these past few weeks, doll, and your dreams might give you some insight. I could help you," she said. I heard her exhale and imagined the smoke from her cigarette circling outward.

"It was just one dream," I said. "I was searching for something and I found the hatbox it was in. I went to reach for it and woke up."

"It was vivid, hey?"

"Yes," I replied. "But as my mom pointed out, I've just been digging through boxes, so ..."

Some commotion erupted in the background. "I need to go," Maude said. "I'll touch base with you later."

Exhausted by the end of our conversation, I wondered if this was a normal thing for people with head injuries or if my Lyme's was acting up.

I spooned the chicken soup into my mouth, its warm flavors popping. Nobody made chicken soup like my mom.

"How is it?" she said, smiling.

"So good, Mom."

She beamed. Such a little compliment made her so happy, which made me a little sad. She'd had a rough life after my dad disappeared, her only comfort the booze. I couldn't fault her for that, could I? But it became a problem. Her showing up at events plastered, embarrassing me—and herself. Her not remembering to fill in school forms or to file her taxes because she was on a drinking binge.

She'd gone through treatment a few years back and had attended AA meetings. I had wracked my brain trying to figure out what could have set her off this last time.

I stared down at my bowl and lifted the spoon to my mouth. With one bite, it was as if Mom had delivered me a magical brew, a potion. The warmth of the soup spread through me along with a bubbling notion: what next?

Forty-One

I slept underneath my worn quilt the rest of the day.

When I awakened the next morning, I took a few blinks to remember where I was and to get my bearings. My familiar mess splayed around me: clothes scattered on my chair, the lighthouse painting by my long-gone cop father, and my dresser with a dusty jewelry box and unused perfume bottles.

I stared up at my ceiling, which was painted sea-green. I'd used money I didn't have to buy the exact color I wanted because it was so calming. But it wasn't working its magic, not today.

My bare feet found the weathered plank floor. First to the bathroom, next to my laptop. All the bed rest had given my legs a rubbery, weak feel.

"Charlotte, you know you're not supposed to be in front of any screens for a while," Ed said as he walked in my room with a tray of scrambled eggs, homemade bread, coffee, and water.

"Yeah, I know," I said. "I don't plan on being here long. I need to send a few emails." Both Justine's agent and editor were waiting on me. Informing Natalie and Lucille of my attack and concussion was the first thing on my task list.

While the computer warmed up, I tried to clear my head. It was like cotton. Was it all the drugs they'd given me? Or was it the concussion? I wasn't thinking straight and didn't know how I would finish the book. Maybe I could get another extension. I'd ask Lucille if it was possible.

Ed walked over and sat the coffee down next to me. I sipped it, strong and good, its heat traveling through me. I glanced over at the bed where the tray sat. "Thank you."

"Of course," he said. "Now, if I can help you get back to bed? I need your blood pressure and to check your pulse."

On the way back to bed I glimpsed my face in the mirror. It stopped me cold. The lump on my head had gone down. But it was a sick shade of green, tinged in deep blue, with yellow around the edges. Stitches sat in the center of it. My swollen and bruised nose matched my black eyes. I resembled a fifty-year-old version of my thirty-two-year-old self.

Ed caught me gawking. "You've had better days, I'm sure. But give yourself some time."

"I guess I have no choice." I tried to make light of it. But both the way I looked and the way I felt were in sync. Stupid and ugly.

Regret plucked at my chest. I should have told Den about the ring and turned it over. Why was I holding on to it, really? Some strange connection that I felt had something to do with the book I was writing? Or was it just the last piece of Justine I could hold in my hand?

The ring was more than a ring, and more than a missing puzzle piece in the case. If I gave it to Den, he'd act on it. And I wasn't sure that was the thing to do.

Ed placed the blood pressure cuff on my arm and pumped.

Did I not trust Den enough to tell him about the ring? Or did I not want to turn over my last piece of Justine to him?

Ed smiled. "BP is good." He tore off the cuff, set it aside, and reached for my wrist.

Den. If I handed over the ring, what excuse could I give for not telling him before? I was withholding evidence, and I appreciated that it wouldn't sit right with him.

My thoughts were slow and hurting my brain. It wasn't good to think so hard when you had a concussion. But I couldn't help myself. I couldn't bear the shame of giving up, after getting so close.

After picking at my breakfast, I fell into a deep sleep beneath my quilt. When I awoke, I understood I had to do two things: tell Den about the ring, no matter the consequences, and somehow avenge Justine and the Jean Harlow look-alike's deaths—the higher calling. I took heart in still believing that maybe all of it was linked.

I'd hold that resolve in my mind and heart, knowing I was doing the right thing even if it would sacrifice what I imagined could be a meaningful relationship with Den, the first I'd even been interested in for years. But then again, the sick look on his face as the boat pulled away from the harbor? That said it all.

Kate called the next day.

"I miss you."

"Yeah, I miss you too."

"Are you feeling better?"

"Yes, a little better each day."

"Have you heard from Den?"

"Nah, I don't expect to."

"Why not?"

"You know why not. He knows about my Lyme, and after this attack he's seen me at my worst. You know what men are like."

"People used to consider me one of them, you know."

I laughed. "I remember."

"I think he's different than other men. Call it a hunch."

The window across the room gave me a good view of the sea. Not for the first time, I'd considered it the one constant in my life. How I'd longed for it when I was in Manhattan.

"It doesn't matter," I said. "I've decided to tell him about the ring, and when I do, it will piss him off."

"You don't have to tell him how long you've had it, do you?"

"I don't know. It feels wrong to lie to him again. Even a little white lie. He's working so hard on this case. And he was so good to me when I was in the hospital." A flicker of a heartbeat trembled in my chest.

"Suit yourself."

It had been two days on the island and no call from Den. Was he avoiding me? Or too busy to call?

I caught myself. I'd told myself I would never be one of those women. The ones who wait for the phone calls. This was why I took solace in controlling my relationships through dating apps. Why I hadn't gotten involved with anyone for a few years. Yet somehow, Den had wormed his way in beneath my well-tended shell. I was glad it would stop now—I had to focus my attention elsewhere.

Forty-Two

"Lucille got another extension on your deadline, but I'm afraid it's the final one, Charlotte. They're threatening to find another writer to finish the book," Natalie said.

"I understand," I said. I couldn't blame them.

"They took pity on you because of the extraordinary circumstances." She paused. "How are you, Charlotte?"

"A little better, but the brain fog is the problem."

"Understood."

Meanwhile, even my battered self was going mad staying in my bedroom. After hanging up with Natalie, I untangled myself from my blankets and opened my bedroom door to the happy mess of our living room. I walked to the couch and sat down.

My mom entered. "What are you doing, Charlotte? Are you supposed to be out of bed?"

"I couldn't stand it a minute more," I said, folding my arms across my chest.

She sat down beside me. "You must be feeling better."

"I'm sore, and, I don't know, groggy, but things are clearing."

"Good," she said. Sheepish, her eyes met mine. "I'm sorry for the relapse, Charlotte. I've been sober since then. I just wanted you to know."

I'd heard that before and still refused to get my hopes up. Yet hope flickered.

"I'm glad," I said, looking around the room. My eyes landed on some packages in the corner. "What's over there?"

"Oh, dear! I'd forgotten about those packages for you."

"For me? Packages?" I stood too quickly and dizziness overcame me. Bam, I was back on the couch.

"Now, stay there and I'll bring them to you." Mom raced off to the corner.

Had I ordered something and forgotten? It took longer for us to get mail on the island, let alone packages. Sometimes I ordered books way before when I'd need them. I also ordered manuscripts and other research materials from libraries and other institutions. What had I forgotten?

"Here," Mom said, handing me the smaller of the packages. No return address. Odd.

I tore the brown paper and found a floral box, which reminded me of my dream of the floral hat box. I paused. Was I dreaming now?

"What are you waiting for?" Mom asked, poking me. Okay, I wasn't dreaming.

I lifted the lid. Inside were manila envelopes labeled "Postcards," "Letters," and "Documents." The handwriting was familiar with its loops and sways.

I dumped the postcards out. There were two of them.

A bouquet of wildflowers graced the front of the card. I flipped it over. *Package delivered with love.* The card was stamped in France and signed *M. Bello.*

Marino Bello. Jean Harlow's stepfather.

Justine! She must have sent these packages to me weeks ago.

And Marino Bello had been in France in July 1932.

I wasn't aware of that. But I hadn't been tracking him in my research. I'd been tracking Jean and her mother. What did it mean? Why had Bello been in France? Two weeks after Jean's marriage to Paul Bern?

"What is it?" Mom asked, her eyes wide and lit with curiosity.

"A postcard from France. From Jean Harlow's stepfather. I don't know who it was sent to or why he was there."

"Did Justine send this to you?"

"She must have." My attention turned to the other postcard.

My head ached more as my pulse rushed. What was going on here?

The other postcard was dated July 14, 1937, a month after Jean's death. Another floral postcard, lavender blooms splayed on the front.

"Success!" Signed by M. Bello, once again.

"What does it mean?" Mom sat wide-eyed.

"It means Jean's stepfather took two trips to France. One a few years before she died and one after she died. I'm uncertain what meaning that has." I didn't even need to study the timeline to place those two events in my mind's eye. Why did Justine send these to me?

It hit me with a bolt. Justine must have been hiding, at that point, which is why her apartment hadn't been lived in. She sent the box of papers to me for safekeeping. But why? What was so important about it?

I opened the envelope labeled "Documents," slid my hand in, and found a space. Odd. Why would she send me an empty envelope? In frustration, I turned it over and shook it.

"Looks like she wanted you to fill it," Mom said.

"But with what? What kind of documents?"

"Justine was an odd bird," Mom said. As if I didn't know.

I reached for the third envelope.

One letter was inside.

A letter from Jean's mother to Bello.

"Dearest husband,

I can't tell you what grief I feel. But I'm comforted by the love of you and knowing we've done right by Baby.

Thank you for being the best husband I could ever hope for.

With all my love,

Jean"

I grunted. Bello was a prick. What was making him seem like a good husband? He'd ripped off his wife's daughter countless times. Invested her money in his schemes and lost it all. Cheated on her.

The letter was dated after Jean's death. The same period as the one postcard.

"It's like a puzzle," Mom said.

"Indeed. But it's a puzzle that makes little sense."

"Not yet, but you'll figure it out." She had more faith in me than I did.

"What's in the other package?" I said, reaching for it.

"It's heavy. Let me open it for you," she said.

Mom opened the side of the box, reached her hand in, and pulled out something cased in bubble wrap. We untangled it. My heart nearly stopped. *Justine's laptop.*

I opened and plugged it in. "Where's my phone?"

"Probably in your room. I'll get it for you." Mom scurried off to my room and brought me my phone.

I dialed Den.

"Brophy," he said.

That voice. It sent shivers through me, and at the same time warmth and comfort. How? How could one man's voice affect me like this?

"Hi there, it's Charlotte Donovan."

"Hey! How are ya? I was just going to call you."

"Why?" Did he expect me to believe that? Sorriest line in the book.

"We've had a big break in the case." He paused.

"Well?" I stared at the blank laptop screen.

"The same poison killed both Justine and Jean."

My skin pricked and hummed. Every pore was alert with anticipation. "So what's next?"

"It gives us more time," he said. "Now we know they're linked, it's a whole new case." Shuffling noises sounded in the background. Hushed voices, phones ringing.

Relief poured through me as my body exhaled. More time. We had more time. I'd been given more time on the book. Den was given more time on the case. I drew in air.

"Why did you call?" Den asked.

"Oh! I almost forgot," I said. "There were a few packages here from Justine."

"At your home?" His voice carried an excited note I'd not heard from him before. "What's inside?"

"The first package contained two postcards and a letter," I said and explained them in further detail. "I'm uncertain what any of this means. It fits on Jean Harlow's biographical timeline, though."

"That's interesting. But I'm not sure it has anything to do with the murder cases. Are you?"

I hesitated. "I don't know. I've no idea what these items mean. It's like what you said. Different pieces of a puzzle that may or may not make sense as part of a whole."

"I said that?" He laughed a little.

"Well, you said something like that," I said, with a smile cracking my face. Ouch. Maybe I shouldn't smile again.

"What's in the other package?"

"Justine's laptop. Now before you get too excited about that...
nothing is on it." I clicked around on the pad.

"Nothing?"

"Yeah, it looks like everything was wiped. I don't know if it happened when it was mailed or some other way. But she mailed it here
for safekeeping, so obviously it had something on it at one point."

"I don't know if our cyber unit can figure out what happened, but
it's worth a shot."

"Do you think they could recover the files?"

"I know nothing about that stuff, but I'm sure they'll try like hell."

I pictured Den with his blue eyes and sideways grin. His wide
shoulders and solid arms. I was feeling too down to tingle, but not
too down for my heart to skip a few beats.

"I'll send someone for the computer," he said.

"I was hoping you'd come," I said before thinking.

"I can't do it." He paused. "It takes too long to get out to Cloister
and back. I need to be here working this case. Bad timing."

"Okay," I said as lightheartedly as I could muster. *Message received.*
The journey took a good hour each way, sometimes longer depending on the tides. Sometimes I wished Cloister Island was closer to the
city; other times I was grateful for the distance.

Jabs of sharp pain moved through my head. Time for another pill.

"Okay, we'll watch for an officer."

After we signed off, I took another pain pill and weariness overcame me. Mom was tidying up, and I wanted her to settle down. It
was all the nervous energy she tried to use when she wasn't drinking.
Couldn't she sit down like a normal person? Sit and read? Sit and, I
don't know, knit?

I made my way to my room and plopped down on the bed. If I
had to watch Mom and all of her nervous tidying any longer, I'd lose
my mind. Peace. I wanted peace.

But even as I lay there, staring up at my sea-green ceiling, my mind raced with the news Den had given me, along with the postcards and letter Justine sent. And just the fact that she'd sent them to me said volumes. She understood she was in trouble. But why? What exactly was going on?

For the life of me, I couldn't believe a sapphire ring could get someone killed. *"People have been killed for less."*

Mom entered my room, breathless. "I received a call from your grandmother."

"And?"

"She says she has him. The collector you warned her about."

I sat up too fast and dizzied. "Has she called the police?"

Mom nodded. Her eyes were lit with excitement. "They're probably there by now."

"I should get dressed," I said, this time moving slower.

"You'll do no such thing. If the cops need to talk with you, they can come here."

"But Mom—"

"No buts about it."

"But how will she explain this?"

"You know your gram. She'll handle it." Mom's mouth spread into a wavy Cheshire-cat-like grin. "She held him at gunpoint while she called the police."

Imagining my sweet little gram holding Chad Walters at gun point made me giggle. Just a little.

What a day. So many things were breaking. The poison connection. The postcards and letter. Now Walters in custody. The pieces weren't connecting, but at least now we had pieces to chew on.

Later, Gram came into my room and filled me in. "I told Walters he had no business in my shop. Then he kind of scowled at me. I told him to leave. He said something like 'it's a free country.' So I pulled out my gun and told him I was glad it was a free country, not to move, and I called the cops. They couldn't hold him. But I don't think he'll be back."

The Donovans were an old family on the island, and even though we were always down on our luck, especially with fathers and husbands, we were a part of this community. Chad Walters didn't stand a chance. Everyone from the ferry operators to the restaurant owners would be watching for him now.

I grinned. "That's my gram."

Forty-Three

I woke up in the middle of the night with a clear head and one racing thought: *I'm not giving up.*

I fired up my laptop, which sat on my desk facing the sea. The same view I'd studied for years in the dark, in the light, and everything in between. From here I'd assisted Justine. I'd written, I'd scheduled, I'd proofread, I'd researched until I needed to go into the city for primary sources, or meetings with Justine, or interviews.

My spot. My seat of power.

I clicked on my timeline document and added the new information. Usually when information surfaced like this, there was a secret baby. Hollywood was full of them. But I'd ruled it out because Jean Harlow was always working and medical records indicated that she'd had at least two abortions, which hadn't taken her out of work for long. There was never a long-enough period of time, where she wasn't accounted for, during which she could have had a baby.

But something was going on around the time of her marriage to Paul Bern, and then right after she died. And it had to do with France. France? Why France?

I had a hunch whatever was going on in France had everything to do with Justine's death. Why else had she sent me those packages? Those items were so important she wanted nobody else to get their hands on them.

I sent off an email to the French embassy in DC, asking how I could find out information on a visitor to their country. How long they stayed and what they were doing there. The press people at embassies were easy to work with. In fact, some of them lived for this kind of stuff.

Next I sent off an email to the Hollywood Museum, who boasted the largest collection of Jean Harlow memorabilia. I already had a contact there. I asked him if there were any notes or letters of Jean's from France.

I wasn't sure any of this had anything to do with the case. If there was something to unearth, I'd do it. And if it helped solved the murder of Justine and the Jean Harlow look-alike, all the better. But I also had to explore this because it absolutely had to do with the manuscript I was working on.

The day Justine met with me at Layla's Tea Room, she was unlike herself—nervous, scared, and secretive. She was getting ready to explain it, and before she could, she died.

I would find out what it was. I owed her.

I opened the manuscript on my laptop and scrolled to the Paul Bern chapter, adding notes and queries. Then I scrolled to the "After Her Death" chapter and added more notes and queries. This was leading me somewhere. I had no idea where. I would need to be careful. I'd been clumsy. And I never should have let Natalie and Lucille make that public announcement that I was taking over the book. But I hadn't been myself then. I was still in the shock of my grief.

But also, I'd had no idea what a quagmire I was stepping into. People coming out of the Harlow woodwork. The ring. The secret room. Being stalked by the look-alike. And finally, attacked.

219

Who would have figured on any of that?

A wash of weariness over came me then, just before sunrise. When the sky and ocean held the color of near dawn. A glow. I pulled the curtains shut and made my way to bed.

I was awakened at nine a.m. by Ed opening my door. "Good morning, sunshine," he said. "Rise and shine!"

The ache in my head was slowly dissipating, but it was still there, low-grade and more than a little annoying. My face and nose still burned from the cuts.

Ed set a tray of breakfast food in front of me and for the first time since the attack, my stomach didn't wave. Coffee first.

"I'll check your BP and pulse," he said.

"I'm feeling better today," I said as he wrapped the cuff around my arm.

"Good," he said. "It's okay for you to move around the house today and see how it works out. Don't leave the house yet, though."

But I wanted to. I needed to. This would not do. I needed to get back to Manhattan, to Justine's apartment, where most of my other notes were—and where there must be further clues. I needed to get back into the secret room, even if it freaked me out.

"When can I leave?"

"What's your hurry?" he asked. "Just relax. You need to take care of yourself. You have me for one more day."

Maybe that's when I would make my case to leave. It would be tough—my mom and gram wanted me to stay. I was feeling stronger, physically, emotionally, and spiritually. I needed to be in Manhattan until we found Justine and Jean's killer.

"I'm serious," Ed said. "Don't push it. That's one of the tricky things about concussions. You start to feel better and then think you're okay. You took a nasty blow to the head. Not to mention the emotional trauma of the attack." He took me in with his keen eye.

"You may feel better, but your coloring is still off. " He reached for my wrist and motioned for me to be quiet, right as my mouth opened to say thanks for his concern. But I understood my body enough to know when it was okay to push it and when not. Call it a gift of Lyme disease.

Then again, one more day away from Justine's place wouldn't hurt. It would give me a chance to contact Kate and plan. Digging through the secret room was something she'd wanted to do since we'd discovered it. Kate loved secret places and stories of finding a lost treasure.

Ed caressed the scratch on my face. "Let's put ointment on it. It doesn't look like it will scar."

My mind rushed to the image of scar face, the person who'd killed Justine and, it seemed, the Jean Harlow twin. His wound must have been deep for his face to have scarred in such a way. How did he get that scar? What had he hoped to accomplish by killing those two women? What in his sick mind could ever justify such a thing?

Two days later I got up, found my old suitcase, flung it on to the bed, and packed. I would have to tell my mom and grandmother that I'd made the decision to leave.

A knock came at my bedroom door, and I opened it to find my mom and grandmother, each holding dishes and bags.

"Mom, Gram, what's up?"

"People sent food," Mom said, motioning for me to follow her to the kitchen, my tiny white-haired grandmother following with her arms full. "Come look."

"What's all this?" I asked.

"More food," Gram said. "Even though you say you're better, you'll need to keep your strength up. Oyster stew." She pointed to a Tupperware container. Oysters had enticed loads of Irish immigrants to this island. "Linda sent you brownies."

"Sweet potato casserole, and there's other stuff here from the ladies at the quilt shop, and some goodies from the bakery guys," Mom said.

The women of this island kept full freezers for just such a time. Tears stung at my eyes.

"But I—"

Mom cut me off by wrapping her arms around me. "Oh my sweet Charlotte," she said. "How awful for you! This whole thing. Come and sit down."

"I'll bring you coffee and a brownie," Gram said. "Do you need anything else?"

I shook my head as my mom lead me to the couch.

"Grief is exhausting. Plus this attack and concussion. You need to keep your strength up." Mom spotted my suitcase sitting on the bed. The door was open and the couch was about four good paces from my bedroom door. "Where are you going, exactly?"

"Uh, well," I said. Normally I'm articulate, but I struggled to find the words to tell them I was leaving again for a few weeks, maybe longer. "I received news, and I have to go into the city and stay a while."

Their heads tilted in interest in almost the exact same way, off to the right, eyebrows hitching.

"Pshaw! What do you need to go back for?" Mom said. Her disdain of the city was clear in her tone. "You need your family right now. You're not strong enough to leave yet."

I leaned back against the couch. "I've gotten the okay from Ed. I'll see my doctor in the city." I paused. "There's more I need to do for Justine. There's news about her case. It's the least I can do." My chest burned.

"Can't you do it from here?" My grandmother asked, handing me a cup of coffee and a brownie on a napkin. "Where will you stay?"

"At Justine's again," I said. Mom gasped and Gram crossed herself. Even though she'd left the church years ago, it was her way of letting us know she was praying for us.

"Are you certain?" Mom asked after a few minutes.

I nodded.

"Well, let's put some of this food in the freezer, then," Gram said, waltzing into the kitchen and opening the cupboards, fridge, and freezer. My grandmother was like most of the women on Cloister Island, moving through the kitchen as if she were a well-oiled robot.

"Leave the brownies out," I said. "I'll take those with me."

My mom sighed. "What are you going to do? Is the Harlow book finished?"

"No, the book's not finished. I've no idea what comes next. I got an extension. Those postcards and letter Justine sent me may add something to the book. I need to follow up with more research," I said and sipped from my coffee.

We three women sat in silence—or, almost silence. Gram was clicking her teeth, a nervous tick. We'd been here before. We knew grief and sickness too well. Three generations of it.

Mom ran her fingers over the quilt that was thrown over the back of our worn couch. "I know you well enough to know your mind's made up. Please be careful and promise me that if you start to feel unwell, you'll come home. Please."

"Okay," I said.

Later, on my way across the sound, I watched my island, with its shops, galleries, and restaurants, fade into the distance. I always hated leaving. And Cloister Island, even with its small-town mentality and people, was home.

The ferry slowed, and I took in the view of the city. As usual, it took me a few minutes to adjust to the pace. As soon as the ferry approached the dock, I rang Den.

"Hey, I was just going to call you," he said. "Where are you?"

"Passing Long Island, heading to Manhattan. I'm staying at Justine's place again."

"The guys have been able to recover some of Justine's files from her laptop. But nothing about Harlow or the case yet." He breathed into the phone.

"Maybe the postcards and letters will help. I don't know what they mean. I'm waiting on a phone call back from the French embassy. The Hollywood Museum has nothing for me so far."

"I gotta go, Charlotte. Stay in touch."

"Sure thing."

I tried not the think about Den too much. My month wasn't quite up yet. But somehow, it didn't seem to matter.

I disembarked from the ferry and called an Uber to the train to Justine's place, grateful for the ride. I hated to admit it to myself, but I needed to ride instead of walk. Just the journey across the sound had worn me out. The first thing I'd need to do was take a nap. Or I'd be sorry later on.

How I hated that. I felt like an old woman sometimes. The stab of the unfairness of my health situation zoomed through me. But it did no good to feel sorry for myself. Not at all.

Riding in the Uber, I took in the people along the streets—the funky Chelsea vibe, then moving uptown through the travesty of Times Square and picking out the tourists, then onward to the Upper East Side, where the crowds were thinner and less frantic. An interesting mix of people populated the Upper East Side—nouveau riche and old wealth. Vastly different on the social spectrum, in everything from what they wore to how they moved through the streets.

The Uber edged along Central Park and made its way to L'Ombragé, wedged between the shadows of two bigger apartment buildings. But its old-world elegance outshone the others surrounding it.

I anticipated digging into my research further, hoping it was leading me somewhere and not down a rabbit hole. Why had Bello been in France? Both before and after Jean's death? None of the Harlow biographies mentioned any of that. And the biggest question of all was what could have been secret enough about these two trips to reach into the future and, perhaps, play a role in the murder of two women?

Forty-Four

Riding through Manhattan, I had turned off my cell phone because the barrage of the calls that had backed up while I was on Cloister Island would come through and it would beep and beep and beep. Hated it. So when I walked into Justine's apartment and switched my phone on, countless beeps erupted, and within minutes I received a call.

"Hello." I set my laptop down on the desk.

"Ms. Charlotte Donovan?" the official-sounding female voice on the other end of the line said. Vaguely familiar.

"Yes."

"Susan Strohmeyer, Justine Turner's attorney."

I'd forgotten about the missing updates to the will.

"I've been trying to call you. I'm so glad to get through to you."

"I went back to Cloister Island. Sometimes my cell doesn't work there." I sat down on the desk chair, the muscles in my legs overjoyed for the relief. "Did you find the updates to the will?"

"Yes, we did. But we couldn't locate you, so we read the will without you. Justine's cousin insisted. She was threatening a lawsuit. I apologize for that."

"No worries," I said.

"Justine left most of her estate to you."

"Come again?" I must not have heard her right.

"She left most of her estate to you."

"Me?" I blinked and scanned the library. The books. The chaise. The delicate rose window. It was all real, not a dream.

"You're aware, of course, she had no family except Judith."

I inhaled and found it difficult to exhale.

"Are you still there?"

"Yes, but there must be some mistake. Everything? To me?" I let out a slow breath. My heart kicked in, rapping heavily against my rib cage. I stared up at the beautiful ceiling.

"Yes, that's the good news. The bad news is that Judith Turner is contesting it."

"Of course," I said. She was a piece of work. Justine had barely acknowledged her. And Judith was a wealthy woman in her own right. What was she about?

"How much is it?" I stammered, somewhat embarrassed by my question.

"I've no way of knowing at this point. As I say, it will take time to sort through. I don't think Judith has a case."

"Okay. What do we do now?"

"We wait for Judith's attorney to officially file the complaint and we go from there."

As we hung up, I told myself not to get my hopes up. I had never imagined Justine would leave anything to me, let alone everything. Did that really mean the apartment? I should have asked. It seemed too much to hope for—the prospect of finally having money, being able to pay of my hospital bills, perhaps helping my mom and gram after all those years of pinching pennies.

No. I wouldn't hope for it. Judith Turner would end up with it all.

I twirled around in Justine's chair to face the wall of books. It didn't matter if I ended up owning any of it—or inheriting all of her money. Tears stung my eyes. Justine *wanted* to leave it all to me. Something in my chest lifted.

I turned back to my laptop with a new sense of determination.

I moved forward on the manuscript, writing into the wee hours of the morning. I was almost there. Almost. Except for the gaping holes in earlier chapters. Why was Bello in France? Not once, but twice?

Still no word from the embassy. I'd gotten a brief email from my contact at the museum. So far he'd found nothing, but he was interested enough to keep pursuing it. He said there was one more place he had yet to check, but didn't have much hope.

I awoke the next morning with the Jean Harlow look-alike on my mind. As far as I knew, her life and death were still a mystery. She'd apparently changed her name to Jean Harlow, but there were no records of the change. Den still had no idea where she lived. When she was found, she'd had nothing on her with an address.

Was nobody missing her? Had nobody called the police to report a missing person? Sadness tugged at me. She must have gone through a lot to reclaim herself as a woman, and not just any woman, but Jean Harlow. Like Kate, she probably had her own story of family struggle, grief, and perhaps violence.

To be a person who'd gone through hell to become who she believed she was meant to be, and then to have been killed so young…it struck me as extraordinarily cruel. But then again, the world was unforgiving and ambivalent. There was little justice.

My phone interrupted my deliberation. It was Kate. "I'm running about an hour late. The Japanese buyers are giving me a hard time. I need to meet with them very quickly, and then I'll be over to help you clean."

"See you then," I said.

I took a deep breath and listened to my messages.

Several from Natalie, Justine's agent.

Several from the Lucille, who was livid. "What is the problem? Why can't you get this manuscript done?" Her voice was sharp and clear and quivering from anger.

The next call from Lucille was full of apologies. "I'm so sorry to hear about what happened to you."

A call from Lizzie the librarian, checking in for my opinion about the clip of Harlow, asking if there was anything else she could do for me.

A phone call from a woman named Crystal, who has a message for me from Jean Harlow's ghost. *Oh no, not again.* "She said she knows about the trinket in your purse. Whatever that means. She's insistent you deliver it to the right person."

My breath stopped. Who was this person? This Crystal? Her use of the word "trinket" led me to believe she was making it up. But then again, the ring was the only possible "trinket" in my purse.

Shivering, I slid my phone away.

What utter nonsense. Nonsense that freaked my ass out.

Forty-Five

After performing my morning rituals, I slipped out onto the balcony for some air. The sky was moonstone gray with the threat of rain. Nobody else in the building minded the rain. Most of them were independently wealthy and ordered everything from groceries to books. They weren't like the rest of us working slogs, hoofing around struggling to carry packages and manage an umbrella.

Kate would arrive any minute so I went back inside, reluctantly. The apartment still needed a good airing out. I was trying my best. But years of stale air were difficult to vanquish.

The scent of Cotillion hit me hard as I walked into the library. The desk lamp flickered off, then back on. I'd noted how the electricity wasn't right. I reached for a blanket and wrapped it around my shoulders. Damn, it was cold in here. I made a mental note to speak with the management about the fluctuating temperatures. Even though I was uncertain of how much longer I'd be living here. Still, this needed to be tended to.

The intercom's buzz interrupted my thoughts. I pressed the button.

"Ms. Kate, here to see you," a voice said.

"Send her up please."

I was happy that Kate would join me in my search through the secret room today. I didn't want to do it alone. It gave me the heebie-jeebies, as we used to say when we were kids. A secret room. Like something out of the Trixie Belden books I loved to read when I was a girl. Secret rooms were never a good thing.

Kate waltzed in the front door like she owned the place. Even dressed in jeans and a T-shirt, she somehow looked more pulled together than I ever did.

"Hey girl," she said and hugged me. "You look great."

"Thanks. I'm feeling so much better," I replied.

"I brought you some cream for the cut on your face. It'll encourage faster healing and prevent a scar." She set her bag down on a chair in the entryway and rubbed her hands together. "Let's get to it, shall we?"

"Do you want coffee?"

"Sure, that would help. It always does. Hey, how's everything at home?" We walked into the kitchen and I grabbed two cups, poured coffee into them.

I told her what had happened with Chad Walters and Gram.

"Good old Birdie." Kate stirred cream, laughing. Then she followed me into Justine's white bedroom, through the closet, and into the secret room. "Well, we have our work cut out for us."

"Where to start?" We stood for a moment among the covered furniture, paintings, and heaps of boxes.

"Okay, we've already searched those boxes," she said, pointing at the stack we'd examined before. "Let's set them aside."

I carried them into the bedroom. "After we search through each one, let's set the boxes out here so we won't be reinventing the wheel."

"What are we looking for?" Kate said. "Anything in particular?"

"Mostly papers. Anything to do with France, Jean Harlow, or Marino Bello, her stepfather. Maybe something to do with the ring?"

"So let's table the paintings and furniture and get started on the boxes." She sat on the floor and reached for a box. "Have you told Den yet?"

"Not yet, but I will as soon as I see him. I plan to hand it over to him." I sat down against a wall to support my back as I reached for a box.

"Nothing in this one but a pair of old sparkly shoes," Kate said, pulling one out. Red and sparkling.

I gasped.

"What?"

"Those are ruby slippers, aren't they?"

Kate's eyes slanted. "I suppose they are."

I hesitated. "I thought all of the ruby slippers were accounted for, but maybe not. I need to check into it. Seems like I read something about a stolen pair that was recently recovered."

"Do you think she stole them? Was Justine a thief?" Kate said after a few moments.

"I never would have imagined that," I said. I was learning more about my boss than I wanted to, perhaps. I'd always considered her one of the most honest people I'd ever known. Could a person be an honest thief?

Perhaps I hadn't known Justine at all. Maybe the person she presented as was nothing more than a charade. I swallowed the disappointment.

The next few boxes all held shoes in them. Some were labeled and some weren't. Ginger Rogers's tap shoes. Shirley Temple's tap shoes. Why tap shoes?

"Oh! Here's a box with papers," Kate said after she took several cartons out into the bedroom and sat back down. She held up the paper. "Looks like this is a will, and it's attached to a deed. It's the deed to this place." She read it over. "Justine's grandmother willed her this apartment."

"I'd wondered how she came to live here."

"Here's Justine's birth certificate, along with her parents and grandparents. They emigrated from Sweden." Kate read over the documents. "That's about it."

"One mystery solved. But not the one we need solved." I opened another box with papers. "Why are all those things in the secret room instead of a lockbox or something?"

"Justine wasn't the most organized person."

No, she wasn't. I was the one who organized her work. The computer files. The emails. The research. Sometimes I even helped organize the books.

I plunged my hand into another box and pulled out a paper with a key taped to it. It was Justine's membership to Club Circe. She was a lifetime member, complete with all privileges. "What privileges do you think those Circe Club members have?"

"Oh, who knows?" Kate said. "But I imagine free drinks and food. They pull strings for one another for jobs, too. Like the old boys club, but instead the old girls club. Why?"

"Here's Justine's membership papers." I held them up. "With a key. Could it be the key to a locker? A lockbox?"

"A room?" Kate said. "A lot of the old private clubs have rooms for out-of-town members. Or entertaining on the down-low if you know what I mean."

My synaptic fibers snapped and crackled. *Justine.* Did she have a private room at the club? Is that where she'd been living before she died?

I left Kate in the secret room as I stepped out into the bedroom to phone Den.

"Sergeant Den Brophy."

"Hi, Den, it's Charlotte Donovan."

"Charlotte, how are you feeling?" He sounded genuinely concerned.

"Better, and I'm back at Justine's place."

"That's good."

"Kate and I have been going through some of her things and we found her membership documents to the Club Circe, along with a key."

"And?"

"Were you ever able to pull financials for the time right before Justine's death?"

"Ah, hold on," he said. The sound of fingers on a keyboard came over the phone as he muttered, "Damn thing is so slow."

I waited a few more beats.

"Okay, here we are," he said. "Yes, and this is why it led us nowhere. The few credit card charges are in the city. There's a period of about eight days where there are no charges to any of her credit or bank cards."

"What do you know about Club Circe?"

"Not much. It's a private club, so we don't get called in there often. They take care of matters on their own."

"Matters? You mean like—"

"Drunks and thieves, things like that. They just kick 'em out of the club, I hear."

"I'm wondering if Justine might have stayed there to write…and to hide."

Silence on the other end of the phone.

"Is it possible?"

"Maybe," he said, drawn out. "If she stayed there, probably all the evidence is gone. It's almost been a month. But it's worth a shot."

"Can we meet at the club today or tomorrow?"

"I could send someone down there," he said. *Message received. Again.*

What the hell? A cop who couldn't take the way a roughed-up woman looked? Even though I'd been preparing myself for this, part of me had hoped he'd be different. But just like that, he was no longer interested?

"You said these people are secretive, so I don't think they'll talk with a cop alone," I said. "If I was there, they might. I was Justine's assistant. They'll trust me before you or anyone else. Should I take care of this myself?" I sounded more zippy than I felt. But one minute he was telling me not do a thing without the cops and the next minute he was trying to send a strange cop to question the ladies of Club Circe. It made no kind of sense.

"I told you not to do stuff like that," he said. "I'm just going to send someone down there to ask about membership, and if Justine had a room there."

"They won't tell your guy anything," I said.

"Look, Charlotte, I appreciate what you're saying. But we have protocol here. So if we get nowhere and need a search warrant, I'll call you. How's that sound?"

"Honestly? Like you're putting me off, Den." Yes, those words came out of my mouth. Sometimes my mouth had its own mind.

"Putting you off? Nah. I'm trying to keep you safe. You're a civilian with no business racing around this city right now. You need to recover."

"I told you I'm fine. I'll just go on my own."

A long silence on the other end of the phone. "Okay, Charlotte. But I'm driving up to get you. You don't need to be on the subway right now."

"I don't need your pity."

"Pity? What's wrong with you? I just care about your well-being."

Did he? How would I know? I hadn't seen him since he'd watched me leave Manhattan in a police-escorted boat.

"Look, I'm a cop," Den went on. "I think like a cop. I'm sorry. Let's do this thing. I'll pick you up around four. Can you be waiting?"

"Sure," I said.

"What was that all about?" Kate said, coming up behind me. I relayed my theory and what had just happened with Den.

"I think you've got him all wrong."

"I doubt it. You know my luck with men."

"You've been involved with some real jerks. But Den's not like that."

"I guess it doesn't matter," I said after a few moments. "I'm not interested in a relationship. Not really. I thought he was, and I was charmed by that. But that's all." I still had to tell him about the ring. The longer it went on, the worse I felt about it. What was my problem?

"So I guess I owe you some money. You've lasted four weeks. Can I pay you next week?" Kate grinned.

"Absolutely," I said.

"You told me a while ago that you'd tell him about the ring," she said.

"I know." I kept working.

We straightened out the boxes, having at the least peeked inside each one and not finding anything more relevant than the key to something at the Club Circe. Next time we would unveil the large objects, but for now we'd made progress.

"What do you think she would do with all of it?" Kate said, standing with her hands on her hips.

"That's a good question. Who knows where it all comes from."

"I can't believe Justine would steal."

"Oh no, me neither. But maybe she bought this stuff on the black market. Just as bad."

"But still," said Kate, flinging her arms out. "She had this all hidden. It wasn't like she was even enjoying it. I don't get it."

I didn't either. And I thought I knew Justine better than anybody. But it was clear she'd gotten herself involved in more than one illegal activity. Who knew what we'd find at the Circe Club?

Forty-Six

I waited in the L'Ombragé lobby, surrounded by marble and soft lights. Kate left, muttering something about my not needing a chaperone anymore.

When Den pulled the police car up to the curb, it was as if all the onlookers had never seen a cop car before. Snappy white with blue strips down the side, it made my breath hitch. Just a little. I drew in air and marched outside. Den was waiting by the door, and he opened it for me with a crooked smile. "At your service," he teased, tipping his blue cap.

I slid into the passenger seat, marveling at the dashboard with its sparkling blue lights and a computer screen.

Den climbed in on his side.

"It's great to have a police escort," I said.

"Yeah," he replied. "This car is one of the new smart cars. It's a prototype. It's full of all kinds of cool technology. Half of which I don't understand, yet." He laughed. "I mean, I'm a cop not a computer geek." There was a hint of disdain in his voice.

"Are you up for some kind of promotion? Didn't you mention that?"

He pulled away from the curb. "Yeah, I applied to be a detective. They have more time to investigate. I get a little frustrated with the paperwork and the chain of command I have to deal with. I always just wanted to investigate crime. Ya know, help people."

Little fireworks exploded in my chest. I gazed off, out the window. It was obvious Den would not pursue our relationship. But the attraction tugged at me.

"What about you?"

"What?" I asked.

"What did you want to be? Did you always want to be an assistant to a writer?" He grinned. We stopped at a red light. I watched the crowd move from one side of the street to the other. Sometimes I marveled at how orderly things were, and how at any minute someone could change all that.

"I always wanted to write," I said. "I worked for Justine right out of college. I've learned a lot from her." My voice cracked. And we left it there. Rode in silence the rest of the way.

Walking into Club Circe was like stepping into an enchanted castle. I remembered being more than impressed during Justine's memorial service. But I'd been in a haze and not truly able to appreciate the many details of the splendor. The ornately carved baluster. The gilded age murals on the ceiling. The huge stained glass window with the goddess Circe's image.

"Sergeant Brophy." A woman approached us. "So glad to see you." She turned. "You must be Charlotte Donovan."

I nodded. I wasn't sure I could speak. Not yet. Her bearing was so precise, confident, and sharp. She was a woman used to having her way. Like Justine. It would take me a few moments to gather myself.

"Follow me, please," she said, and lead us into an office with a huge fireplace flanked by the plushest leather chairs I'd ever seen.

Gorgeous red oriental carpets were well-placed throughout the room. Instead of sitting behind the massive desk, the woman took a position in the chair. There was a table with a set-up tea service.

"Please sit down," she said.

Den and I took our seats.

"Tea?" she asked as she poured. Her nails were perfect and smooth, but she didn't wear nail polish.

"No thank you," Den said.

"How about you, Charlotte? I won't have to have my tea alone, will I?" she purred. And she was catlike, slinking about the hallways and now pouring the tea. So graceful but with a hint of edge, as if she was ready to pounce.

"Sure," I said, taking the delicate cup and saucer, Limoges, I was sure.

"Justine was a close friend of mine," she said. "She thought highly of you, Charlotte."

Air left my lungs as I tried to smile. I lifted the tea to my mouth and sipped.

"Ms. Collins," Den said, "was Justine staying here during the last few weeks of her life?"

She drank from her cup, set the cup back in the saucer, and held it. "Yes, she was."

I sat the tea cup and saucer down on the table. As I did, my hand trembled. *We were right.*

"We have private rooms for the exclusive use of our members. Justine was a lifetime member. She had a suite," she said.

Den looked at me and sort of rolled his eyes. Disappointment seemed to be lodged there. "Can we see the suite? It's imperative to the investigation of her death."

"I'm sorry, Sergeant Brophy." Ms. Collins held the tea cup to her perfectly lipsticked lips. "This is a private club. And as such, I cannot permit you to enter any of the rooms."

I swallowed. "But Justine was murdered. There may be something in that suite to help us find her killer."

Den held up his hand to quiet my blabbing. "We can get a search warrant. Private club or not. So, why not let us look today?"

The woman smiled a stiff smile. "I'm sorry, Sergeant Brophy. I cannot allow you to enter that suite."

Den stood in a huff, chest out. A shock of excitement, fear, and attraction moved through me. *Damn. He was all male.*

"Fine, you'll hear from us soon," he said and turned toward me. "Charlotte?"

I stood. An awkward moment as my eyes met hers.

"I'm sorry," she said.

"Okay," Den replied. "We'll be back with the search warrant. In the meantime, I trust nobody else will be going inside that room. Because that would be tampering with evidence."

"I can assure you, Sergeant, nobody has been inside since Justine's death," she said, standing. "Let me show you out."

"Nah, don't bother." Den waved me to walk in front of him. We headed toward the opulent entryway, opened the door, and exited Club Circe.

"What the hell?" I said. "Why wouldn't she let us see Justine's suite?"

"These society types," he muttered.

But these women were more than society types. They were learned and powerful. Several judges and congresswomen were members. You'd think they'd have a healthy respect for the law.

I followed Den to the car. He opened the door for me and I slid in. He walked around the back of the vehicle. When he was inside, he pulled out his cell phone and pressed his finger on the screen.

"This is Den Brophy. I need a search warrant for a suite in Club Circe. Has to do with the Justine Turner case. She was living there

the last few weeks of her life." Pause. "That's right. Club Circe."
Pause. "No, man, I'm not kidding. Club Circe. Get it done."

He put his phone back in his pocket and glanced at me. "This
won't be easy."

But I wondered if it would have been easier if I had gone alone as
Justine's assistant, without Den. I made a mental note to call and ask
Ms. Collins. In the meantime, I sank into the car seat and watched
Den drive, enjoying my view, perhaps a bit too much.

Forty-Seven

After Den dropped me off, I headed to a nearby deli for food. I ended up with two bags filled with meat, cheese, olives, two kinds of bread, and wine. A feast for a queen.

When I entered L'Ombragé, I stopped cold. There stood Judith Turner, glaring at me with evil spewing forth from her beady, made-up eyes. I started to walk by her and she grabbed me, almost causing me to drop my groceries.

"Let go of me." I jerked my arm away from her.

"Don't tell me you're still staying here," she said, with a sweep of her eyes up and down my person. With one glance, she communicated exactly what she thought of me. I regretted that. After all, she was Justine's cousin, her only living relative.

"I am," I replied. "I'm still cleaning and sorting her apartment. And then there's my work. I'm finishing the Harlow biography."

"You need not live here to write," Judith said.

I shifted my weight. How could she appreciate anything about what I needed to do to finish the book? I shrugged. "I'm sorry?"

"Why don't you move out? And leave the place and all of its belongings to someone who was actually related to Justine."

"According to Justine's will—"

"Pshaw! I'm certain you coerced her."

I couldn't help myself. I laughed. "If you think I could talk Justine into anything, it shows how little you knew your cousin."

The security guard eyed us.

"I know she loved me," Judith said.

The bags were getting heavy in my arms. "She only mentioned you once to me."

"You are the help. Why would you know anything at all about the real Justine?"

I wanted to say that no, I don't know much, but I'm learning more every day. Justine has a hidden room full of stolen Hollywood memorabilia and art. She hid out at Club Circe for weeks before her death.

I wondered how much Judith Turner actually understood about her cousin.

"When I'm done with you, you'll wish you'd never heard of Justine Turner," she said.

A sharp, chilling prickle traveled up my spine. I wanted to smack Judith, but my arms were full. And God only knew what she'd do if I hit her. I needed to escape to the elevator and get back to the apartment.

I started to walk by her, but I stopped. "You know what? I already wish I'd never heard of Justine. Do you think I like any of this? Do you think I like cleaning up her mess? Finishing the book she didn't finish? Trying to figure out who killed her? Have people chasing after me because of it? No, lady. Being Justine's assistant was never a picnic. Especially not now."

Judith's mouth flung open, as if in shock. I headed toward the elevator in tears. I pressed the button for the fourteenth floor.

It was all true, wasn't it? Justine could anger me like no other person, except perhaps my mother. I was pissed. The messes she'd left me with were difficult to clean up. In fact, she hadn't made it easy for me at any turn. We'd now solved one mystery: she'd stayed at Club Circe in the weeks before her murder. But the members wouldn't let Den and me inside to explore. It could take days if not weeks to get the search warrant.

And she'd left me with a pile of illegal Hollywood crap to deal with.

What was I going to do with all of it, let alone the ring in my purse I had yet to tell Den about?

Yeah, Justine had educated me about publishing, and she gave me a chance when nobody else would, but damn, I was angry with her. Why hadn't she trusted me enough to take me in to her confidence?

The elevator stopped and opened to Justine's floor. I sat the bags of groceries down while I rummaged for the key and opened the door. I'd been anticipating my little feast. But now my stomach had soured. I stashed all the groceries in their rightful places and opened a bottle of wine.

My Saturday night would be wine and work. I poured myself a glass and headed into the library, flipped open my computer, and wrote. Damn, I needed to finish the book and get people like Judith Turner, Severn Hartwell, and Chad Walters out of my life—for good. Let alone scar face.

My phone beeped. It was my Tinder account. One of my favorite cops asking if I could get together tonight. Such late notice. I glanced at the clock. I considered it. After all, my month was up and I could use a zesty diversion.

But Den Brophy plucked at my mind. I didn't see why. He'd sent signals of his disinterest. Perhaps I was even more attracted to him because of his lack of interest. When I was attacked in the park, he'd been there for me, but from the moment he'd placed me on that boat, his sour expression and sick stance had said it all.

I wrote back to Zach. *"Not tonight. I'm sorry. I'm on deadline."*
That was true. I needed to stay focused. Words were flowing.
And it wasn't because I was hung up on Den. No. *I don't get hung up on anybody.*

Forty-Eight

I didn't know how much longer I could put Lucille off. She called me at least twelve times within the next two-day period.

Finally, I answered the phone.

"Charlotte, where have you been? Are you feeling better?"

"I'm fine. I've just been very busy," I said, and told her about Justine's suite in Club Circe.

"All very interesting, but what does it have to do with the book?"

"I'm not sure. But Justine may have found a new twist to the Harlow story," I said, hunching over the desk with my head in my hand. Was Lucille going to buy any of this?

"The Harlow story has no twist," she said. "This book is the definitive Harlow story. With a few new pictures, a few new remembrances, and that's it. Harlow led a brief life and most of it was very much accounted for. What's new under the sun?"

I paused before telling her more. I didn't want her to think I was chasing clouds even though I might be. "When I was at home recovering, two packages arrived that Justine had sent before she died."

Complete silence on the other end of the phone.

"One was her missing laptop. Unfortunately, it was wiped clean, though the police have been able to recover emails. They've already been looking at emails we accessed through her desktop computer. She was being threatened by several people."

"Nothing new there, I'm afraid."

"She wasn't being warned about a lawsuit, but for her life. And she was murdered, so there is something to all this."

Lucille sighed an impatient, get-to-it sigh. "Look, where are you going with this?"

"It's possible Justine's killer came after her because she was exposing a secret about Harlow, or because of the star sapphire ring."

"What secrets are we talking about?" Lucille was interested. Her voice inflected upwards.

"I think it has something to do with Marino Bello."

"Her mother's husband? What? Did he make a pass or throw himself at Harlow? What?"

"I wouldn't put it past him. But that's not what I'm saying." I explained the postcards and letter Justine had sent to me.

"All very interesting," Lucille said. "But it appears to be leading nowhere. I've got a production schedule to maintain. We've already let it slide a few times."

There was bite in her tone, which sent my heart racing. This woman had worked with Justine for years. She was one of the best editors out there. I wanted her to think highly of me.

"But then again," she continued, with another sigh. "Justine always said you were a kick-ass researcher. I can give you a few more days. If there's not a story here, you'll have to get me that manuscript ASAP. Do you understand?"

Justine had told her about me. "Yes. I won't let you down," I said. *And I won't let Justine down either.*

"I hope not."

248

"I contacted the French embassy. They were able to confirm that Bello was there. And it worked out with the Harlow timeline. But what we don't know is what he was doing there."

"It sounds like there may have been a secret baby. Wouldn't that be something?"

"Jean Harlow's movements are well accounted for. She was on-screen or rehearsing so much, she couldn't have been out for any length of time. Every time she gained weight her mother placed her on a strict diet. There are records about it."

"Plus she had two abortions, didn't she?" Lucille asked. Papers shuffled in the background. "Just a minute." She covered the phone and came back.

"Yes, she had two we know of," I said. "All of her medical records are available."

"Hmmm," Lucille said. "Stay in touch, Charlotte. We're cutting it very close. I don't want to have to track you down."

"Understood," I said.

"I heard from Severn Hartwell, you know, and he's just waiting for us to drop the ball on this book."

"What? I wish he'd mind his own business."

"He has no business. The man is broke. And no editor or agent will work with him. He's not earned out his latest advances and he's deeply in debt."

"That's surprising," I said. But it made sense now why Hartwell had been hanging around me. Perhaps he considered the Harlow book his last chance. He was desperate. But was he desperate enough to kill?

"Justine was one of the few writers I ever knew who could make more than a living at this profession. Hartwell is more typical of authors," she said. "Are you certain you want to be a writer?"

"I'm afraid there's no turning back now."

There comes a time in everybody's life where you have to be honest with yourself. Defining yourself is difficult. But I'd always wanted to write, and now I wasn't qualified to do anything else but research and write. I might be broke the rest of my life pursing my dream, and I'd made my peace with it. I didn't need much, anyway. I wasn't into expensive clothes, makeup, or any frivolity. I needed a small apartment and my computer, and enough food to get by.

Funny. I'd never even thought about all of that before. Until that moment. Few authors ever reached Justine's fame and fortune. But most writers, like me, didn't care. You had to do it, because you loved it, and no other reason sufficed.

Forty-Nine

*N*ow that I'd told Lucille about it, I had to discover what was going on with Marino Bello in France. Maybe it would lead nowhere. But I had to find out.

I called the embassy again and left a message.

I walked into the kitchen and sliced bread and cheeses, poured myself a glass of wine, and took a plate into the library with me.

I mulled over what had transpired over the past few days. We'd found out Justine was staying at the Club Circe and that it wouldn't be easy to get a search warrant. I drank from my glass. The wine was fruity and sweet. I bit into a slice of cheese, a good, hard blue cheese. The flavors mingled in my mouth.

So Justine must have been hiding at the club, suspecting she was in danger. She was getting ready to tell me something.

Lucille was more agreeable to my ideas than I'd imagined, which was a good thing. She was also a font of information concerning Severn Hartwell. I could visualize him killing Justine, but why would he have killed the Jean Harlow look-alike? The cops seemed pretty certain the two murders were linked.

And I also confirmed that Judith Turner was a piece of work. Grabbing me in the lobby? Why was she so concerned about Justine's money? Was it greed or some other sinister compulsion?

With each sip of wine, I sank further into my chair. The cheese, the bread, the wine lulled me. My reflections were dripping through me, giving me plenty of time to consider each thought. Which was better than having racing thoughts.

My cell interrupted my meditation. I glanced at the screen. It was my grandmother.

"Hello," I said.

"Charlotte, it's about your mom," Gram said, her voice wavering. She was upset, which rarely happened. "I found her passed out in a pool of blood. I don't know if she was drinking or not. But we're at the hospital."

"Which hospital?" My reverie spun into prickling alertness. My mom!

"Mercy."

Mom was probably airlifted, then.

"I'll be right there." I set my glass down and reached for my purse.

I cabbed it to the hospital. I couldn't deal with the subway. Not tonight. My heart was racing and the food in my belly soured. I walked into the main reception area. A few people gathered around the front desk. I shuffled in behind them.

"I'm sorry," the receptionist said to the man standing there. "She's in ICU and can't have visitors."

"That's my mother," he said.

"Please have a seat or I'll have to call security." The receptionist was a plump, brown-skinned woman, made up to the hilt, with a strong manner and tough voice.

The man wandered off, hanging his head.

I stepped up, knowing that the woman was not in the mood for pleasantries. "Hi, I'm here to see my mom. Mary Katherine Donovan. She was just brought in."

"One moment please," she said, her fingers moved across her keyboard. She glanced up at me. "She's in room 410. The elevators are just around the corner." She pointed me in the correct direction.

"Thanks so much." I thanked my lucky stars I didn't have her job. I could imagine the crap she had to put up with.

I found the elevator and pressed the up arrow. What had my mother done? Was she drinking again? She'd promised she wouldn't drink another drop of alcohol. Disappointment jabbed at me. She had vowed that before, hadn't she?

I exited the elevator and found my way to her room. I opened the door to a mostly dark space. One small light shone. Gram sat next to her.

"Charlotte!" Mom said with a raspy voice. Although she was in her fifties, remorse had taken away the years. Ashamed, she looked like a child. "I'm sorry. I tried."

I leaned over and kissed her forehead. "It'll be okay."

Gram's eyebrows lifted in surprise at my reaction. We'd been here before. I'd railed and lectured at my mother. Why couldn't she stay sober? But I didn't have it in me that night. Not with the way my mom looked. Not knowing she'd been bleeding.

A tear escaped from Mom's eyes. "Oh, Charlotte. I thought I could just have a glass of wine with my spaghetti. Just one glass. The next thing I knew...I finished the bottle and threw up."

"And passed out," Gram said. "Could've choked on her own vomit. Good thing I checked on her."

Just then a doctor came in the room. "Mrs. Donovan. And you are?"

"I'm her daughter, Charlotte. This is her mother, Brigid."

The doctor walked over to my mom and reached for her wrist, took her pulse. Then he listened to her heart.

"You've got a good ticker, Mrs. Donovan. But your liver is another matter."

Mom's chin lifted. "What do you mean?"

"I mean psoriasis of the liver. It's in terrible shape. As is your stomach. What are we going to do about that?"

Mom shrugged. "You're the doctor. You tell me."

"Stop drinking alcohol. It might take one drink or it might take twenty, but it will kill you."

Gram reached over and took Mom's hand. Her mouth was moving slightly, whispering a prayer.

"To that end, I'm having a social worker check into some rehab options for you. Get some help, okay?"

Mom nodded, looking shell-shocked. But I remembered the times we'd done this before. Twice. She'd been in rehab twice over the years.

"There are some new approaches, new therapies that might work for you," he said as if reading my mind.

"Mom? What do you think?"

She nodded, tears streaming. I handed her a tissue. How had she gotten to this point? How did anybody get to this point? Was the pain of my father's disappearance still too much for her? Had she never gotten over it?

I'd tried to help her as best as I could, but I admitted to losing patience with her and probably making it worse. The whole situation made me angry. Why couldn't I have a strong mother? A mother who said, "Forget him. I'll do fine without him." Mom had tried to wear that mask for years, but it had worn down with each passing day.

Her pluck had vanished. My mom, her head on the white hospital pillow and covered in a pilled tan blanket, was so small, so delicate, it broke my heart.

Fifty

*G*ram and I both stayed the night. Mom's stomach still bled, and they gave her something to stop it. Gram lay on a lounger and I lay on a cot next to Mom. Tossing and turning. With each nurse's check-in, I sprang awake.

The next morning, we ate breakfast together. Mom's coloring was coming back into her face. Whereas before it was grayish, now it was more pink. A priest visited, which thrilled my gram, but not so much me and my mother.

My cell phone beeped. It was Den.

"Hey, Charlotte," he said when I answered. "We've got our search warrant. Usually we don't allow civilians to come along on these things. But you might be able to help us make sense of what we confiscate."

My heart fluttered. But my stomach sank in regret. "I'm sorry, Den. I can't do it."

My grandmother sat up, her attention on me and what I was saying.

"What? What do ya mean?"

"I'm at the hospital with my mom. There's been an incident."

"Incident?"

"Yeah, she's in bad shape. I can't get away."

There was a pause. "I'm sorry, Charlotte. I hope she pulls through."

"Oh, she will for now," I said. "It's complicated." Mom was sleeping, so I tried to speak quietly.

"Hmph. I imagine we'll be at Club Circe all day, and even tomorrow. So just come by when you can. Or not."

"What will happen? I mean, what will happen to whatever you find in those rooms?"

Gram stood and stretched. She pretended to not pay attention, but she was straining to hear every word. Call it a granddaughter's intuition.

"We'll bag up and label everything. Nothing will get thrown out. Not yet," he said. "So don't worry, Charlotte. You do what you gotta do, y'know? It's your mom."

I nodded. "Yeah. I'll get there when I can."

"Charlotte?"

"Yeah?"

"Take care." He clicked off.

It wasn't the first time I'd had to miss something because my mom was sick or drunk. But it was the first time I didn't care.

Oh, I cared about getting into that room. But it could wait. As Den had said, the stuff wouldn't disappear. And as I looked at my mom, the fresh memory of losing Justine reminded me of the fragility of life. One day here, the next day gone. I was in the right place, with the right people.

"Who was that?" Gram asked.

"The police officer working on Justine's case." I lay back on the cot, weary.

"What's going on?"

"They've got a search warrant to check out Justine's private room at Club Circe." My head sank into the pillow. "They wanted me to come and help them sort it all out."

"And?"

"I told them it could wait. And it can."

"Club Circe? Isn't that one of those fancy private clubs?"

"Yeah," I said. "It'll take them a few days."

The room quieted. Gram went into the bathroom and I closed my eyes.

I awakened to Mom and Gram laughing. *I Love Lucy* was on the television. I sat up and eyeballed them. Mom was smiling, a rosy touch in her cheeks.

"They'll spring me tomorrow morning. Got a place for me at a rehab center in Jersey."

"Jersey? Could they have picked a worse place? It'll take hours to get there," I said.

"We are not allowed to visit," Gram said, shrugging. "It's going to be quite a vacation for your ma."

"Yeah," Mom snorted. "A vacation in Jersey without my family and without the booze."

"Let's hope so, Mom. You don't want to end up here again." I stood and leaned over her bed, brushing away a cluster of gray hair on her forehead.

"I'm so sorry, Charlotte. For everything," she said with authenticity in her eyes and voice.

"Me too, Mom," I said, warmth spreading through me.

"You need to know something," she said. "Yesterday, I received a letter in the mail." Her voice cracked.

What could it have been? A bill collector? Another package from Justine?

"It was a note from your father."

"Come again?"

"He's alive. Your father is still alive."

Air whooshed from my lungs. "It can't be."

"That's what I thought. I assumed someone was messing with me." Her lips formed a straight line.

"And?" I prompted.

She shrugged. "I don't know, Charlotte. It looked like his handwriting. He wrote about things that only he would know about."

No wonder Mom took that first drink. My dad had vanished twenty years ago without a word. We thought he was dead.

I had a million questions rushing through my mind. But only one came out. "Where is he?"

Mom's eyes turned to blue pools of sorrow. "He didn't say."

Fifty-One

*T*he next day, after we packed Mom off to her rehab facility and Gram off to Cloister Island, I hailed an Uber to Club Circe.

Gutted by the news that my dad was alive but hadn't bothered to reach out to us until now, and with my energy as sapped, I didn't have much left within me for investigation. Even though I was keeping up with my meds, I required rest.

But I needed to be in the space Justine lived in the last few weeks of her life. It was more than a nostalgic compulsion. It was a need to know, to dig through the things she'd left behind for some answers. What and who was she hiding from? Was it the person who killed her?

Did she have files pertaining to any of this? I'd found no juicy research on the Harlow book in her apartment. I decided they must be in her Club Circe suite.

A grim Ms. Collins opened the door to the club and directed me to the elevator. "Tenth floor, Suite A."

As I made my way to the suite, I contemplated Club Circe, the missing files, and Justine. There were only two suites on the floor, and

I assumed the one with the door open and police inside was Justine's. But I was unprepared for the well-ordered chaos, and it took me a moment to get my bearings. Plastic bags, labeled, held Justine's things. Uniformed officers walked around, bagging and labeling. The scent of sharpie markers and cheap plastic filled the luxurious room, making for an odd scene when combined with the Oriental carpets, crystal chandeliers, and original paintings. A forensics team was examining every nook and cranny of the place and working with the police.

"Charlotte," Den said, lifting his chin toward me. He was crouched down on the shiny floor bagging up a dress. I inspected it further, my heart skipping a beat. It was the same pink dress that the Harlow impersonator had worn when she came to the apartment. The day Justine's computer was stolen.

"Den, that's—"

He stood. "She was staying here with Justine."

I clutched my chest. "What?"

"Whatever they were involved in, they were in it together," he said.

Justine had been living with the Harlow look-alike here? At Club Circe? Why didn't she tell me any of this? What exactly was going on?

Several other officers were in the rooms, placing shoes, clothes, and such in bags and labeling them.

"What are you going to do with that?" I asked as someone carried off one of Justine's outfits. A black-and-white Chanel suit.

"It's evidence," Den said. "Don't worry. We'll get her things back to you when we can."

"Why is it evidence?"

"Everything in here could be evidence. We'll examine each piece for any clues as to who killed Justine and Samuel."

"Samuel?"

"The Harlow look-alike. Her name was Samuel Bello Stone." Den handed me a passport. "Her name before she transitioned."

Did I hear that right? "Wait. Did you say Bello?"

He nodded. "Yeah, why?'

My mouth dropped. Could it be? Could she be from Jean Harlow's stepfather's line somehow? How could it be? My brain clicked into action. Had Marino Bello gotten someone pregnant and taken the baby to France? Is that why he was there?

"Ah, Charlotte?" Den's left eyebrow cocked and his voice held expectation.

"Bello was Jean Harlow's stepfather's last name," I said.

Den blinked several times, as if trying to process the information. "Do ya think?"

"I don't know." My heart thudded against my rib cage. "But it's possible. He cheated on his wife frequently. Perhaps he fathered an illegitimate child."

"Hey, Sergeant Brophy," a uniformed officer interrupted. "Guy's got a question for you over here."

"Be right back," he said.

I was going nowhere. My feet were firmly planted on the black-and-pink tiled floor as if frozen. Had Bello had a child?

An illegitimate child of Jean Harlow's stepfather would be considered quite an embarrassment. The Hollywood studios would have done anything to keep her reputation pristine. She was highly regarded in Hollywood. One of the best to work with, always had a kind word for the guys on the crew. People loved her. But any whiff of scandal in those days could ruin a young rising star. She'd already suffered one almost-scandal with the suicide of Paul Bern. Would her stepfather siring an illegitimate child have led to concern with the studio?

These days, I couldn't see why anybody would care. But in the 1930s, it would have been viewed in a different light, even though he was her stepfather, not her father.

Den brought me an armful of files. "Would you like to sort through these? We'll take them with us. But you can go through them and label them. And if there's anything you need for your book, let me know and we'll get you a copy."

I took the files from him and sat at a desk with them. I glanced over at a dressing table holding a mannequin head with a red wig on it. The very wig the impersonator had worn at Justine's service. But why had she been stalking me if she was a friend of Justine's? It made no sense.

The first folder I opened contained copies of Jean Harlow's official documents. Birth certificate, marriage and divorce certificates, and death certificate. I'd wondered about these. The next folder was chock-full of magazine clips about Harlow. Standard stuff for a biographer.

The next folder contained Justine's interviews with experts about Harlow. I already had those files on the computer. I placed it on the stack of folders I'd already examined. The next folder contained a bad copy of Samuel Bello Stone's birth certificate: mother Grace Harcourt, father Luther Stone. Luther was from France and Grace was from Great Britain. One of the attached sheets was Luther's immigration paper for England. The other was a listing of addresses where the couple had lived in London.

So, Marino Bello's love child must have been Luther or Grace. No, wait—the numbers didn't add up. It must have been one of their parents. But even if that was the case, it would only be worth a sentence or two in the Harlow book. Hardly a huge secret, and not worth all the fuss. There had to be more.

I set the folder aside and moved on to the next one, which was full of information about the star sapphire ring. The very ring I still carried in my purse. Official papers about its worth in the 1930s, where Powell had purchased it, and so on. He was cheap. We already understood that. I flipped the page over and saw, written in Justine's handwriting: *"Current owner Sam/Jean Harlow, who claims the piece was handed down in the family. Says the real Jean Harlow gave it to her stepfather to hand over to the child in France."*

What? Why would Jean Harlow have done that? Why would she want her stepfather to give her ring to his illegitimate child? I would think she'd be pissed—he'd cheated on her mother and had a child with someone else. Why would Jean entrust him with her ring? The ring given to her by the love of her life?

I stared at the words. *Sam/Jean Harlow claims.* Justine was a wordsmith. She purposefully used the word "claim," which meant she had no solid evidence. And that Sam didn't either. They were trying to find proof—and in doing so, got themselves killed.

The police surrounded me as I searched through the folders. I barely heard their shuffling around because I was deep in thought.

"Have you found something?" Den came up beside me. "Hey," he said poking me.

"What?" I raised my face in his direction.

"What have you got there?"

I explained to him what I'd uncovered.

"Is it relevant?"

"The fact that Bello had an illegitimate child is a blip. I mean, it warrants a mention, not a chapter. It's not a twist in the Harlow story. But it's odd she would have sent her ring to the child. I'm not sure Justine believed that. I think she may have been trying to prove it."

"Would that warrant a chapter?" Den's eyebrows shot up.

"Probably. Because there's been so much speculation about the ring for years. It's taken on mythical qualities," I said and laughed.

A pang of guilt shot through me then. I gazed into Den's blue eyes. Okay, so he wasn't attracted to me anymore, but he was a good cop and a good guy. I'd been holding on to the sapphire far too long. Maybe handing it over would help solve Justine's murder in some way. It wasn't my last link to her. It wasn't. She'd left everything to me. I wouldn't get it all, due to Judith, but still, the fact that she wanted me to have it? Well, that meant more than the sapphire ring I was hiding.

"Den, I have something to tell you."

He pulled up a chair close and sat down.

"I have the ring."

His head tilted in interest and he leaned forward. "The ring?"

I nodded. "The very ring."

He sat back and crossed his arms and appeared deep in concentration. "Where did you find it?"

"In Justine's apartment."

"Where is it now?"

"In my purse." Sweat was pricking at my forehead.

"As a cop, I should ask you to hand it over, but then it would become a matter of public record and I think that might be dangerous."

"Dangerous?"

"Look, you've been stalked, attacked, and it probably has something to do with this ring. Nobody knew where it was and you're still being attacked. I care about you, but I can't protect you twenty-four-seven."

My heart fluttered. "You care about me?"

"Yeah, yeah. I told you, you know, after this case is solved. You and me. You still up for that?" he said in almost a whisper.

"I've been getting mixed signals, Den. I didn't think you were interested anymore." I closed the folder and placed it on the already examined pile.

"Whadya mean?"

"The day you put me on the boat to head back to Cloister Island. And then you didn't come to the island to pick up the computer. I just assumed."

His face fell and eyes slanted. It was the same expression that was on his face as I'd jetted off across the water. "Look," he said. "You may as well know."

I leaned in. "Know what?" Was he married? Engaged?

"I don't do water."

"What do you mean?"

"I have a type of aquaphobia. I don't like water," he said. "I don't do boats and I don't do islands."

I blinked. Den, a sergeant in the NYPD, didn't do islands. But Manhattan was an island. I was confused.

"What I mean is, I don't leave my island to go to other islands." He sat back. "I don't like to talk about it. But none of this shit had anything to do with you, okay?"

I nodded. "Okay. What do I do about the ring?"

"Keep it. Let me think about the best thing to do here, okay? I don't want to put your life in danger, so we need to proceed with caution. Tell nobody. I mean, not even Kate. Understood?"

"Kate knows. She was with me when I found it."

An officer walked by with several plastic bags in his arms. One held the silver pumps the Harlow look-alike had worn when I first spotted her.

"Okay, tell her to keep her mouth shut."

"Will do."

A few moments passed of awkward silence. "Den? I'm sorry I didn't tell you right away. About the ring."

"S'okay. I think your instincts are solid. I think the ring might be the key to solving both murders. But I need to think."

"Understood," I said. "I need to think, too. I don't understand why Jean would have sent her ring to Bello's illegitimate baby in France. Doesn't make sense."

"Could be a ruse."

"Yeah, could be."

"Or maybe the baby was hers."

"It can't be. She was on-screen, working, all the time. If she'd been gone from the scene long enough to have a baby, I'd know it."

"Maybe it wasn't Marino's kid," Den said after a moment. "Maybe it belonged to someone she cared about."

"Makes sense," I said, making a mental note to call the French embassy as soon as I could.

"So between this baby in France and the missing ring, which is now found, you may have something new to add to your story," Den said.

Out of the mouths of cops. But how to prove or disprove any of it? My fingers tapped on the last few folders to sift through. Documents could be forged. Hollywood was a master at it. They loved to create backstories for their stars, especially those who had something to hide.

The fog in my head was taking over. A throbbing crept into my temples. My arms heavied. Torn between staying and reviewing the files and going back to the apartment to rest, I asked Den if I could take the files with me.

"I can't let you do that," he said. "But what I can do is have them copied and sent to you. How's that sound?"

"Perfect," I said, standing, trying to brush off the weariness in my legs. "I'm off, then."

I rustled up whatever energy I had left and exited Justine's suit, made my way to the front door of Club Circe, and caught a cab back to L'Ombragé.

Fifty-Two

The next day, I woke up to the buzzing of my cell phone. I picked it up. Kate was calling.

"Hey," I said.

"Where've you been?"

I told her about my mom, leaving out the news about my father, then informed her about going into Justine's private rooms at Club Circe.

"Oh my gawd. What did it look like? How was it decorated?"

"You know what? I noticed nothing at all except the red wig on one of those heads."

"Charlotte Donovan! What about the bedding? What about the paintings? I'm sure there must be several wonderful paintings in her rooms! How about the books?"

"Nothing, I'm sorry. My mind was struggling to concentrate on what I needed to focus on." I yawned.

"Are you still in bed? It's almost noon. I was going to ask if you wanted to meet for lunch. I'm on your side of town. But why don't I just bring you something to eat?"

"Okay," I said.

"See you in a few."

I lay on the chaise for a few moments before trying to lift myself off of it, remembering what I'd learned yesterday, wondering when Den would send the files. I sat up, feeling as if I were moving through water, which was typical when I felt Lyme-ish. I took a deep breath and made my way to the bathroom, then to the kitchen where I prepared coffee.

As the scent filled the room, I sat down at the kitchen island, scanning myself. Was my grogginess because I was just now getting up or was another Lyme episode setting in?

The buzzer sounded, and I pressed it.

"Kate to see you," the gravelly voice said.

"Okay, send her up." I unlocked the front door and went back into the kitchen to pour myself a cup of coffee. I heard the elevator and a slight rapping at the door.

"Yoo-hoo!" Kate said.

"I'm in the kitchen!"

"There you are," she said. Her arms were full of bags of food.

I took a swig of coffee and helped her unload.

"Chinese food," she said. "I know what you like."

We set all the food out and heaped our plates with chicken chow mein, egg fu yung, and egg rolls.

I sat down and drank more coffee.

"Wow, you slept all morning. Are you okay?" Kate said, eyeballing me.

"Just tired. I needed to get caught up on my sleep after everything with Mom."

She nodded while shoveling eggs into her mouth with chop sticks.

I took my chop sticks and slid the food around on my plate, finally lifting chicken chow mein to my mouth. "Listen, I didn't tell you about my father."

She dropped her sticks. "What?"

"Yeah, he contacted Mom. Wrote her a letter. He's still alive." I ate more chow mein while Kate gaped.

"Wait a minute. He's alive and he just now contacted her? What a shit."

"Exactly. I think it's what set Mom off. What made her drink. She won't admit it. But I have my strong suspicions."

"Speaking of strong suspicions, how is the murder case going?"

I filled her in on what we'd found out, though none of it seemed helpful to the actual case. More helpful to the book, perhaps. I'd have to add new information, if verified, which wouldn't be a problem at this point.

"Bello had an illegitimate kid, heh?"

I nodded. "So it seems. I'd not be surprised if he had a few out there."

"So if Harlow sent this kid her ring…"

"That's a big if. I mean, why would she send her stepfather's child her most beloved possession?"

"You said she was a nice person."

"Too nice, probably. She should have gotten rid of William Powell, her mother, and Bello. But she was sweet. If crew members were sick, for example, she'd notice and send flowers. One time when a studios executive cut the crew's coffee breaks, she stood up for them. She told them either the crew gets a coffee break or she'd not work."

"So, a nice woman like that would definitely send something to a baby she knew about."

"Her ring?"

"The baby must have been special, or maybe sick. You know how celebs will sometimes do 'make a wish' appearances?"

"You'd think she'd be mad if her stepdad cheated on her mother and had a child." But we were talking about Jean Harlow, who had an inferiority complex and a huge heart.

"You need to find out more about the baby," Kate said.

"Yeah," I said, swallowing a bit of egg roll. "I also need to find out more about Sam, aka the Jean Harlow look-alike."

We ate in silence.

"When is the book due?" Kate asked after a few minutes.

"The editor gave me another few weeks, so it's due in a month."

"Not much time to investigate and work into a manuscript."

When I thought about it, I felt tired, but inspired. My gut instinct told me this thread would give the Harlow story an interesting spin. And it might help to solve the murder of Justine and friend.

I drank more coffee. "Do you want some?"

"Nah, I never drink the stuff after noon. Keeps me awake. I need my beauty sleep."

I was slowly waking up with the coffee and the food. I wondered why I didn't have Chinese food for breakfast more often. It seemed the perfect way to start the day.

The buzzer sounded again.

"Who could that be?" I said, more to myself than Kate.

I pressed the button. "Sergeant Brophy left a package for you. Shall I send it up?"

"Yes, please," I said.

"A package? What kind of 'package'?" Kate said, using air quotes.

"Not the fun kind, Kate, I assure you."

Fifty-Three

*A*fter Kate left, I took to the floor, spreading out the timeline. Jean married Paul Bern in 1932. Her mom and Bello were at the intimate wedding. But three months earlier, where was her mother? I glanced over at her timeline. Her mother and Bello were traveling and came back in time for the wedding.

A few weeks after that, Bello was in France, according to the postcard and to my sources at the embassy. He was "delivering a package." Was it a baby?

It made sense. But whose baby was it?

Certainly not Jean Harlow's.

My head hurt. This was the same spot I'd gotten to each time. How to unearth this answer?

"When you're stuck, move on to something else. Works every time. Or take a shower. I get all my answers and ideas in the shower."

I set aside the Harlow timeline and her mother's timeline and examined Sam's. I read over my questions scribbled on it. Now we had a few of those answers.

Had the look-alike connected with Justine while she was in New York? Yes.

When did she come here from Hollywood? Six months ago.

Where was she before she lived in Hollywood? London.

What did she do to make a living? Entertainer.

Family? Father: Luther Stone. Mother: Grace Harcourt.

Boyfriends? Nothing here.

Girlfriends? Nothing here.

I dialed my contact at the French embassy and left another message. Would he ever return my call? Or was I going to get on a train and visit DC? I hated the place and avoided it as much as possible.

Just when I set my phone down, it buzzed. It was Den.

"Hello," I said.

"Hey, how's it going?"

"Not good," I said. "I'm getting nowhere."

"Nothing here either, except we've been able to rule out that the killer was sitting in the center of Layla's. He was nowhere in that section."

"How did he even get in there anyway? It's a members-only teahouse, right?"

"Yeah, but that's not significant because they were having some kinda membership drive that day. We've gone over the list of visitors and I've had guys calling and interviewing those folks. So far, nada." He took in a breath. "Something's gotta give soon, y'know?"

"Where did you say she got her implants?" I asked.

"London. That's where she mostly lived. Where we've found out most about her. But she didn't live there consistently. Like, we have addresses for six months, then nothing."

"Like she was going off the grid?"

"Yeah, kinda like that."

Unfortunately, transgender people were often forced to live off the grid as much as they could. But I imagined if she was estranged from a violent father, she'd have taken great care not to leave a trace.

"Why did she come to the US? To Hollywood?"

"That's the million-dollar question."

Then I remembered something I'd seen scribbled in the corner of the sheets in the folders. The word "Hollywood" poked me. Memory was an odd thing, the way it held things, and only let them out when it was damn good and ready to.

"Hold on, Den," I said, reaching for the folder. I opened it and, yes, there it was: *"Hollywood Genetic Labs."*

My heart nearly exploded in my chest.

"Den," I said, my voice quivering, "I think she was here to get genetic testing. There's scribbles on one of the sheets in the folder. Hollywood Genetic Labs."

"Genetic testing?"

Then, like a curtain being lifted from my eyes: "Maybe she was sick? Or maybe trying to prove her relationship to someone."

"Maybe Harlow?" Den said after a few moments. "Think about it. She looked like Harlow and was trying to make a career out of it. Money in the bank if she could prove a genetic link."

"But Harlow had no children." My brain raced. He was right. He had to be.

"Who else in her family could have? Her biological dad? Her mom?"

My brain circled around the facts and attempted to make connections. Her father had remarried, but he didn't have any kids. Was Jean Harlow's mother too old to have had a baby in 1932? I added the figures. She'd have been around fifty. People were having babies these days at that age. But then? I didn't know. Was it possible?

"Den, you're brilliant."

He laughed. "I am?"

"It think it was her mother. Her mother and Bello must have had a baby they sent to live in France. That has to be it."

"Then that baby would be Jean Harlow's half sibling," Den said.

"It makes sense she'd send her ring to a half sister," I said. My heart was fluttering in excitement and awe. Good old Jean Harlow, so genuinely nice, thinking of her half sister even as she lay on her death bed.

"Okay," Den said. "Interesting theory."

I remembered the pleading emails. *"Please don't go public with this story. He will kill me."*

Those emails must have been from Sam/Jean. "He" must have referred to her father, Luther Stone.

Somehow, Justine had found the look-alike and protected her from her father by bringing her to stay at Club Circe.

Was this the big secret?

"Charlotte? You still there?"

"Yes, yes I am," I said. "Things are making sense."

"Okay, okay. Get more sources on this before you go half-cocked," he said.

"I'm a researcher, Den. I never go off half-cocked. In fact, I believe nothing until I have three solid primary sources."

"Oh? Good. Me too," he said. "I'll give the lab a call and get back with you."

After we hung up, I reached for my laptop and keyed in "Hollywood Genetics." Its specialty was the genetics of the stars. Of course. I clicked on the "News" tab and scrolled through. I saw nothing about Harlow. I kept scrolling—and there, eight months ago, was a news item stating they'd been able to get a sample from Jean Harlow. She'd left her DNA on clothes, brushes, cosmetics. It there were any relatives of hers around, it could now be proven.

There you had it.

Fifty-Four

*M*y head was buzzing with this new revelation. I needed to focus but I was too excited. I needed to walk this off. I changed into my yoga pants and T-shirt and slipped on my shoes. The same shoes I'd worn the day of my assault. A brief wave of panic moved through me. *Calm down, you've been in Central Park thousands of times and were attacked once.*

I slipped the small bag over my neck that contained my keys, phone, bank card, and pepper spray. I practiced reaching in and pulling it out, several times. Okay, perhaps I was getting paranoid. But it couldn't hurt to practice.

We still had no idea where my attacker was, or if he was the same person who'd killed Justine and Jean.

He could still be watching me.

Waiting for me.

But would he attack in the same place twice? Would he have the audacity to show his face in Central Park after attacking me there so recently?

I sucked in air, trying to calm my racing heart.

I couldn't let him scare me. Couldn't let him rule my life. Being outside was one of the few joys I had. I'd not let him take it away from me.

I opened the door and pushed myself toward the elevator, "Fuck him, fuck him, fuck him." It was my new mantra. It became part of my rhythm as I walked.

No running, though. Not today. My ribs were healing and I didn't want to jeopardize it. It would be foolish. Besides, it was painful to move my arms. I knew better than to push it.

As I walked past a falafel vendor, smelling the spicy scent, I mulled over what we'd just learned and tried to piece it all together. Justine had been trying to help the look-alike. Evidently she had an inkling she was in jeopardy.

The look-alike probably gave Justine the ring for safekeeping. It made sense.

If Marino Bello had taken a baby to France, and it was Jean Harlow's half sister, it also made sense that Harlow would send her the ring rather than take it to her grave. Although it was romantic to think she went to her grave with it, she'd swelled to almost double her size and couldn't have kept the ring on her finger.

But why the secrecy about the baby? That was the big question.

I walked along the sidewalk and noted a shadow coming behind me. I stepped aside, trying not to panic. I stood in the grass and let the innocent passerby go along. I was paranoid. But who could blame me? I turned around and headed back to the apartment.

The air and sunshine were a healing balm. But it seemed just a little would suffice. My legs wearied and my mind and heart were healing, but slowly. Would I ever be able to walk or run here without thinking about that day? The way he snuck up behind me and pushed me? His hands on my back. My head hitting the bench. The feeling of helplessness. Of not being in control.

"None of us are really in control, hon. Consider it a good thing."

I exited the park and stood at the corner, waiting for the walk sign. I was alone in the crowd of strangers surrounding me. I should be used to the feeling, but today it bothered me. Today, the awareness of it frightened me.

We crossed in unison, the strangers and me. I often pondered the orderliness of humanity in situations like this. What kept people from not obeying the signs? Oh yes, you heard about those who disrupted order   wild shooters, for example. But for the most part, most of us were content to follow signs, follow the rules. It might be our saving grace.

I ducked into a café. I didn't want to go back in the apartment. Not yet. I paid for mint iced tea and a lemon scone and took a seat in the corner. I needed to think. Thinking had always gotten me where I'd wanted to be. My body sometimes let me down. And sometimes my mind was cloudy because of the Lyme disease, but when I was healthy and in control, thinking helped.

If Jean Harlow had a half sister in France, I'd write a new chapter. Maybe two. Depending on the reason the baby was taken there. People viewed babies and children differently back then.

"Children are to be seen and not heard" was the dictate of the day.

Adoption was hush-hush.

Babies out of wedlock were still scandalous.

Babies born with Down Syndrome, blind, or deaf, for example, were often shoved away in homes and schools for the "handicapped."

Is that what had happened with the Bello baby?

Or had Hollywood gotten wind of it and deemed it bad for Harlow's reputation for her fifty-year-old mother to have a baby?

This was the same studio system that probably covered up Paul Bern's murder, by claiming it was a suicide because suicide was less scandalous. In the meantime, the woman who most likely killed him made off scot-free. Her name was Dorothy Millette and she was

Bern's common law wife, who he'd thought was safely tucked away in a hospital. She found out about his marriage to Jean and showed up in Hollywood to find him. According to Jean and Paul's domestic help, there was a woman on the property that night. Many signs indicated Paul was murdered. They found Dorothy's body a day later, after she took a river cruise, washed up on the banks. Either she'd killed herself or someone suspected she'd killed Paul. Her hotel room had been ransacked. Many items were stolen, including her personal journal.

Twisted.

So what did this have to do with the look-alike and Justine?

If the look-alike was descended from Harlow's line, who would care?

Why would someone kill not just one but two women over it?

It made little sense.

But then again, the person who killed them wasn't about making sense. The person was disturbed. A chill moved up my spine. I sipped my iced tea.

I examined each person as they came into the café, searching for a familiar face, a face with a scar. Would I always be searching for him?

After going back to the apartment and showering, I sat down at Justine's desk, surrounded by all those books. They were calling to me—my writer's monkey mind. Once it settled, focus was my bitch.

I pulled up the manuscript and re-examined the places I'd marked in the text. The note about Bello and Paris. I added space and more notes.

My cell phone buzzed. I picked it up. It was Lou from the French embassy.

"Hi, Lou, how are you?" One must always be polite to the French.

"I'm well, and yourself?"

"I'm fine," I replied. Those formalities out of the way, I wanted answers. "So what do you have for me?"

"I've been able to verify that Bello brought a baby into the country."

"Good. Can you email me the documentation on that?"

"Absolutely."

"Do you have anything else for me?"

He hesitated. "How much would you like to know?"

"Everything."

He laughed, then quieted. "It's not pleasant."

I think my heart jumped into my throat and squeezed. "What? What do you have for me?"

"The baby was taken to the St. Agnes Home for Orphans."

"Orphans?"

"Yes, Charlotte. The man who brought her to France—Marino Bello—signed her over to the sisters."

My heart split. "But there must be more to the story."

"Yes. The child, a girl, had a disease."

"So they gave her up? That's ludicrous."

"In the 1930s, many people didn't know how to handle children with what is now called cystic fibrosis. It didn't even have a name. The nuns took children in with these and many other conditions."

"Do you have any documentation about the baby? Who the parents were?"

"I'll have that soon. The papers are being faxed. I'll forward them to you."

"Thank you, Lou."

"Certainly."

After we hung up, I sat for a few moments in disbelief. If this was the truth—that the baby had Jean Harlow's DNA, along with cystic fibrosis—this news would take more than a chapter in the book.

My mind circled back to the ring. Pieces were falling into place. If Jean Harlow sent the ring to her half sister, in care of the nuns for safekeeping, and it was handed down through a few generations, it might be one of the few items proving the Harlow line had continued.

Who would be threatened by that? The look-alike's father? But why? It made no sense. After all this time, who cared?

It was a legacy of shame, certainly, to have given up a child because it was ill—and to secretly have taken it out of the country. But the people who were involved were all long gone. And Harlow, the person I assumed Hollywood and Mama Jean were trying to protect, had outclassed them all by her final gesture.

What gives?

Okay, perhaps my imagination was running away with me. Maybe this was all a set-up by some crazed Jean Harlow freak. I needed to calm down. I needed the proof.

The door buzzer interrupted my thoughts. I pressed in the button. "Yes?"

"Officer Brophy here to see you."

"Send him up, please." I was finding this procedure annoying. Den had been here countless times, and he was a cop, for God's sake. Why did they have to ask every time?

When I opened the door to Den dressed in his uniform, all angles and solid maleness, a fluttering in my belly awakened. "Come in." I gestured with my arm toward the library.

Den had a briefcase hung over his shoulder and a huge sparkly handbag in his hand.

"What's that?" I pointed to the bag.

He freed himself from the briefcase, placed it on the chair. "This belonged to our Jean Harlow impersonator. There's nothing in it except an envelope addressed to you."

"Me?" I clutched at my chest. "Really?"

"Makes me wonder."

"What?" I reached inside the bag and pulled out the envelope.

"Maybe she wasn't stalking you in the way we thought she was."

"What do you mean?"

"Maybe she was trying to give you the envelope."

Something in my chest cracked, filled with a fluttery lightness. The look-alike had been trying to give me something, and that something was in this envelope. She wasn't chasing me to kill me. She was trying to find a good time to deliver it without being seen. Her odd gestures, especially in the hallway of the apartment, made sense now. She was watching to see if anybody was around to witness her handing the envelope to me.

I stood in the moment, feeling a shifting sensation. A paradigm change. Could it be?

The envelope had my name written on it. In Justine's handwriting. I lifted the envelope to my nose and breathed in the scent. Cotillion.

"Charlotte? You okay?"

I turned to face him. "I'm good. I'm very good."

"Why were you smelling that envelope?"

"It smells of Justine's perfume."

He was quiet as I ran my fingers over the handwriting.

What was in here? Was this going to solve the mystery of the ring and our Jean Harlow impersonator? Was it going to help us solve the murders? I didn't know. I was transfixed. This envelope had been held by Justine and she'd written my name on it. *Oh, Justine, I miss you.*

"Are you going to open it or what? I've got to make a copy of it and get it into evidence. Pulled strings to get it to you."

I tore the envelope open and pulled out the papers. I spread them out on the desk, with Den at my side. They didn't answer all of our questions, but they answered most.

Fifty-Five

The first paper was the original copy of Samuel Bello Stone's birth certificate. The parents, as on the copy I'd seen before, were Grace Harcourt and Luther Stone. The paper stapled behind it was Luther's original birth certificate. His mother was Agnes Bello. No father was named.

"St. Agnes was the name of the orphanage where Bello took the child," I said.

"Orphanage? What?" Den said.

"My source in France just called with information. Bello took a baby to St. Agnes's Orphanage. They specialized in children with disabilities or illness. If you had the bad luck to be born with a problem, it was considered reasonable to send you away."

Den whistled a low whistle. "Christ."

"Agnes must be the baby girl Bello took over there. She really might be Jean Harlow's half sister."

"How do we find that out for sure?" Den said after a minute. "It was such a long time ago. Adoption laws have all changed. Things were much more hush-hush back then."

"I'm expecting an email from the French embassy any minute," I replied, setting aside the birth certificates.

Den cocked his head. "Agnes must not have been that sick if she had a baby."

"She had CF," I said. "Back then, few people with the disorder lived past the age of twenty, but she could have had a baby before that age."

Another stapled group of papers documented Samuel Stone's official name change, which had taken place in Sweden. No wonder we hadn't been able to find any record of it.

"I still think it's strange to change your name to a well-known movie star's name," Den said. "Something wasn't right there."

"I agree. It's like Sam was obsessed with Jean Harlow and wanted to become her." I made a mental note to check in with Maude about this. About the mental health question.

Den shrugged. "Maybe it was the only thing she had in her life. Sounds like the dad was a nut job."

He handed me Luther "Lucky" Stone's record. As I glanced it over, he made a call to the precinct to issue an APB for him. "It's gotta be him, right?"

Luther had quite a record, everything from attempted murder and manslaughter to theft of valuable art and jewelry belonging to movie stars. But he was slippery, either serving small stints in jail or weaseling his way out of it by hiring good lawyers.

Jewelry belonging to movie stars.

So he was a collector. And he must have been after the ring.

Knowing Justine, I understood that she'd never hand it over to a man like that. So she'd gotten herself embroiled in protecting the look-alike and the ring. And it's what got her killed.

But what to do with this information? Den was still on the phone, and my mind was flooding with possibilities.

I glanced over at the last paper, which was a handwritten note on a torn yellow sheet.

"My darling Baby,
One day you will ask many questions. You probably won't find many answers. But one thing you must know is you were loved. We couldn't take care of you. I have another daughter and it's very complicated. But you were loved."

It ended there. At the tear. It could have been written by anybody. There was no signature. No names. Someone had torn this paper or it was destroyed some other way. I sifted through my mind to remember the name of a handwriting expert we'd used for another book. I had to have his name somewhere. I had to verify this note before I could use it.

"Sad, isn't it?" Den said as he came up beside me.

I nodded.

"So we'll search for Luther. Maybe he's our guy."

"Perhaps," I said, sitting down in front of my computer, pulling up my email. There was my email from Lou. It had an attachment. I clicked on it, with Den's breath on my neck.

An official document, written in French. But there was Marino Bello's name under "father." No name under "mother." *No name.* They never gave the name of the baby's mother.

"Shit!" Den said.

"That was the document that would provide a genetic link to Jean Harlow, so we still don't have one. There's only a link to Bello."

"What about this note?"

"I can get a handwriting expert on that. But those results are never one hundred percent."

Den stood and paced in front of the delicate rose stained-glass window. "It doesn't matter for me. For my purposes. I think we've got our guy. I just need to find him."

"If he's in the city, I'm sure the NYPD will get him," I said, confident.

Den snorted. "I hope so."

"You don't sound optimistic."

"It might be cold. Luther's trail, I mean. It's been a while. It's been well over two weeks since your assault. If it's the same guy, he could be back in London, or in Sweden, or God knows where else by now."

I mulled it over for a few minutes. "He's gone to a lot of trouble to get the ring. If he's our killer, I don't think he'd give up until he's got the ring."

Den continued to pace. "Could the man have killed his own son or daughter?" He stopped. "It makes no sense. I've seen some messed-up things, but to kill your kid over a ring?" His voice rose a decibel or two.

"I agree. It's disturbing. It makes little sense. But we're not dealing with a normal person. Who knows what he's capable of?" I shivered, remembered his hands pound into my back, pushing me. *It had to be him. It was the only answer.*

Now the only question that mattered was, where is he?

In a city like New York, people disappeared every day. Some killed, never to be found. Or their remains were discovered years later. Sometimes people broke, lost their way. I suspected it happened a lot here. It was a tough city to live in and it wore people down. If you didn't have the resources, and had a fragile disposition, you ended up homeless or in a hospital somewhere.

There were also those who had resources who wanted to disappear. New York was a good place for it. Especially if you had connections. Like Justine, harboring the Harlow look-alike in a private club filled with moneyed, educated woman with gravitas. They kept secrets.

Finding Luther "Lucky" Stone in this city would be like finding a needle thrown off a skyscraper. Den didn't seem to have much confidence in it. There were too many places to hide, especially if you had unlimited resources, which apparently Luther Stone had.

My fingers flew over my keyboard, hunting for any reference online to him.

"Jesus," Den said when the long row of websites listing entries about Luther "Lucky" Stone came up. Den turned back to his phone, barking orders for someone to do internet research on the man who had amassed his fortune as a gambler and art dealer. According to one website, he had one of the largest private collections of Hollywood memorabilia, with a particular interest in the movie stars of the Golden Age of Hollywood, especially Jean Harlow.

"It's all right here," Den said, looking over my shoulder after he hung up his phone.

I clicked on one website that had a photo of him. A damned good photo. Those lizard-like eyes stared back at me, and the scar on his face nauseated me.

"There he is." A chill moved through me. My hands reached to my mouth. Even though we hadn't gotten a decent picture of the killer from the security footage, the rendering the police artist had drawn was spot on. Distinct eyes, scar, and a pointy shape to his chin.

"I think you need a break," Den said. "We need a break."

He was right, but I wanted to continue. I needed more answers. This mad man was somewhere out there. I'd bet on him still being in the city. How could I stop searching? How would I be able to sleep, to eat, to live?

"We need to find him," I said. My voice came out a harsh whisper. My fingers moved over the keyboard.

"We won't find him by researching on the computer any more today," Den said, crouching down beside me and grabbing my hands. "Let's go get something to eat. Okay?"

I gaped at him in disbelief. He wanted to eat?

"Look, ah, it will be a long night for me. And you need to get out of this apartment. Okay? I know this is upsetting. But the best thing you can do right now is get away from your screen and fuel up." His voice reached into the center of me, as it had ever since the day I first met him. Soothing. Comforting. Yet strong and in command.

He opened his arms and I fell into them. Awkward, as I was sitting on the chair and he was crouching, but we found our way to a standing position and he didn't let go. I buried my face in his chest as he stroked my shoulders, my hair. I pulled away just enough to glimpse his face, lifted my chin, pressed my lips on his.

Currents of white-hot lust waved through me. He met my kiss with soft lips, with a demanding pressure.

Wrong, so wrong. Even though the bet was over, Den had felt strongly about us not getting together while working on the case. But this molten heat sparked my insides. Raw. Want. The sweet rush of the yield.

When we came up for air, he lifted an eyebrow. "Wow."

I met his gaze.

"We haven't solved the case yet," he said, yet he kissed me again.

When we pulled away from one another, heat coursing through us, I gazed at his eyes. "When we solve the case, you know where to find me."

He pulled further away from me. "I think we better go." His voice lowered, smoky. "Or I won't be able to leave this place." He took me in. "Maybe for days."

I laughed. "Days, huh?"

He chuckled. "Okay, guess I'd need to find vacation time for that. But seriously, the next few days are likely to be crazy." He tugged at my hand. "Let's go eat."

We exited the apartment and found our way to an Italian place two blocks over.

I remembered my fear and anxiety when I'd returned to the park. I was glad Den was with me. If Luther was anywhere around watching, he wouldn't bother me while I had a police officer with me. At least I didn't think so.

We sat at a small table in a corner, complete with a red-checked tablecloth. The server brought menus. And where I'd been queasy walking down the street wondering if I could eat, the moment I walked into the place and smelled fresh rosemary, garlic, and tomato sauce, my queasiness disappeared.

After we ordered our meals, Den the manicotti and me ravioli, his phone buzzed. "Excuse me," he said. "Brophy." Then, "I'll be in. Give me two hours."

He clicked off. "Shit's flying." He laughed. "I knew that call was coming. Suddenly there's a lot of research to wade through and we've gotten a few calls on the APB, people think they've seen him. I gotta get with my partner and check each one of those leads out. Who knows? Maybe it could lead somewhere."

"What are the chances?" I asked, trying to tamp down my growing hope.

"Sometimes leads pan out, but sometimes not. You never know." He shrugged. "But we have to check each one."

Our server brought our salads and we tucked in, not chatting a lot. What more was there to say? We were each lost in our own reflections. Drained, with a full stomach, I yawned.

"So," he said, and cleared his throat. "How much of this are you going to put in your book?"

"I need to speak with my agent and editor, but I'm thinking, everything," I said and took my last bite of ravioli.

"I think you should think about it. Look at everything you've been through. Is a story worth your life? If I were you, I might not write about it."

"The Jean Harlow story hasn't had any new twists since the David Stenn biography in 1993. If I can add more to her story, it will help my career tremendously."

"But what will it matter if you're dead?"

He had a point.

"Point taken," I said. "But after the police get Stone, I'm in the clear, right?"

Den appeared thoughtful as he paused. "I suppose. I just don't want anything to happen to you."

I warmed. "It won't. Because the police—you and your NYPD—you'll get Stone. Right? He can't continue to evade us. He just can't."

I sounded more confident than I felt. I was trying to cheer myself into believing the guy would be caught—and soon enough that I could include everything in the book. Was I kidding myself? Time would only tell—even if I didn't have much of it.

Fifty-Six

Two days later, Lucille tracked me down. As in, she came calling at the apartment. I hadn't answered her phone calls or her emails. Knew she was curious and checking up on me, but I didn't know what to tell her. The story was still unfolding, and even in its current state, it was unfinished.

I'd half been expecting Den or Kate, so when the buzzer sounded and it was Lucille, dread came over me. *This is it*, I thought. She'll tell me they found someone else to write the book. Or they've given it to Hartwell or some other poor schmuck wanting to make it in publishing.

"Lucille Everheart to see you," the voice said.

"Okay, send her up, please." I was in yoga pants and a long-sleeve T-shirt. But she couldn't expect me to be dressed for a business meeting. Not when she popped in like this.

When she knocked, I opened the door.

"Hmm," she said. "This is interesting. This door didn't use to be here. It was all open, you see. The elevator came right into the apartment." She seemed perplexed.

"I didn't know that," I said. "Please come in."

She was not at all what I expected. I'd imagined her more like Justine, dressed to the hilt in designer clothes. She wore black pants with an argyle sweater thrown over a white cotton blouse. Argyle? I hadn't seen that in years. The sweater must have been ancient.

"Come into the library? It's where I'm working. Can I get you anything?"

She followed me into the library and took a seat in one of the plush chairs. "Do you have any beer?"

An argyle-wearing, beer-drinking editor? I might like her. This woman was one of the most powerful editors in New York. But it didn't seem like she flaunted it. It could be a ruse. A way to make me feel comfortable, and then she'd drop the bad news.

"I have stout. Is that okay?"

She nodded. "Better than okay," she said with a flat note to her voice. "Just bring the bottle, I'm fine with it," she yelled after me as I went in the kitchen to fetch our beers.

I'd join her. Yes, I would.

While I was in the kitchen, I made up a plate of cheese and meat and slices of bread.

"You didn't show up for our lunch date," she said when I set the plate down on a coffee table.

"I'm sorry. I didn't know we had one."

"I received your invitation." She looked me square in the eye.

"What invitation?" My heart was skipping around in my chest. Had I made a lunch date I forgot about? I'd never done that before.

"Well, it was an email," she said. "Don't you remember?"

"I'm sorry," I said. "I've not checked my email in days. I'm in the thick of writing. Email is a distraction."

Her head tilted. "Odd."

"Are you certain it was from me?" Great. I'd made an appointment with an editor I hoped to impress and forgot about it. She wouldn't work with me again.

"It was from your email address," she said and reached into her bag, pulling out her phone. She fingered the phone and pulled up the email. Sure enough, it was my email address.

I sucked in air. Someone had hacked into my account. "Jesus," I said. "Someone hacked me. I need to let the police know."

"Why would they hack you? What exactly is going on?" Lucille's voice rose, and her eyes slanted as she took me in. She didn't trust me. Why would she?

"I'll explain everything after I text the police," I said.

"You're damn right you will. I sat there for at least half an hour waiting for you." She lifted the bottle to her mouth. No wonder she was miffed. I'd be miffed too if I thought I'd been stood up for lunch.

I texted Den, then kept my phone close by waiting on his response, which came in a few seconds. *"On it, but in the meantime, change all of your passwords,"* he texted. I wasn't sure what "on it" meant. But probably he would go to the cybercrimes unit.

I turned back to Lucille, who was picking over the food, fashioning herself an open-faced sandwich of sorts.

"Thank you," she said. "I'm more than a bit peckish."

"Please," I said. "Help yourself."

She took a few bites, then focused on me. "Well?"

My mind raced. How to start? Where to start?

"You know that Justine was murdered. We think the same person killed another woman, a woman who looked like Jean Harlow, and then came after me."

She took a swig of her beer. "What does any of this have to do with the book?"

292

"I need you to promise you'll keep an open mind about this," I said, standing. I paced the floor. "We've got most of the proof we need. We're just waiting on a few more sources to come through."

She set her stout down with a thud and huffed in exasperation. "Stop that infernal pacing. Sit down and tell me what the hell is going on."

I sat, even though my nervous energy was raring to go. I forced myself to be still and reveal the story to her.

She was expressionless through most of it, eating, drinking, nodding.

At the end, her mouth dropped open. "Jean Harlow had a half sister? A half sister with CF? She sent her ring to her on her deathbed? And you have this very ring in your possession?"

My turn to nod.

"Jesus Christ, woman. We've got a hell of a story here. Make sure your sources check out."

"They do. Well, most of them. I'm still waiting on a few sources to check in, especially the DNA lab."

She set her empty beer bottle down on the table. "We need to arrange a pre-release tour. This will work out for publicity and sales. We're going to have a hit on our hands."

"Wait. This man, this Luther Stone, he's at large. The police are still searching for him. He's dangerous. I'm not sure about putting myself out there yet. I allowed you to use me during Justine's memorial service and it started this whole thing."

She sank back into her chair with a thoughtful demeanor. "Maybe we can kill two birds with one stone. Luther Stone."

"What do you mean?"

"If he wants to kill you, and he wants the ring, what better way than to give him what he wants?"

"Excuse me?"

"Hold on. Let me explain," she said. "We hold a huge press conference. Very well publicized. All over the place. This is exactly the kind of thing publicists live for." She took a breath. "We let the world know you've got the ring. You'll be wearing it that day. Collectors will come, and so will Luther Stone."

Was she suggesting what I thought she was? Using me as bait? "Hold on. That guy is nuts. He killed his own daughter. He'd not think twice about killing me."

"Precisely," she said. "It will pull him out of where ever he's hiding. We'll have the place booby-trapped with police and security. You'll be safe. Safer than you've ever been in your life."

Fifty-Seven

"You can tell your editor that the NYPD does not use civilians as bait to catch a killer," Den said over the phone, which left me only somewhat relieved.

I left it alone. "Have you gotten anywhere?"

"Not yet. None of the leads have taken us anywhere." He paused. "But police work is like that. Sometimes just when I'm ready to give up, something happens."

Which reminded me of my dad. Odd. I barely remembered him. I mostly recalled parts of him. His hand cupping my hand. The nook between his arm and shoulder where I'm told I'd crawl and lie. I remembered the feelings he left me with when he held my hand or hugged me.

We had given up on him a long time ago. You presumed a person dead when he was gone for such a lengthy period.

Why had he written to Mom after all these years? Didn't he know what he'd put her through? Let alone his only child? I tamped down my confusion and anger and concentrated on the moment.

Den. On the phone. "We've learned that Luther entered the country seven months ago," he was saying.

"Soon after our Jean Harlow look-alike arrived in Hollywood."

"Yeah," he said. "He was tracking her. I can't believe it. Her own father."

Den kept coming back to this. A cop who'd seen just about every form of deviation in human behavior. This part disturbed him. I didn't know him well. Maybe he was troubled a lot. Perhaps he was too sensitive for it not to bother him. Most cops didn't talk about their worst cases, but I had a hunch they were more like Den than not.

"Families can be complicated," I said, once again, thinking of my own. My dad, gone for twenty-eight years. Husbands killed wives. When a woman showed up dead, the husband was always the first suspect. And, of course, they murdered their own kids. "But usually when a parent kills a child, it's when they're young. Or even as a teenager. In the heat of passion. To chase one down across the world, now that's a different kind of killer all together."

Den laughed a little. "Have you been investigating again?"

"Of course. I looked more into Luther. I know you guys are researching him, but I'm trying to understand him at least enough to write about him. I'm meeting with Maude later."

"Who's that?"

"She's a psychoanalyst we often work with to help piece together personalities of people we never knew. Like Jean Harlow."

Den grunted. "Let me know if she tells you anything helpful. I'm worried we'll never get that first date."

My turn to laugh. "We need a deadline."

"Don't you think we've both had enough deadlines?"

We signed off, and I hurried to dress to meet with Maude. It would be only the second time I'd see her in person. We usually worked over the phone.

She sat at a table studying the menu. Short cropped gray hair surrounded her slightly chubby unmade-up face.

"Hello," I said. "Nice place."

"I come here often. Too often," Maude said, glancing up at me. "How are you?" she asked after I sat down.

I shrugged. What do you say when a psychoanalyst asks you that question? Was it loaded? "I miss Justine, I'm stressed about the book and everything going on with it, and I'm finding it difficult to leave the apartment because I know the killer is out there. He could be here. He could be just outside the door waiting for me."

Maude cracked a compassionate smile. "What you're describing is normal. Your stress will go away when the book is done. You'll always miss Justine, but it will lessen with time. And Christ, you were attacked. Everybody deals with that in different ways. You've gotten back in the saddle. That says something."

The servers approached us. We ordered drinks and beet salads. We were saving room for dessert. This place had the best cheesecake in the city.

"So what you're describing is not a typical father killing a son. Many times when that happens, they're what we call family annihilators. Something has gone wrong in the marriage. Custody is an issue. It's a threat to his masculinity," she said as she sipped her Bloody Mary.

"So what about this guy?"

"I think his masculinity was also threatened, but for different reasons. His son identified as a woman. For some that would be difficult."

I remembered Kate's dad beating her when he found out she would get the operation.

"In my practice, I see more of the dads trying to be supportive and come to terms with it. They reach out to me for help. That says something about their character. But these other men? Very vengeful."

"Small penises?" I said after a minute.

"Who knows? Let's not go there, doll." Maude paused, taking another long drink. "So you say he's traveled around the world chasing his son for this ring his son supposedly had? It belonged to his mother's family? Is he estranged from his wife as well?"

"Dead. He gallivants." The beet salad was excellent. I ate every bite.

"From the picture you paint, I think he felt betrayed. His son turned into a woman, which was a threat to his masculinity. Not only did he become a female, he became Jean Harlow. Another blow. Deeper. Then she came here, bringing the ring with her to Hollywood to prove her relationship with Harlow. It's like she was obsessed with starting over and shedding her past. Once again, betrayal."

"And she ran to Justine," I said. "Gave Justine the ring for safekeeping. Somehow he figured it out. And Justine wouldn't give the ring to him."

The server came along and took away our plates. "Desserts?" he asked.

"Cheesecake for both of us," Maude said. The server nodded and walked off carrying the plates. "But it seems you've also got a man who may suffer from extreme delusions of grandeur. Many of these art collector types and wealthy guys exhibit similar traits. Not only does this guy think he has the right to do anything he wants, but he also thinks he has all the answers. If people don't live his way, in his mind he's justified in killing them."

I drank my Bloody Mary. A cold tingle traveled the length me. His hands had been on my back.

"Simply put, you're dealing with the worst kind of psychopath, someone who has no empathy for others, including his own child."

Fifty-Eight

*L*unch with Maude left me more frightened than I'd been before. But it gave me a better sense of who we were dealing with. I didn't have access to police specialists, like Den did. And he was so busy that our conversations were few and brief.

One thought kept occurring: What if we were wrong? What if Luther wasn't the man in the security video, not the guy who attacked me? Could we be wrong?

Chad Walters was mean enough to murder someone. But he was not the individual in the security footage. He was a pudgy guy. The guy in the recording was slender. Severn Hartwell was still a possibility, though. He was slim and his chin was kind of pointy. He was desperate. But was he desperate enough to kill?

I walked along Fifth Ave, the lunch crowd dwindling, and a sudden cold crept up my back again. Was someone watching me? I stepped over to the nearest shop. Ann Taylor. I'd never been in one before—too pricey and too vanilla. I peered out the window, my breath as uneven as the heart pounding in my chest.

I searched faces and found nobody remotely suspicious. But this nagging sensation wouldn't go away.

"Can I help?" a woman said from behind me.

I gasped and turned to her.

"I'm sorry," she said, smiling with her shiny pink lips. "I didn't mean to startle you."

"No, no, I'm sorry. I thought someone was following me," I said. "I'm a bit paranoid. I guess."

Her smile vanished. "My mom always said to trust your instincts. Maybe someone *was* following you."

Dressed in a smart little blue dress, with jewelry to match, her name tag read Rhonda. She fingered her necklace. "Can I show you some clothes? Are you interested at all?"

I met her eyes. "Not really. I ducked in here because it was the closest shop. I'm sorry."

"That's okay," she said with a lighter voice. "I'll let you be, then. Good luck."

"Thanks." I turned back to the window, which is when I saw him, standing between a lamppost and a trash container, dressed in all black, shifting his weight and turning his face from side to side.

Luther Stone.

I pulled out my cell phone and tried to dial Den, but my hands were shaking so much that I wasn't sure who I was calling.

"Brophy," his voice said. Thank God.

"Den, Luther Stone is standing right outside of the Ann Taylor shop on Fifth," I said, my voice low and raspy. "Den, he was following me. I'm inside the shop now."

"Stay where you are," he said and hung up.

I turned back toward the window. He was gone.

"Fuck," I said out loud.

"Are you sure I can't help you?" Rhonda came up beside me. "You're shaking! Can I get you some water?"

I nodded.

"Why don't you come with me?" She wrapped her arm around my shoulder and lead me to a chair outside the dressing room. Rhonda. So nice.

I melted in to the armchair. My knees and thighs soupy, shoulders and arms frigid. I was cold. So cold. Luther had been following me. For once I'd listened to my guts, and it paid off. The scent of Cotillion breezed by me as Rhonda brought me water and a jacket to wrap around me. Was she wearing Cotillion? My mouth wouldn't form words to ask.

Two uniformed officers entered the store. One of the other sales clerks led them to me.

"Ms. Donovan?"

"Yes," I said, chattering.

"How are you?"

I sipped water, hands shaking. I nodded. "Luther Stone was standing right outside. He was between the lamppost and the trash can. I think he was following me."

The cop's head tilted. "You think?"

"Yes, I just had this horrible feeling of apprehension," I replied. "So I ducked into the shop."

He scribbled something on to his pad. "What was he wearing?"

The sales staff was now more concerned with me and the cops than their store. Even the customers were gathering around.

"Okay, people," the other cop said. "Just go about your business."

"He was dressed in all black. Black jeans, I think, and a black jersey, plain."

The cop lifted his shoulder and spoke into his device. "Suspect wearing all black. Last seen on Fifth Ave. Over."

"How are you?" he asked me again.

I didn't want to answer. I felt like shit. But it was more than that. I was feeling ashamed of myself. Ashamed for allowing things to get this far. Ashamed I hadn't done something more to help nab this guy. The man who'd killed Justine and the look-alike. A part of me understood it was a ridiculous way to feel. I mean, what could I do, right?

But he'd been right behind me. Following me. He was after me now. The attack in the park wasn't enough. He wanted to finish me off. I swallowed the water.

"I'm shaken," I said.

He nodded. "You got every reason to be. We're taking you home. That okay?"

Luther had evaded the cops once again. A city full of police couldn't seem to track down one slippery man.

As I walked into Justine's apartment, my stomach settled, my heart calmed. A feeling of serenity came over me. If I could stay inside here for the rest of my life, this wouldn't be bad. Of all the things I could imagine, stepping outside was not one of them.

I'd be fine here. A recluse. Den and Kate could bring me whatever I needed. Mom and Gram could visit from time to time. I'd order food and incidentals online. I could continue to work from here.

As I walked into the library, books all around me, the chaise where I slept, the delicate rose stained-glass window, I was certain staying here was the answer. I might never leave.

Fifty-Nine

A fever came over me and leveled me. For a night and a day, I did nothing but sleep, sometimes eat. I had no choice. I often had strange dreams when I was in the thick of a Lyme flare-up, but I didn't think this was Lyme.

I imagined the fever cleansing me, getting rid of my unhealthy impurities. On the last day of my fever, I dreamed about Justine.

She was here in this room with me, looking twenty years younger.

"Why don't you take the guest room? Sleeping on the chaise in the library can't be comfortable. You need to take care of yourself so you can get the book done."

I was stunned. She appeared to be there, right beside me. She reached down and brushed my hair off my forehead. "Poor girl," she said. Comfort filled me.

"You've taken a long rest," she said. "You've used your smarts to figure everything out. I'm proud of you."

Her soft features morphed into something almost animal-like. "Now, get up and do something!"

A cold whoosh of air pressed on me and I woke up shivering. I picked up the blanket from the floor and wrapped it around me. It was just a dream. Justine wasn't there. It was just my subconscious talking to me in the form of Justine. But that's not the impression that lingered in the air, a tiny shift filled with mist and memory. Gram was right when she'd said grief does strange things to people. I could have sworn Justine was there and we were talking. Gram swore she'd seen my grandfather frequently.

"Is it a trick of the mind? Or just something we don't understand?" she'd say, shrugging.

I lay on the chaise, thinking about everything Justine had said in my dream. Perhaps it was time to move into the guest room. But then again, if Judith had her way, who knew how much longer I'd be allowed to live in the apartment? I guessed it didn't matter. I should venture out and explore the apartment in any case. I hadn't been in half of the rooms, I was sure.

I wrestled myself out of the blanket. My skin had cooled, which meant my fever broke. I made my way to the kitchen and brewed coffee. As the scent filled the room, I continued down the hall and opened the door across from Justine's room.

In the center sat a king-size bed covered in a deep blue silky spread. The room bore all the hallmarks of the rest of the place. Art deco lamps, lighting fixtures, and dresser and chairs. I opened the door to the closet and slipped in. It was bigger than my room on Cloister Island.

The room needed a good dusting and vacuuming, and stale Cotillion wafted here and there. Justine had been in this room countless times. It was her home.

I flitted across the floor feeling lighter, as if my fever had shed a part of me that had been weighing me down.

I moved into the kitchen and made myself some coffee and checked my phone. Three calls from Den, eight calls from Kate, one from Gram, and one from Natalie.

I called Kate first.

"Why haven't you answered your phone? Den told me what happened. I was sick with worry," she said.

I drank my coffee. "Calm down. I was sick, had a fever. I've just been sleeping."

"Sleeping? All this time?" Her voice rose a decibel or two.

"That's right."

"Are you okay? Are you getting sick? I'll be right over." She hung up, not giving me a chance to explain.

Next I called my gram and explained to her what was happening. I should have explained everything from the beginning, but I hadn't wanted to worry her.

"So you have the ring?"

"Yes, I do."

"It may not be hers, you know? That's going to be difficult to prove. Documents can be faked. So can jewelry."

As usual, Gram hit the nail on the head. All the documents in my possession were copies. I wasn't sure I could rely on them to tell the Harlow story. What the book called for was an addendum or an afterword, along the lines of *"This is what may have happened to the ring, and this is what may have happened with Marino Bell and Jean Harlow's mother."*

Next, I phoned Den.

"Hey," he said. "How ya doing?"

"I've been sick. Have you caught our guy yet?"

"No," he said after a few beats. "It might be ready to go cold soon. We're using way too many resources, ya know?"

A roaring sensation filled my chest and spread through my body and into my skin and throat. "Do what you want, Den. I'm planning to call Lucille and tell her it's a go."

"What's a go?"

"We'll announce it, have a press conference, with or without the help of the NYPD."

"Now, hold on—"

"I've played by your rules most of the time. But it's not working. We need to turn the tables. Lure him out of hiding. It's the only way to do it."

I surprised myself by the decision, formed there and then. It was as if I'd made it sooner and my mouth was now ready to say so.

"It's too dangerous. I can't let you do this."

"I'll ignore what you just said about letting me do this. For now. We'll talk about that later. My publisher will hire a good security outfit. It will be fine. I will be fine. I promise." With those words, confidence and calm spread through me, even though fear dwelled deep down in my bones. This was something I would never have dreamed of doing before Justine's death. But then again, I'd imagined none of this at all.

Sixty

We planned the press conference down to the most minute details. We publicized it, announcing that the public would be allowed as room permitted, figuring most people couldn't care less about Jean Harlow or her ring.

Only the press and the Jean Harlow "kooks," as Justine had hailed them, would care. Lucille wrote a speech and planned to do most of the speaking. She assured me this was her kind of thing. "I'm ready for my close-up," she joked as we sat in what they called a green room. Dressed in a classic blue suit, evidently leaving the argyle behind for official functions, Lucille seemed ready for anything.

"Jean Harlow didn't say that, you know. Some people think she did, but it was Gloria Swanson."

"I thought it was Mae West." She glanced at herself in the mirror.

"No." I'd eaten a large breakfast, which was unlike me, and now I regretted it. "Ladies' room."

"Again?" Lucille said as I left the room.

When I returned to the green room, Jonathan, the head of the security detail, stood there, along with Den, who was not officially there but working with the security because of his knowledge of the case. Police officers, however, were scattered around the block on alert.

Den handed Jonathan photos. "This is our guy, though he's known to disguise himself."

"Got it," he said, then took photos with his phone and I presumed sent them to his crew.

I took the ring out of my purse and slipped it onto my finger.

"That's it, huh?" Lucille said. "It's really quite gaudy."

I agreed. There was nothing pretty about it. It resembled smoky blue marble, and it was difficult to wear. I'd seen photos of Harlow wearing it and the ring didn't even suit her.

"Changing times and styles, I guess," I said.

She stood and motioned for me to stand. This was it. Pulses of something like a fluttery electricity shot through my center. Nervous one minute, the next, impatient to get this over with. This was our last shot. If it didn't work, the case would slow down, making it even more difficult to nab the slippery Luther Stone.

Den grabbed me by the shoulder. "Good luck," he said. I nodded back at him.

"It's imperative you follow our instructions," Jonathan said. "We need to keep you safe."

Sweat beads pricked my forehead. Was I going to do this?

The three of us—Jonathan, Lucille, and myself—walked out onto the platform. Jonathan said something into his shoulder mic as Lucille stood behind the podium.

Flashes from cameras went off, and then it settled down as Lucille spoke about the Harlow book and the ring.

I studied the audience and spotted Natalie. A sea of faces focused in our direction, some in the light and some in the shadow. They were bobbing between one another, trying to get the best view or camera shot.

Nobody there even remotely resembled Luther Stone, but more people appeared to be entering, as was always the case with press conferences. People came and went.

I intently scanned the audience and wasn't listening to Lucille. One face popped out at me. It wasn't Stone, but it was Severn Hartwell. What the hell was he doing here? Had Den told Jonathan about Hartwell? I didn't think so. They'd focused on Stone. I tried to hail Jonathan, but it was no use. He was fixated on the room. I finally tugged at his sleeve and he looked at me with a question on his face. "What?"

"There's someone here you should know about," I whispered into his ear. "He's dangerous."

He leaned forward, confused.

I didn't want to point, which would alert Hartwell.

"And so I give you Charlotte Donovan, who is wearing Jean Harlow's blue star sapphire ring," Lucille said with excitement.

All eyes turned toward me.

Jonathan gestured for me to move forward behind the podium. The bullet-proof podium.

As I took my spot, more people came into view.

"Getting to know Jean Harlow and her family has been a remarkable experience," I said into the microphone, as rehearsed. My heart thudded against my rib cage, unrehearsed.

Severn Hartwell moved ahead, breaking from the crowd. There was more movement in another part of the flock and a familiar face came forward. Chad Walters. Shit. Did the security people know about Chad Walters? Two of the men I'd had run-ins with were here, but not the killer.

I didn't even know where to gaze next. There were two of them, both edging their way forward. Had security noticed? Had Den? He'd recognize both of them.

"So many facets of her life remain a mystery. But we are all entitled to some mystery and privacy in our lives. Even if you are the original blonde bombshell." I attempted to smile. A few people in the throng laughed.

Hartwell was closer than Walters, who was stuck in the pack. I watched Hartwell and then watched Walters. I willed Den to pay attention, to recognize these two men. They might be every bit as dangerous as Stone. *Please, Den.*

"One of the many mysteries about Jean Harlow has been solved. The blue star sapphire ring that the great love of her life gave to her now sits on my finger." I held up my hand, and the flock hushed as photographers snapped away.

Den appeared next to Hartwell. Thank God. Thank God he'd spotted him.

Security had closed the door and weren't allowing anybody else into the room. That was part of the plan if Stone was identified. But where was he? Was he in the crowd? *He must be here.* I tamped down a jolt of panic.

Just then, Hartwell lunged forward, making a dash for the podium. Gasps came from the crowd as the press snapped pictures. Den apprehended him and dragged him off.

"You bitch!" Hartwell yelled. "The ring should be mine! The story should be mine!" His words became garbled as he was led away.

The crowd simmered down, and I cleared my throat. But something was wrong. Where was Walters? I'd lost track of him.

Just as I thought I'd spotted him again, a man jumped out of the crowd onto the platform and grabbed me. He poked something hard into my ribs and yanked me backward, just as Jonathan lifted his hands as if to say he wasn't armed.

Luther Stone!

As Stone wrapped his arm around my neck, my gaze fell to the object sticking into me—a gun.

This is not happening. This is a nightmare. This is not happening. I'll close my eyes, and when I open them, this will all be gone. Close. Open.

Still he was there, his arm wrapped around my neck making it hard to breathe. I gagged.

"Just give me the ring," he said.

I didn't care about the damn ring. "Take it."

"Hold on just one minute," a voice said from the side. It was Chad Walters, who also had a gun. "If anybody gets that ring, it's me." He was unnervingly calm.

Walters moved forward. Luther reacted by pulling me in harder. "I'll shoot her."

Walters smiled a vicious smile. "Do you think I care?"

I glanced up at Jonathan. What the fuck good was he? What was he doing, standing there with his hands up?

What were members of the press doing, milling around watching this? Was nobody going to help me? *"You can only help yourself, honey. Nobody else gives a shit. Not really."*

Walters's face grimaced in pain and he fell forward. Blood spread across his back. What the—?

"He's been shot," Luther Stone said, realizing there was a shooter out there. He dragged me backward and stumbled enough to let go of me for just a few seconds, but it was sufficient for me to shake loose of him, twist, and grab for his gun.

The weapon was now in my hands. I held it and found it heavier than I imagined. It was moving. Why?

Luther's hands rose. "Now, now Charlotte. You don't want to shoot me."

Within a nano-second, Den was by my side. "Give me the gun, Charlotte."

Why would I do that? I pointed the gun at the man who'd killed Justine and the Jean Harlow look-alike. I had him. A welling of power surged in me. The voices of the crowd behind me hushed. Security took control of the swarm, escorting them out. I stood with the shaking gun aimed at Luther Stone. His evil hooded eyes filled with fear.

"Charlotte," Den said with firmness.

I heard him. But I also heard other voices. Justine. Jean Harlow. The look-alike. Other women. Other men. How many others?

"You don't want to do this," he said.

Yes I do.

I lowered the gun, aimed, and pulled the trigger.

Sixty-One

I still don't regret shooting the man. But remembering that day, I admit, there were a few things I could have done better. Like aim. I wanted to shoot his groin. Instead, the bullet grazed his inner thigh and, from his yelps, I gathered his pain was considerable. In that regard, I was a success.

The incident held the ambiance of a weird dream, almost as if I were a different person at the time. People often say that, right? But in reality, it's beyond description.

"You don't feel bad at all for shooting him?" Kate asked over lunch.

"No. I probably should. Maybe I'm a sociopath," I said and popped a fry in my mouth.

She grunted as her fork twirled her spaghetti. "I know you. I know that's not right. You're probably still in shock. But thank God you didn't kill him. Then you'd be going off to prison."

"Not necessarily."

"I don't think Den could stretch that bogus self-defense plea if you killed the guy," Kate said.

Was it bogus? The man had a gun pressed up against my side. I'd just taken advantage of his clumsiness. Of course, I'd had time to make a decision.

"So, after all this, was your look-alike related to Jean Harlow?" Kate said.

"We have no idea yet. We've contacted the genetics lab in Hollywood and the results are on the way. So we'll see," I said. "I just want to get this book finished, and I can't quite do that until we know."

"Your publisher should kiss your ass," Kate said. "You shouldn't feel any pressure at all to finish the book."

It was true. The pre-sales numbers had skyrocketed. It was so good, I was thinking maybe I could make a living at writing these types of books, ones with my own added twist, a little more depth into my subjects. Eventually I might work my way into writing exactly what I wanted. But I was still in Justine's shadow on this book, which was fine with me.

"Do you hear anything from home?" Kate asked with a note of sorrow in her voice. She was homesick even though she'd never admit it.

"Gram is fine. Mom is still in rehab. Neither one of them have heard anything else out of my dad," I said. "Why don't you and I go back for a weekend. Stay with us. Just like when we were kids."

Kate brightened, then frowned. "I don't know," she said, gazing off into her own distance.

"Think about it," I said.

She nodded and frowned. "When I think about the look-alike it makes me sad. She had no real family. Her mother died and her father despised her. Maybe by becoming Jean Harlow, she'd hoped he'd approve. Or maybe she was searching for a family of others like her, which is why she worked as an impersonator, why she needed to prove her relationship."

After lunch I made my way back to Justine's apartment, still barely believing I could reside in such elegance. I laughed out loud, and the sound echoed. I'd gone from my bedroom in my family's dilapidated beach home to this. I was still uncertain about what Judith would do, but I felt more comfortable. Which was probably not a good thing. I braced myself for the inevitable letdown. Still, how many people could say they'd even been in a place like this, let alone lived in one?

I opened the French doors onto the balcony and soaked in the sun and fresh air as I took in the view of Central Park and the West Side of the city beyond, with the grand buildings sprouting from the trees. I felt good, better than I had for a long time. Lighter. Freer. I missed Justine still, and always would.

I wished I'd gotten to know the Jean Harlow look-alike. Maybe Justine was planning to tell me about her that day at Layla's tea room. I would never know. In a way, it didn't even matter if the look-alike was blood-related to the real Harlow. She believed she was. She became obsessed with the star, so much so she'd had plastic surgery to make herself look more like her famous relative.

Was she so haunted because of her father's obsession with Harlow? That held a kind of logic. But there was more to it.

Luther "Lucky" Stone had taken his son's identification as a woman personally. As if it was an assault on his own manhood, like Maude had suggested. He felt it was his failure as a father. The fact that his son had the ring once belonging to his mother only added insult to injury.

Harlow's reputation also preoccupied Stone. He wanted to keep the story hushed. In some twisted way, he imagined he was protecting her honor by keeping the story secret. It was almost as if he was in love with her. In love with a woman long gone. In love with his mother's half sister. Way out of reach. And more than a little creepy.

Family. How did it get so twisted in some families?

I ambled back into the apartment just as my cell phone buzzed and the still-cracked screen said it was Susan Strohmeyer.

"Hello," I said.

"It's Susan Strohmeyer," she said. "Justine Turner's lawyer. I've got good news and bad news."

I braced myself.

"Judith has conceded the apartment."

"What does that mean?"

"It means the apartment and everything in it is yours. You can stay there or sell it. It's entirely up to you."

Heat traveled up my spin. I stopped myself from squealing. The apartment!

"That's incredible," I said. "I can't believe it!"

"Congratulations!"

There was an awkward pause. "Wait. You said there was bad news?"

"Judith is still contesting the rest of the will. The money. The stocks."

"How much longer until we know?"

"It could be a long time. Sometimes these cases go on for years. I don't think that will be the case. But brace yourself, it could get ugly."

"Okay," I said. "I hear you. What comes next?"

"Come to the office and we'll transfer the deed to the apartment into your name. That's the first thing you need to do," she said. "We'll discuss Judith when you get here."

I could do that. I could go to her office, sign papers, chat about Judith. Right now, I sensed my own strength, as if I was ready for anything.

Sixty-Two

Tonight was the night. Den was coming over for dinner. I was surprised he accepted my invitation, given that I'd shot Stone. I kept hearing the tenseness in his voice as he said my name those few moments before I fired. I hadn't listened to him. But I couldn't. The other voices were stronger. They'd compelled me toward revenge.

So I hoped our evening would not turn into one long discussion of the incident. I wanted it to be a celebration. And whether or not Den and I moved forward with a relationship, I craved time with him.

Earlier in the day, I'd received the results from the lab in Hollywood, which were sitting on my desk. I didn't want to look at them without Den. It seemed appropriate.

When I opened the door to Den, the sweet rush of temptation almost overcame me. He was dressed in nicely fitted jeans and a blue shirt, which made his blue eyes pop. And what was in his eyes was a smoldering passion. Or at least that's what I gleaned.

"Come into my new apartment," I said, definitely in my come hither voice.

"What? You're kidding me, right? This place is yours?" he said.

"Yes!" I squealed and flung myself into his arms. One hand was holding a wine bottle, so it was an awkward one-armed hug. But still, it quenched my hunger for comfort. For now.

"That's amazing," he said as he pulled away. "I'm so happy for you."

"Thanks for the wine," I said when he handed it over. "I have champagne on ice. I hope that's okay?"

He grinned that cute sideways grin of his. "Yeah, sounds good. We can drink the wine some other time."

Some other time.

"I've gotten good news myself," he said, following me into the dining room. It was the first time I'd used it. The chandelier was turned down low and several candles were lit. "Wow, what a room."

"What's your news?"

"I got that promotion. You're now looking at a detective." He grinned.

"Congratulations!"

Den sat down at the table. "I guess this is where you want me."

It's one of the places I want you. I nodded. "I'll just get the salad."

We laughed and chatted through dinner as if we'd known each other for years. We'd been through an intense time, gotten to know one another in our worst moments, um, er, my worst moment. His best, I suppose. Justine and the look-alike's murder case had finally gotten him his promotion.

"Such a good dinner. Thank you," he said, reaching out and caressing my face. "You are just so beautiful."

My face heated. "I'm glad you think so."

Why did him saying I was beautiful embarrass me? I'd heard it before, but it had never had affected me like this.

"I didn't mean to embarrass you," he said. "I thought it was clear I like you." He sat back, removing his hand from my face.

My heart became a ticking clock, with soft, brief beats against my rib cage. "It's okay," I said. "I like you too." *And I need more champagne.*

I stood and started to clear the dishes. He reached for me and pulled me to his lap. "You remember that kiss?"

"What kiss?" I played stupid and coy.

He pulled my face to his with gentle determination and showed me.

I lost all sense of time in that kiss. Or should I say those kisses? I was a puddle of sweat and molten heat when we finally stopped kissing. I gazed at his face, eyes lit with passion, and I pulled away, standing up. I cleared the dishes again. Den helped me.

"I have news for you," I said.

His head tilted in interest.

"Let's drink the rest of the champagne in the library."

"Sounds good," he said, and grabbed the glasses while I carried the bottle.

When we entered the library, I picked up the envelope with the results of the genetic testing results and moved to the chaise. Den followed my lead with excitement and curiosity.

"What's that?" He put his arm around me. So warm. I wanted to stay there. Suddenly my plans to ravage him gave way to something else. I didn't know what. But somehow, it didn't matter if we made love tonight, the next night, or next week. The comfort I found with Den was deep.

"The genetic results," I said.

"The answer?"

I nodded. I leaned into him. His eyebrows lifted in interest.

"Shall I open it?"

"Right now, I'm not sure I care." He ran his fingers along the inside of my arm, tickling me. "I mean, what does it matter? It doesn't matter to the case." His voice was soft and deep.

"It matters to the book." I willed away the delicious sinking feeling overcoming me, drawing me to him like a magnet.

"Okay then, open it," he said, pulling away.

I did. As I read the results, disappointment and sadness pinged through me. The Jean Harlow look-alike had been a perfect match to her famous ancestor and had died trying to prove it. She'd almost made it. But almost doesn't count.

"You seem disappointed?" Den said.

I nodded, swallowed tears. "It's silly. I know. But two lives were lost. Countless others were affected. Who knows how many? Our Jean Harlow almost achieved her dream. But she was killed."

We sat in the quiet for several minutes. Den poured champagne. "I'd like to make a toast."

"Really?" I said with a small grin. "How formal of you."

"Don't get used to it." He raised his glass. "To the best damn researcher, and maybe best person, I've ever known."

I batted my eyes. "Who's that?"

"You," he said, and we clinked glasses. "And oh, one more thing."

I held my glass up.

"To us," he said.

"To us," I said.

We clinked glasses and drank.

"But please don't shoot anybody else, Charlotte."

"I can't make any promises, Den," I said. The champagne was going to my head. But I felt good, warm, and safe, and all of my senses were on fire. Burning.

"Well, I can," he whispered and drew me into him.

Turns out, Den was a man of his word.

Afterword

*I*n 1943, my mother, Saranna "Sandie" Lee Carpenter, was fortunate to be adopted by Paul and Irene Carpenter. Sandie's father was a cousin of the famous, long-gone Harlean Carpenter, otherwise known as Jean Harlow. Growing up, I heard bits and pieces about the Hollywood star, but it was never made a big deal over. My grandmother Irene often said the best thing about Jean Harlow was that she was a friend of Clark Gable. Also, my grandmother didn't think much of Jean and the fact that she wore no underwear. Irene was a woman who believed in layers of proper undergarments.

Fast forward to 2015. I'd written a blog post about being related to Harlow, and a German game show contacted me to be on their show. Contestants ask questions about your famous relative and try to guess who it is. It was a free trip to Germany, so of course I took it. My personality being what it is, I researched Harlow. I wanted to be well-prepared, and I knew nothing about my famous relative except the rumor of her death, which claims her mother didn't seek medical help for Jean as she lay dying. Absolutely false.

This incident was what prompted me to think about Jean Harlow, and, of course, she crept into my writing. And because I'm mainly a mystery writer, I wanted to write a mystery. I toyed with the idea of a historical mystery, but I wanted a contemporary take on her life, from the eyes of a character who on the face of things is the opposite of Jean Harlow. Enter Charlotte Donovan, dogged researcher and wannabe writer, struggling with Lyme disease, money, and men issues, whose life is turned inside out when her boss dies. She's not one of those superhero kickass sleuths or PIs. Her superhero power is her mind. She's a modern woman with modern struggles and, when pressed, finds she's stronger than she imagined. I like to think most of us are.

The book is set in New York City, but all of the establishments, apartment buildings, clubs, and even Cloister Island are fictional. Of course, all of the biographical information about Harlow is accurate. But the narrative about her ring is fiction, along with her sending it to a secret baby in France. Jean did own a huge star sapphire ring, which was given to her by William Powell, but it has never been found. From my research, I learned that Harlow is one of the most mysterious and misunderstood Golden Age actresses. A great deal of misinformation has been passed off as biographical. I hope I've set some of those rumors to rest, even though this book is a work of fiction.

If you're interested in reading more about Jean Harlow, a couple of the best well-researched books are *Bombshell: The Life and Death of Jean Harlow* by David Stenn and *Harlow in Hollywood: the Blonde Bombshell in the Glamour Capitol, 1928–1937* by Darrell Rooney and Mark Vieira. There are countless Facebook, Twitter, and Instagram feeds about her, some actually using her name as if Jean Harlow herself is Tweeting. I also found a podcast chock-full of fascinating information called "You Must Remember This." It's a must-listen to if you're into old Hollywood.

Other historical notes about the story include the film clip where Jean stood up nude during a break in shooting a movie. That is true. Whatever happened to the clip is anybody's guess. Also, as strange as the incident with her second husband is, it is also true. If you'd like to read a good book about it, check out *Deadly Illusions: Jean Harlow and the Murder of Paul Bern* by Samuel Marx.

Getting to know my great aunt once removed has been an honor and a pleasure for me, and I hope you feel the same way.

Acknowledgments

A deep, heartfelt appreciation to Terri Bischoff for loving this book enough to publish it, and to my agent Jill Marsal for all of her steadfast belief in this book and my writing. Special thanks to beta readers Mary Sproles Martin, Rosemary Stevens, and Matthew Kelland. A big hug both to Jess Lourey for reading the book and blurbing it and to Hank Phillippi Ryan, who spoke with me a few years ago about the book when it was just a nugget of an idea—and very nicely refused to let me give up on it. Thank you to Emma Bryan, my oldest daughter, now living in New York City, who helped me with my questions about directions and the logistics of getting around the city, and to Tess Bryan, my youngest daughter, who came up with the title *The Jean Harlow Bombshell*.

And thank you, dear reader, for choosing to spend your time reading my book.

About the Author

Mollie Cox Bryan is the author of the Cora Crafts Mysteries and the Cumberland Creek Mysteries. Her books have been selected as finalists for an Agatha Award and a Daphne du Maurier Award and as a Top 10 Beach Reads by *Woman's World*. She has also been short-listed for the Virginia Library People's Choice Award. Mollie is distantly related to Jean Harlow.